I0736908

CHASING WISHES

(CAPTURING MAGIC, BOOK 1)

JESSICA SORENSEN

USA TODAY & NEW YORK TIMES BESTSELLING AUTHOR

JESSICA SORENSEN

CHASING WISHES

CAPTURING MAGIC

Chasing Wishes
Jessica Sorensen
All rights reserved.
Copyright © 2017 by Jessica Sorensen
This is a work of fiction. Any resemblance of characters to actual persons, living or dead, is purely coincidental. The author holds exclusive rights to this work. Unauthorized duplication is prohibited.
No part of this book can be reproduced in any form or by electronic or mechanical means including information storage and retrieval systems, without the permission in writing from the author. The only exception is by a reviewer who may quote short excerpts in a review.
Any trademarks, service marks, product names or names featured are assumed to be the property of their respective owners, and are used only for reference. There is no implied endorsement if we use one of these terms.

ISBN: ISBN: 9781939045881
For information: jessicasorensen.com
Cover design by Qamber Designs

❋ Created with Vellum

CHAPTER 1

MY PARENTS ARE FIGHTING. They rarely fight. But tonight is different. The air is toxic with anger and fear. I should go to bed and give them some privacy. Instead, I hunker down near the outside of the doorway and spy on them. Maybe I'm a terrible kid for doing so, but I'm curious. Not about the fight, but about what's perched on the cracked kitchen table.

"What have you done? This is what you've been looking for, for the past month? This is what you've been doing while I've been working fourteen hour shifts at the club? Going off and playing treasure hunter?" my mom yells at my dad as she paces the length of the small kitchen.

They've been arguing since my dad came home this

afternoon from a month-long trip, bringing home a silver, emerald-trimmed genie lamp. I can't quite figure out why my mom's so mad. My dad didn't steal the lamp. Plus, it's so pretty, all sparkly and covered with jewels, carrying the power to grant wishes. I've never seen anything so powerful in my life.

My dad lowers his head into his hands. "I'm sorry. I'm so sorry. But I couldn't think of any other way to get out of this magical-damned world."

"Using magic to survive isn't the way to fix this world," my mom seethes. "We aren't any better than *them* if we use magic to put this broken world back together. And if the legends are true, then we'll still be more damned if we use that stupid thing." She thrusts a finger in the direction of the cracked table where the lamp is perched.

"We don't know if the legends are true." My dad carefully picks up the lamp. "Legends rarely are."

"Tell that to all the humans who were around when the paranormals took over our world," my mom spats. "They all thought the stories and rumors of paranormals wanting to take over were just legends. Now look where we are." She gestures around the narrow, cramped space of the kitchen.

The walls are cracked, the floor is browned and rotting with age, and the ceiling leaks every time a rainstorm passes through the city. But, at least we have a roof over our heads, which is more than most kids my age can say.

My mom also has a job, another rarity in this world known now as Endlessland. Here, humans struggle to live from day to day, starving, poverty-stricken, and homeless. Or the really unlucky ones are forced to be prisoners and servants to the magical creatures.

Life hasn't always been this way. A long, long time ago, paranormals coexisted harmoniously with humans until a group known as the Five Smoke Magic corrupted that disorder and overthrew the human ruler, taking over our world. Then they put the idea into the rest of the paranormals' minds that they were better than humans because they were more powerful. And so began the downfall of human life in this world and the uprising of magical creatures.

We're trapped here, the only species not allowed to world travel. We're also at the bottom of the food chain and are forced by laws to rely on paranormals for almost everything, including jobs. And they don't let humans obtain those very often, at least not the good, decent paying, moral jobs.

My mom has had a job for a while, but I don't know much about what she does, other than she works for paranormals and hates her job. I've heard her crying at night to my dad about how disgusting and ashamed she feels inside. I wish I could help her, but there's hardly any jobs available for human adults in the city, let alone an eleven-year-old human girl.

I do know how to read and write, though, which is another rarity. And, according to my father, the skill will come in handy when I'm old enough to start job searching.

His ability to read is what landed him a job at the Rare Magic Books City Library. Unfortunately, after working there for over a decade, he was accused of stealing a book. Since there was no proof of the alleged thievery, simply accusations, he was only fired and sentenced to one month in the electric cells, instead of being executed.

I know he stole the book. I once found it hidden underneath the floorboards beneath his bed when I was snooping around. That's a secret I'll take to my grave.

"I can't believe this. I can't believe this," my mom chants, her eyes manically wide. "We need to get rid of it. Right now. Throw it in a lake or something."

"Look, I know you're upset, but … but throwing something this valuable away … something that could possibly change our lives and the entire world's …" He shakes his head as he stares at the lamp. "Imagine if I made a wish to return the world to its rightful place. Imagine how many humans I could save from starvation, poverty, and executions. And you wouldn't have to work for them anymore. You could be free. You wouldn't have to … sell yourself anymore. Can you imagine that?"

Sell herself? What exactly does my mom do? When I asked her once, she told me she was a dancer.

One of my friends once told me about how their older sister sometimes made money by doing things for paranormals. Dirty birds and bees sorts of things. Is that what my mom does?

"And think about what this could do for Harlynn," my dad adds. "She could have a real future. One where she won't have to sell herself someday."

"Harlynn knows how to read. She's a smart girl. She can do better without us using that damn thing to make a wish."

"We don't know that for sure. And even if she does manage to land a decent job, anything can happen. This world is too unstable. All she has to do is smart off to the wrong paranormal or get accused of stealing something and her life will be ruined."

"I know that," my mom whispers with confliction. "But if we make a wish and choose the wrong wording, we could end up being even worse off than we are now. Plus, there's always a price in exchange for every wish, and the genie gets to decide that price." She eyes the lamp warily. "There's a reason no human has been able to wish the world back to what it was before. No such wish exists. The genie will twist whatever we say into something else, and then make us pay by cursing us double." She slumps into a chair across from my dad. "I hate that you even brought it into this house. It feels like we're cursed already."

"I know you're worried, but I went through a lot of trouble to get this." My dad rubs his thumb alongside the lamp. "It was sheer luck I was even able to find it without getting myself killed. Some of the men who were with me were less fortunate." He swallows hard. "They didn't make it back."

A beat of silence ticks by.

"I'm sorry, but I'm still not happy you found it." Her anger is softening, her gaze fixed on the lamp.

"The fact is that I did find it, and it'd be a waste not to try to wish the world back." He clasps his hand over my mom's. "Let me try, please. I won't ever be able to forgive myself if I don't at least try." He grips the lamp with his free hand. "Please, dear, let me wish away the corruption in this world and replace it with good."

Poof!

A cloud of purple, hazy smoke funnels from the floor and swirls around the kitchen, shaping into the figure of a tall man with heavily tattooed arms and raven black hair. He's dressed in all black, metal cuffs wrapped around his wrists, and thick, buckled boots cover his feet.

His eyes are what's most frightening, like a bluish-purple tint, mirroring the bottom of a flame.

I know what he is immediately. A genie.

My heart slams against my chest as I crouch down lower to better hide myself.

At the sight of his smoky presence, my mom gasps and my dad jumps to his feet, toppling the chair over. He reaches for my mom, but the genie snaps his fingers and both my parents freeze, hands outstretched, worried features carved into their faces.

"So, you're the human who stole my lamp?" The genie steps from the smoke and assesses my parents with his head tilted to the side. "I have to say, I expected you to look a bit more … What's the human word I'm looking for …?" He drums his fingers against his silvery lips. "Stronger, perhaps." The genie smacks my dad in the forehead then stares at the lamp in his hand. "And maybe a bit brighter than to utter the word *wish* while holding my lamp." Magic sizzles from his fingertips. "Then again, if you were brighter, then I wouldn't get to play now, would I?"

Fear lashes through me as he raises his sparking finger toward my dad's forehead. I've heard the stories of genies. How they curse and break humans whenever they get a chance. Heard tales of their cruelty, even against their own kind. I may be terrified out of my mind, but I won't let some wish-granting creature hurt my parents.

"Leave them alone!" I shout as I jump to my feet and storm into the kitchen.

A grin curls across the genie's face. "I was wondering if you were going to be brave enough to come in here. Well, brave might not be the correct word. More like stupid."

"I'm not stupid for saving my parents." I cross my arms and raise my chin, although my legs shake.

He keeps his sparking finger aimed at my dad as he turns his head toward me. "You think you can save them?" He laughs. "Then you must be stupid."

"I'm not stupid. I know he didn't make the wish, so you can't do anything to him."

"Oh, but he did. Maybe not intentionally, but he used the correct wording."

I gulp as I recall what my dad said right before the genie appeared in the kitchen.

"Please, dear, let me wish away the corruption in this world and replace it with good."

"He said *dear*," I point out in desperation. "Not genie."

He lifts a shoulder. "He could've easily been calling me dear."

I narrow my eyes at him. "You know that's not true."

"What I know and what I want are two entirely different things." As if to prove his point, his fingertip showers sparks across my dad's face.

"You can't just do whatever you want," I snap. "That's not how things work."

"You don't think so, huh?" He nods toward the window, where outside, the street is lined with collapsing homes and shacks. "Take a look around you, little girl. That's exactly how things work for paranormals."

My pulse quickens as I realize how right he is. "But you can't just steal a wish from someone."

"It's not stealing. He made the wish. Now it's time for you to be quiet." With a grin, he snaps his fingers.

I open my mouth, but no words come out. I stomp my foot and soundlessly scream. He only laughs.

"Time to grant a wish." He cracks his knuckles and adjusts the cuffs on his wrists before facing my father. "I think your exact words were 'let me wish away the corruption in this world and replace it with good.' You weren't very specific about what sort of corruption you wanted to replace or what you wanted to replace it with, other than something good, so I'll have to go by my standards." Fizzling magic crackles from his fingertips. "There's nothing more corrupt than a human who steals from a paranormal … twice, if the records are correct. So, since you committed two corrupt violations of the law, I'll be removing you and your wife from this world and replacing both of you with something I deem good."

A wave of maddening anger thrashes through my veins as I rush forward, slamming my fist into his side.

He tenses, his jaw ticking. Then, with a flick of his wrist, I'm flying backward into the wall.

"Stay put. You'll get your turn." He places a sparking palm on each of my parents' foreheads and shuts his eyes, his lips moving as he whispers words in a foreign language.

No. No. No!

Tears spill from my eyes as I stagger to my feet. But every time I get my feet under me, a spout of dizziness overcomes me and sends me right back to the floor. I keep fighting, though, refusing to let him just take my parents. Refusing to let a paranormal take something else away from this world. In the end, it doesn't matter.

As hard as I fight, as much as I silently beg, my parents still fade into grains of sand that blow away with his whispering exhale.

I open my mouth and silently scream until my lungs ache, until I can't breathe, until I almost die. If I had my way, I would. My body, however, reacts on pure instinct, forcing oxygen into my lungs.

I gasp for air, my rage flaring potently as the genie turns toward me.

"Now, what to do with you." He crouches down in front of me, and I kick at him. He captures my ankle, his eyes flaming and his fingers digging into my skin. "I was going to let you get off easy and send you away with your parents, but I've changed my mind." He tugs hard on my leg, dragging me toward him.

I lift my hand to smack him, but he snags my wrist, too, and grips tightly enough to nearly crack my bones. The cruelest smirk possesses his face.

"You should know better than to try to harm a genie. And now, I'm about to take everything from you."

Tears spill from my eyes. *You already have.*

Holding my wrist, he leans into my face. "The first time you fall in love, and I mean, really and truly fall in love with someone, they're going to be taken from this world, just like your parents. And you *will* fall in love; I promise you." An eerie grin consumes his face. "With someone you hate at first. That way, you won't even know you're falling in love with them until it's too late." He places his electrically charged hand against my forehead.

A cry rips from my lips, my voice returning, as heat violently scorches my brain and rips at my insides. Then, just as swiftly, the pain abruptly stops.

"Fuck, what did you do!" the genie growls as he jerks back, his skin igniting in flames.

I cower back against the wall as flakes of his singed flesh float to the floor, screaming, "I didn't do anything!"

He glares at me through the whirlwind of ash and smoke flooding the kitchen. "You'll pay for this!"

"I didn't even do anything!" I cry, coughing as the smoky air hits my lungs.

Snarling like a rabid beast, he vanishes from the kitchen, taking his lamp with him and leaving me lying on the floor in an empty, rotting house, with nothing but my tears and whimpers to fill up the silence.

That's when I realize I'm truly alone in this world.

That my parents are never coming back.

CHAPTER 2

PRESENT...

IN THIS WORLD, some humans believe history repeats itself. My mom used to ramble on about that theory all the time. Me? I've never been a big believer in it ... until now. Because, what I'm about to do just might land me in the same position as the day that fucking soulless genie took everything away from me and cursed my future. Then again, I have no other choice. Not unless I want to lose the only person left in this world I care about.

That's what I remind myself as I stare down at the garbage can in front of me, piled with trash and doused with a bottle of everlasting flame I stole from a witch's car parked in the arena's parking lot near multiple bands' world jumper vehicles, vehicles that can transport to different worlds. My pockets are stuffed with potions, a dagger, and a few magical herbs. Again, stuff I stole.

After years of surviving on the streets, I've learned how to become quite the thief. I used to hate the idea of stealing, but then I became homeless and orphaned, and quickly discovered that, in order to survive, I have to do things I hate. Just like I'm about to do now.

If I get caught, I'll likely be sent to the electric dungeons again ... or executed. Or worse, I'll be sentenced to the Human Binding Department where I'll be sold to the highest paranormal bidder.

I've heard horror stories of what happens to humans when they're sold to paranormals. Of how their souls are bound to their masters by magic, and they're forced to obey every command. I'd rather die than become a plaything for a paranormal, so I'm taking a huge risk being in the arena parking lot, surrounded by world jumper vehicles filled with paranormal musicians. But I need to be here so I can pay a debt to the underground mafia, who are human, yet they have enough power over the city to be almost as scary as the paranormals.

Taking a deep breath, I dig my lighter out of my pocket and adjust the staff badge clipped to the front of my jacket. If things go according to plan, I should be able to pay off my debt to the underground mafia by tonight. Well, not my debt, but Jason's, my best friend since we were twelve after we both spent a month in the electric dungeons.

He had been imprisoned for stealing a fey's motorcycle, and I had been thrown in for trying to assault the genie who I thought had been behind the disappearance of my parents—huge emphasis on the *trying* part. The really sucky part? It wasn't even the right genie. Luckily, I only got my ass fried by magic and my arms covered in magical wish burns that left behind a couple of gnarly scars. My sanity was also a bit shaky due to the temporary chaos wish he blasted into my brain, but that eventually faded.

I'm sort of glad the incident happened, though, because it gave me Jason. Knowing he has my back, that I have someone who's there for me, makes the darkness and sometimes hopeless part of life easier to bear.

But then our friendship hit a rough patch about six months ago when Jason got addicted to faerie euphoric dust. When he could no longer afford to buy the magical drug, he started stealing it from the mafia and got caught. The leader was going to kill him, but I made a deal to save Jason's life.

At first, I tried to entice the mafia leader with a vow that I'd get enough money to pay off Jason's debt. But no, the leader didn't want money. He wanted something way more valuable in exchange for Jason's freedom.

A gods damn genie lamp.

Under any other circumstance, I would've said *hell no*. But Jason is the only person I have left in this world that I care about. If I could without losing him, I might have even fallen in love with him by now. So, I told the mafia leader I'd steal the damn genie lamp, and he gave me a name and a location of where I could find a genie and his lamp.

Ashton Wynterford—aka Asher—lead singer and guitarist for the Ash East Arrow, who is currently in the city as part of a music tour. Only paranormals and some of their human servants are allowed to attend the concert. However, humans are allowed to apply for two job positions. One is to work as a bands' staff team, and the other is to be part of one of the bands' "special after-show," which means you have to fuck the band members after they perform.

While some human men and women are into having sex with paranormals, I'd rather cut off my right arm than give my virginity to a soulless, evil monster. So, I applied for a staff position, and here I am, about to break all sorts of laws and start a fire in the midst of the bands' vehicles.

I hunker down between the front of one large, metal, world jumper vehicle and the rear end of another, repeatedly flicking the lighter. My heart is a mess inside my chest, and my skin is damp with sweat. If the wrong human or paranormal sees what I'm about to do, I'm beyond screwed.

You have to do this to save Jason. He's all you have left in this world.

As if sensing where my thoughts are heading, my earpiece begins to ring with an incoming call. I fumble around in my pocket for the receiver the mafia leader gave me and push the answer button.

"Hello?" I whisper, peering around nervously to double-check that no one is watching me.

"Harlynn," the mafia leader, or Lead as he likes to call himself, greets me cheerfully through my earpiece. "So, what's the update? Do you have my lamp yet?"

"Not yet," I whisper, crouching lower to the ground. "I'm about ready to go get it, though. Just setting up a distraction."

"Good, good," he mumbles with less cheerfulness. "I don't need to remind you what's at stake, right?"

"No, I remember pretty clearly," I reply through clenched teeth, my hands fisting into balls.

"Sometimes reminders help motivation, don't you agree?"

"Sure." I really fucking hate this guy. Normally, I'd tell him how moronic he is, but pissing him off right now means risking Jason's life.

"Good. Then let me send out a reminder."

A holographic screen illuminates in front of my face, revealing Jason bound by electric cuffs and surrounded by a group of men dressed in black, hooded uniforms and armed with various weapons.

"Jason?" I reach out like I can touch the screen.

Lead only allowed me to see Jason once when I made the bargain, and I was never allowed to speak to him directly.

Jason lifts his head and peers around with his good eye, the other too swollen to open. His lip is bleeding, and his nose is crooked and bruised. He looks awful, beaten, and sickly. My heart is breaking at seeing him so fractured.

"Harlynn?" he whispers, his eyes finding mine on the screen.

"Hey." I fight back the tears threatening to pour out. "How are you holding up?"

"I'm doing okay," he promises. "I'm just worried about you."

"I'm fine. I promise. In fact, I'm about to go in and get the lamp so I can get your sorry ass freed." I force a smile.

He hastily shakes his head. "I don't want you to do it, Har. It's too dangerous. And this ..." He glances around at the men. "This is my mess, not yours."

"I'm not going to just let them kill you."

"I'll be fine." He flinches as the men begin to close in on him. "In fact, I'm working on a different deal with Lead. One that doesn't involve you ... You need to leave. Get away from wherever you are and forget about that lamp—"

The screen vanishes, leaving me staring at the back of a vehicle.

"Hello?" I whisper as tears roll down my cheeks. "Jason, can you hear me?"

"I've cut off the connection," Lead's voice fills my ear again. "Once you get the lamp and send me a visual of it, I'll let you see him again."

I dry my eyes with the sleeve of my shirt. "How do I know he's still okay?"

"You have my word that no harm will come to him as long as you bring me the lamp."

The word of an underground mafia leader. How reassuring.

"And if your thieving reputation precedes you," he continues, "I have no doubt you'll have no trouble pulling this off."

I want to argue with him, insist that I'm not a very good thief. But the truth is, I am. Even before I lost my parents at eleven years old, I was always able to sneak around and find objects and secrets no one wanted found, like the book my father stole. The trait probably came from him.

While my dad wasn't a thief, he was a tracker, or what some call a treasure hunter. He was the best of his time. That's why he was able to find a genie lamp.

"All right, but just know that, if any more harm comes to Jason, I won't hand over the lamp," I dare say to Lead.

"You're in an awfully vulnerable position to be making such demands," he warns.

"I could very well say the same thing to you, since I'm

the one who's about to get this genie lamp you want so badly." Yeah, I'm being a bit bold, but I can't stand the thought of more harm coming to Jason.

He gives a short, unnerving pause. "I can't decide whether you're extremely stupid or completely brilliant."

A slow exhale eases from my lips. "Perhaps a bit of both."

"Perhaps." He pauses. "No more harm will come to Jason, just as long as I have that lamp in my hands within seventy-two hours. That gives you more than enough time to pull this off."

It takes a lot of effort, but I manage to get out a, "Thank you."

"Don't thank me. Just don't let me down. If you do, Jason dies."

"I won't let you down."

"Good."

The line dies.

I swear to the skies, it feels like a hundred-pound weight drops onto my shoulders.

If I fuck this up, Jason dies. If I succeed, I could still screw everything up because, if there's one thing in this world that I don't trust, it's a genie and his lamp. I have no other choice, though. I'm going to get that lamp, even if it kills me.

Summoning a shaky breath, I glance from left to right, scoping out the parking lot. A handful of staff members are wandering around, along with a few punked-out paranormal band members. Between the world jumper vehicles and the greying darkness of the sky, I'm pretty well hidden.

After double-checking to make sure no one is watching me, I flick the lighter and drop it into the bin of trash and gasoline. Then I run away as the flames swoosh toward the greying sky before pausing to momentarily stare as the fire blazes.

The great part about using everlasting flames is that only a witch can put it out. Since the only witch around is currently performing on stage, the fire won't be easy to extinguish. And while everyone is distracted, I'll sneak onto the genie's vehicle and steal the lamp.

At least, that's the plan.

Please let this go down smoothly.

Tearing my eyes off the hissing flames, I shuffle a few more steps back as smoke funnels through the air.

"Fire!" I shout, pretending to lose my shit.

A few paranormals and humans glance in my direction, but the panic factor I was anticipating never happens.

I try again, pointing at the flames. "Holy shit, there's an everlasting fire and it won't go out! The bands' vehicles are going to blow up!"

That statement unleashes a wave of panic. Staff and band members rush over to try to put out the flames with human devices and magical spells. Then fire only blazes brighter.

Perfect.

"Someone should probably evacuate these vehicles as a precautionary measure," I tell a younger staff member whose eyes are wide with panic.

His gaze flicks to my staff badge. "Yeah, yeah, you do that," he mumbles as he picks up his radio device.

Fuck, I wasn't planning on being the one to do this part of my plan.

I ball my hands into fists, knowing if I knock on that world jumper vehicle door, I very well may cross paths with the owner of the lamp I'm about to jack.

Think of Jason, Harlynn. You have to do this. You have to be brave. And the genie on that vehicle didn't kill your family. He's just some genie. He's nothing.

Yeah, other than a powerful creature who can cast spells and wishes that can shatter your life into pieces.

Lowering my hood, I march over to the world jumper vehicle and pound my fist against the door. I hear cursing on the other side, followed by laughter. Then the door swings open. Standing on the other side is none other than Asher Wynterford.

He looks just like he did in the photo Lead gave me—tall, lean, and around my age. Although, with paranormals, it's hard to say for sure what age they are. He has short, cropped brown hair, pierced lips and brows, and these crazy blue eyes framed by thick eyelashes and smudged eyeliner. He has on the jinn's trademark wrist cuffs, isn't wearing a shirt, and his black jeans hang low on his hips, giving me an eyeful of the intricate tattoos weaving and curving along his scarred flesh.

Scarred flesh? Since when do genies have scars?

Ripping my eyes off his scars, I blink up to meet his piercing blue eyes. And when I say piercing, I mean *piercing*. His gaze nearly tears me to shreds as he scrolls over my unlaced boots, torn jeans, black T-shirt, and plaid overshirt. The only makeup I have on is some lip balm and kohl eyeliner, and my long brown hair is swept to the side in a tangled mess of waves. I can see the disapproval in his eyes, but I don't give a shit. I'm not here to dazzle some arrogant, soulless genie.

"Hey." I sound a bit breathless from the adrenaline overload the situation is causing.

His eyes briefly widen in surprise, then a pucker forms at his brow. A strange reaction, even for a paranormal. Then his expression promptly alters to indifference, and yep, that seems about right.

"Nope. Not interested." He slants against the doorway with his arms crossed, a smirk playing at his lips. "A little word of advice, human girl. Next time, put a little more effort into your presentation. This whole flannel shirt, holey jeans, and whatever the hell is going on with your hair"—he pulls a face as he motions at my head—"isn't going to get most paranormals to fuck you, let alone a paranormal like me." He braces his hands on the doorframe, muscles bulging as he stares down at me with a malicious gleam in his stupidly pretty blue eyes. "You could try the band next to us. They're not as picky with their aftershow women. My band likes top-shelf quality."

My blood scalds, along with the scars on my skin.

Before I even know what I'm doing, my lips part. "Thanks for that little speech, but I'm not here looking to get fucked. And if I was, I sure as hell wouldn't have knocked on *your* door. I just came to tell you that there's an everlasting fire burning at the back of your vehicle and you might want to get off until it's put out, or else you're probably going to get smoke inhalation. But hey, maybe if you do, it'll give your bland, average voice that raspy sound. That will at least bump up your below-average sound to middle-shelf quality, right?" I bite down on my tongue.

Oh, my hell, what did I just do? He's going to curse me where I stand.

As his eyes darken with smoke, my breath gets lodged in my chest.

"You know what? I think I might want to retra—" His gaze darts to the flood of people gathering around the flaming trash can and billowing smoke. "Fuck." He leans back and shouts, "East, Arrow, get everyone off the vehicle. There's a fucking everlasting fire burning outside the vehicle."

"Oh no! Not an everlasting fire! Wait. Maybe it's me? I am pretty fucking hot!" a male voice amusedly shouts back, followed by a burst of giggles.

Asher sighs heavily. "Just get off the vehicle, okay? You know everlasting fire can spread fast and the smoke can be toxic."

"Yes, boss, sir!" the same voice yells back.

Asher shakes his head in frustration.

His annoyance makes me very happy.

When his gaze lands back on me, his eyes narrow into slits. "Did you need something else?"

I cross my arms and carry his intimidating gaze, even though my pulse is soaring "Yeah, to make sure you get your ass off the vehicle." I tap my badge. "I don't want to lose my job because who I'm assuming is your bandmate thinks his"—I resist an eye roll—"fucking hotness caused the fire."

Instead of getting more agitated, Asher heaves a sigh. "Look, he's not as moronic as he sounds. He's just ... drunk?" It sounds more like a question.

"Whatever. All I'm here to do is make sure you guys' dumbasses use the safety exits and get safely off the vehicle." I sound bored, while inside, I'm a nervous wreck.

Why, oh why, did I use the word dumbasses? It's like I have a death wish. And he could very well grant that.

Please just get off the vehicle so I can sneak inside and steal your lamp.

Asher meticulously eyes me over. "You're awfully brave for a human. Or stupid. I'm trying to decide which."

"Maybe a little bit of both," I joke nervously, trying to ease over the situation.

"Maybe." He continues to intensely study me. "How old are you?"

Why does that matter? "I'll be nineteen in a few weeks."

He gives me another once-over then rubs his pale blue lips together. "After they get the fire put out, come back to our vehicle."

I blink at him. "What?"

He wets his pierced lips with his tongue. "I might need a little entertainment later."

Is he kidding me? After telling me only moments ago that I wasn't good enough, he expects me to come to his vehicle and do what? I don't even want to know the answer, nor do I have any intention of coming back. At least not while he's in the vehicle.

I open my mouth to say who knows what—something that would get me into a lot of trouble—when a fey appears behind Asher and thankfully distracts him.

I know from the records I hacked into, needing to find

out more about Asher, that the faerie known as Easton is the bassist of their band and also sings sometimes. I haven't seen much fey in my time, but I have caught glimpses of what most humans refer to as the creatures of trickery and glittery beauty. The nickname seems fitting for him.

Tall, with chin-length blond hair, mischievous emerald green eyes, and full, pierced lips, there's no denying he's gorgeous. He's also not wearing a shirt and has his glittery wings spanned out, all sparkling magic and iridescent light. I find myself wanting to touch his wings, trace my fingertips along the edge and see if it sparkles brighter.

But I also want to keep my fingers, so my hands remain at my sides.

Easton peers over Asher's shoulder and out the front window of the vehicle. "Aw, so there *is* a fire."

Asher folds his arms. "You thought I, what, made the story up for fun?"

Easton shrugs. "You seemed pretty bored earlier. Thought maybe you were in one of your moods and trying to break up the party."

"Well, I'm not," Asher says flatly.

Easton's lips quirk. "If you say so."

When Asher's jaw ticks, the faerie's grin expands. Then he turns to exit the vehicle, but freezes when he spots me.

"Well, well, what do we have here?" His jewel-colored eyes sparkle with mischief and curiosity.

With what I hope is a disinterested expression, I tap my badge. "I'm just part of the staff."

"Staff, huh?" His gaze devours me as he skims me over from head to toe. "You should've applied for the aftershow."

I roll my tongue in my mouth, willing my lips not to part. Unfortunately, I've never been good at keeping my mouth shut.

"Why? So I can have the privilege of whoring myself out to a bunch of paranormals? Yeah, I think I'm okay with the staffing position. Besides, I'm too low-shelf quality to be part of the aftershow." I don't bother glancing in Asher's direction, but I can feel his fiery gaze burning a hole into the side of my head.

Easton studies me with his head cocked to the side. "You're awfully sassy for a human."

"Most humans are sassy by nature," I point out. "They're just too afraid to show their true character to paranormals."

"Is that so?" His eyes glimmer with amusement.

I fear I might be walking into a trap. A trap I set up for myself when I decided to open my damn mouth and challenge a faerie.

Time to shut up, Harlynn.

"Look, I didn't come here to argue," I tell them. "I

came here because it's my job to get you guys off the vehicle safely."

"Oh, don't try to back out of this now." Easton steps toward me. "Keep going. I was enjoying our little banter."

From my peripheral vision, I note the flames are still blazing in the trash can. Someone could figure out how to extinguish them at any moment, so I need to get them off this vehicle pronto.

"I never should've done it to begin with. It's unprofessional." Any other day, I probably would've gone toe-to-toe with the cocky faerie, which is why I've spent more than a handful of occasions in the electric cells.

"No, you definitely should've." He takes another step toward me. "In fact, I think, after they get the fire out, you should come back here so we can pick up where we started."

I aim for a bored tone. "No thanks. I'm super busy."

He cocks a brow. "With what?"

"With anything besides coming back here." I bite down on my tongue hard.

Shut up, Harlynn, just shut up.

"What's your name?" His smile is all trickery and wickedness.

Shit. The last thing I needed was is to draw more attention to myself. It'll make me easier to track down after I jack the lamp. "I'd rather not tell you."

"Just your first name," he urges, leaning closer and crowding me.

"Tell me yours first," I quip, even though I already know it.

"Easton. Or, well, most call me East," he says with a flick of his wrist. "Now you go."

I open my mouth, preparing to tell him my mom's name, when the lampposts enclosing the parking lot illuminate with purple, magical flames.

"Attention, paranormals. It has been brought to our attention that an everlasting fire is burning in the west parking lot," a formal, robotic tone echoes through the air. "As a safety precaution, we ask that all paranormals please evacuate their vehicles and proceed to the upper section of the stadium until the fire has been put out. Thank you for your patience." The voice fades, along with the flames.

"Come on; let's get this over with." Asher signals for East to get a move on.

With a sigh, East seizes my wrist and tows me with him into the mob of staff and paranormals making their way toward the stadium.

"Hey, what the heck?" I dig my heels into the asphalt

"You heard what the announcement said." East's eyes sparkle like starlight. "Everyone inside."

"No, it said all paranormals inside," I say. "Not staff."

"Yeah, so what? I'm not about to let you go. It's too

dangerous." His eyes glimmer for the tenth time in the last couple minutes. I still can't tell if he's joking or not.

"I have to work." I wiggle my wrist, trying to get free of his grip. "If I don't, then I don't get paid at the end of the night."

He practically drags me with him as he starts walking again. "I'll pay you three times as much as you were going to make with your staffing position."

"I'm not a whore," I growl out.

East eyes me over curiously. "I never said you had to be."

I glance back at his world jumper vehicle as two leggy blondes, along with Asher and a cyborg, wander outside. "Let me guess. You also told those two pretty blondes the same thing."

He shakes his head. "Of course I didn't. They signed up for the aftershow position."

"You're disgusting," I say. "You really are."

"Why?" he questions. "I didn't make them sign up for the job."

"No, but your rulers did by making every human in this world desperate for money." The words pour off my tongue and spill into the air before they actually register in my brain.

Lovely, Harlynn. You're really on a roll tonight.

East's fingers twitch on my wrists, the glow in his eyes dimming. "They're not my rulers."

Huh? Did he just insult Five Smoke Magic? There's a first.

Heavy silence hangs in the air as he pushes his way through the mob, towing me along with him.

"East, why are you dragging a human girl with you?" Arrow, the cyborg and drummer of Ash East Arrow, steps up beside me.

Like the rest of his bandmates, he's wearing low slung black pants and no shirt—seriously, it must be their signature look or something—so I get a full view of his body. Half-man, half-machine, his arms, neck, and muscular chest are spun of flesh and bronzed gadgets. His fingers are purely mechanical, and his abdomen is inked with small pieces of steel. But his face is human, all full lips, short black hair, and the most beautiful silver eyes. Many cyborgs roam the city, so I know the drill. They rarely show emotion. Rarely speak. Rarely interact with anyone.

"Because I'm keeping her for the night," East replies, hilarity ringing in his tone, his bad mood gone like human civilization itself.

"No, he's not." I jerk my arm, as if that somehow proves a point.

East just chuckles. "Don't pretend you don't like this bantering foreplay."

"How many times do I have to tell you that I'm not a whore?" I spat, trying to wrench my arm away from him again.

East throws me a smirk. "And how many times have I told you, maybe I don't want sex from you? Perhaps I just want to keep playing our little bantering game all night long."

I cock my brow at him. "Are you being serious right now? Because I genuinely can't tell."

He nods with a wink. "It's my secret wish."

Asher suddenly materializes by East's side. "Careful throwing around the word wish," he warns. "My lamp's too close by. You might accidentally set it off."

East rolls his eyes. "Like I'm worried."

"I know you're not, but I am." Asher stares up at the sky, his muscles tense. "You know how much I hate granting wishes."

A genie who hates granting wishes? Huh, never heard that before.

"I know." East's voice is soft, no amusement evident.

It makes me wonder what the story is behind Asher's hatred for wish granting. But not enough to ask. No, I need to get the hell away from these guys before we reach the gates.

Asher's gaze strays from the sky and lands on East. "So, you're keeping the girl?"

"No one's keeping me," I huff with exasperation and stomp my foot.

Asher exchanges a look with East, and then the two of

them bust up laughing. Even the emotionless cyborg chuckles.

"She's cute, right?" East says to Asher.

The corners of Asher's lips twitch as his gaze collides with mine. "Perhaps just a little bit."

"No, I'm not." I flail my free arm around in a pathetic attempt to escape East's hold. "I'm not cute. I'm just a plain, ordinary human girl who's way less entertaining than those pretty blondes you had in your vehicle. I mean, think about it. Do you really want me over them?" I raise my brows.

Asher rubs his lips together while East laughs and Arrow stares at me with his bronzed brows creased.

"Yep, I'm definitely keeping her," East announces then releases my wrist and drapes an arm around my shoulders, pulling me against him so my arm is wedged against his side.

His skin is warm and smells of spun sugar and strawberries. I subtly breathe in his scent, almost getting lost in his magical scent. Then he chuckles and the sound jerks me back to reality.

Big mistake letting my wrist go, asshole.

Time to escape, go find that damn lamp, and save Jason.

Lifting my foot, I kick East in the shin. His arm falls from my shoulders as he cries out in pain. If I ever do get caught, this moment will come back to bite me in the ass.

But that's a future worry. Right now, I'm only concerned about the present.

I push my way into the throng of paranormals and run away from the band. I don't look back. Don't want to see if they chase me.

I just focus on the forward.

On getting that damn lamp.

CHAPTER 3

TEN MINUTES and at least fifty panting breaths later, I'm sneaking up to the door to Ash East Arrow's world jumping vehicle. I check the handle but, no surprise, it's locked. Fishing around in the pocket of my jacket, I dig out my lock pick and unpick the lock. When I try the door handle again, the damn thing still won't open.

Hmmm ...

I trace my fingers around the edge of the doorframe and note a layer of silvery dust.

Fey magic.

"Shit. East must have sealed the door with magic."

A quick check around the area lets me know the everlasting fire is still blazing brightly and the parking lot is now fairly cleared out.

Inching closer to the door and deeper into the shadows, I dig a can of fey magic repellent from my pocket. One spray of this and the door should unlock. The problem is, the repellent only lasts for about five minutes before the fey magic resurfaces. Since there's only enough repellent in the can for one use, if I'm not off the world jumper vehicle by then, I'll be locked in.

But I really don't have another choice.

I'll have to move fast.

I give the bottle a few quick shakes then tap my finger against the top of the can. A pungent mist spritzes from the nozzle and sprays all over the front of the door, causing the silvery dust to evaporate. I check the door handle again …

"Jackpot," I whisper as the door opens.

I step onto the world jumper vehicle and close the door behind me.

The area inside is far bigger than what the size of the vehicle should hold, more than likely due to magic. To my right is a large sitting room, fully stocked with leather sofas, a fireplace, a hologram television, and an array of guitars, speakers, microphones, and a drum set. To my left is an open kitchen with the biggest fridge I've ever seen, shiny marble flooring, and glass countertops filled with mini water fey.

"Crap, I hope they can't see me." I squint down at the

sparkling miniature water fey and cringe when a glowing pink one makes eye contact with me.

It *tsks* me with its tiny finger before swimming deeper into the counter, urging the rest of the miniature water fey to come over. Once they're all gathered in a circle, they huddle together.

I don't know much about mini water fey, but I have a feeling they're plotting against me right now.

Time to wrap this plan up.

The information Lead gave me about Asher stated that the lamp will probably be hidden in his room in a magically sealed trunk. I cross the living room and head down a wide hallway lined with lanterns and shut doors. Unsure of where to start, I open the first door on my right.

Inside, everything is made of bronzed metals and gadgets, all the way from the orbed chandelier to the gleaming metal floor. If I had to guess, I'd bet the room belongs to the cyborg.

Shutting the door, I move on to the next room. It's also a bedroom, with black hardwood floors, a massive king-sized bed, and winding metal trim covering the ceiling. My first guess is that the room belongs to Asher, but a shimmering coat of fey magic covers almost every piece of furniture and the walls.

No, this has to be East's room.

I back out of the room and open the next shut door.

Behind it is the biggest bathroom I've ever seen, with a bathtub large enough to fit ten people.

I grit my teeth. Here, the world is filled with starving, poverty-stricken humans, and these asshole's world jumper vehicle is better than most human's homes.

Suddenly, the idea of stealing the lamp seems way more appealing. I can almost picture Asher fuming when he discovers it gone.

I hurry onward and throw the next door open.

"Yep, this has to be his room," I mutter as I inch inside the largest room I've stumbled across yet.

The area is spacious, the ceiling domed and painted with a white, black, and grey skull mural. The walls are dark grey and nearly mesh with the black hardwood floor. The bed is lavish and covered with a velvet comforter. Perched in front of the bed is a steel trunk engraved with obsidian.

I resist a happy dance, knowing I still have to get the trunk open, and cross the room to the foot of the bed. I kneel in front of the trunk and examine it. The lock on the front appears to open with a key, but I doubt it's going to be that simple. I give it a go anyway, trying to pick the lock. No luck.

Setting my trusty lock pick aside, I search the trunk's sealing for traces of fey magic. The outside is squeaky clean. I can't spot any other locks anywhere. No magical inscriptions. No scanning pad. Nothing other than the damn key lock.

I sit back and rub my hand across my face. "How the hell are you sealed?" My gaze travels to the bottom of the trunk. "Hmm …" I grip the sides and, with a grunt, tip the trunk upward to peer underneath. Nothing besides a smooth, flat surface resides.

"Dammit." I lose my grip as one of the obsidian jewels cuts my fingertip and the trunk crashes to the floor.

"How the hell is that thing so sharp?" I mumble as I press the bleeding wound to the front of my jacket.

I glance at the jewel that split open my skin. The edges are smooth, so how did it cut me? I brush my finger along the jewel—

"Crap." I wrench back as a needle snaps out of it, but not fast enough before the needle embeds into my skin.

Panic sets in as I fumble to dig the needle out, only to realize it's attached to a thin tube filled with green, bubbling liquid.

A green, bubbly liquid now pumping into my fingertip.

Shit. I know what that liquid is.

Jinn death poison.

My pulse soars as I yank the needle out of my finger. The tube ravels back into the jewel as blood pools from my skin. My eyes water as pain pulsates from my now green fingertip.

Poison. I've been poisoned by jinn death poison.

I'm going to die.

Right as the thought crosses my mind, the lid of the trunk pops open, as if to say *ha, ha, go ahead and take the lamp now. You're going to die anyway.*

Gods dammit, I really hate genies.

CHAPTER 4

I HAVEN'T FELT this shocked since the day the genie made my parents vanish, and that's saying a lot, considering how many crazy situations I've put myself in. I have only a handful of hours before my entire body resembles my finger, before the poison completely fills my veins and begins eating away my body. It's going to be a painful death, one that'll hurt like a bitch.

Tears burn the back of my eyes as reality crashes down on me.

I'm going to die.

My life is over.

Just like my parents.

And just like my parents, a genie has taken my life.

Anger, fear, and sadness sweep through me. I almost lose my shit. I want to hurt Asher for doing this to me. I want to scream. Cry. Then I remember I have a friend to save. I'll be damned if I give up now.

Sucking back the tears, pain, and rage, I peer into the trunk. Inside is a polished silver lamp, trimmed with the same obsidian jewels that decorate the exterior of the trunk.

Not bothering to check for more booby traps—it's not like it matters anymore—I scoop up the lamp and tuck it away in my pocket. Then I shut the lid, stumble to my feet, and check the time on my watch.

One more minute until the repellent on the door wears off. If I'm not outside by then, I'll be locked in.

I rush out of the room and down the hallway, doing my best to disregard the wooziness stirring through my mind. The closer I get to the door, the more my adrenaline courses.

I can't believe I pulled this off.

I can't believe I'm going to die soon.

At least Jason will be okay.

At least my death won't be for nothing.

At least he'll get to live—

"What the hell? Why is the door unsealed?" East's voice floats from the other side of the now cracked open door.

Fuck.

I spin around and hightail it for the living room window. When I throw back the curtains, however, instead of a window, there are a series of holograms showing a fake view of spacious mountains and glistening lakes.

"What do you mean the door is unsealed?" Asher asks as the door creaks open more.

"I mean exactly what I said," Easton says. "The door is unsealed."

A beat of silence ticks by, then the door flies open and smacks against the wall. I duck down to the floor, crawling away from the window and hiding behind the sofa as the sound of stomping footsteps fills the air.

"Where are you?" Asher calls out. "Whoever you are, know that when we find you, you're going to be punished for whatever it is you were trying to take. And the punishment will be cruel and painful. No electric cells for you. No, this punishment is going to be handled by *us*."

He makes it seem like the electric cells are some sort of fantastic punishment. I guess, considering he's a genie, it might be.

"What do you think they're after?" Arrow asks in a much softer voice than Asher's. "Your lamp?"

When the living room floorboards creak, I press myself closer to the back of the sofa and hug my knees to my chest.

"Either that or our little rebellion collection," East replies cautiously.

Little rebellion collection? What the hell is that?

"Do you hear that?" East asks from the other side of the sofa.

"Heavy breathing," Asher states. "A scared, little thief is still in this room."

"The water fey said a girl came in here," East states with puzzlement.

"A girl?" Asher asks, sharing his confusion.

I roll my eyes at their surprise. What? Do they think a girl isn't capable of breaking into places or something?

When the room grows unnervingly silent, my heart begins to thunder in my chest. I place my hand over my mouth and hold my breath. Then I wait to be caught, because I know it's going to happen. I have no way out. And while I'm currently on death row, I'm still scared shitless of the torture that awaits me when they find me. Not to mention I won't make it out of here with the lamp.

Jason, I'm so sorry I failed you. Just like I failed my parents.
My eyes begin to water.

No, I'm not giving up yet. There has to be a way.

Think of something, Harlynn! You've gotten this far. Gotten the lamp ...

I reach inside my pocket with my green hand—the poison is spreading more rapidly than I expected—and brush my fingers along the cool steel of the lamp. I made a promise to myself the day my parents were stolen from me to never use a genie lamp for anything. But, since I'm practically a dead woman sitting, that vow really doesn't matter anymore.

Sucking in a breath, I spring to my feet and whirl around, keeping my green hand tucked into my pocket, along with the lamp.

East is standing near the sofa, and his eyes pop wide at my sudden appearance. "What the …?" He gapes at me.

Arrow, who is leaning against the kitchen counter, seems less surprised, but that's a cyborg for you. And Asher is standing in front of the sofa, looking the exact opposite of Arrow. A mixture of emotions crosses his face, ranging from surprise, rage, to something else, something that looks an awful lot like being impressed, but I highly doubt I'm right.

"You're the one who broke in here?" Asher asks in confusion.

I lift a shoulder in a lazy shrug. "You guys told me to come back, right?"

His eyes narrow. "How did you get in here?"

I shrug again. "The door was unlocked."

"It shouldn't have been. I sealed it with my magic." Burning suspicion pierces from East's eyes. "Who are you, human? And how did you get past my magic?"

"I didn't," I lie. "Like I said, the door was already unlocked when I got here."

"And you just let yourself in?" East assesses me with skepticism.

"I didn't want to stand outside with all the everlasting smoke," I say innocently. "It's toxic."

East exchanges a look with Asher, then they both glance at Arrow. Arrow heaves an exhausted and oddly human sigh, then pushes away from the counter and enters the living room. He positions himself in front of the coffee table while Asher moves to the right of the sofa and East to the left, blocking all my escape routes.

"We know you're lying, so you might as well fess up." Asher stalks toward me with his lean arms crossed over his solid chest. "Why are you here? Who sent you?"

"I'm here because you guys invited me." I hold my ground, even when East closes in on me, too. "Sorry if I misinterpreted your invite. I guess I'll leave since I'm clearly not wanted." I step toward East to move around him, but his arms span out, blocking my path. I twist around to swing past Asher, but he wraps his fingers around my arm.

Smoke funnels in his eyes. "You're lying. I can smell it all over you."

I sniff the air out of pure instinct, but only the scent of sugary strawberries kisses my nostrils. "No, I'm pretty sure that's just East's faerie scent."

Asher's lips twitch as he leans in. "You have about ten seconds to fess up before I start blasting you with curses that'll leave your skin scarred and your mind veering toward insanity."

Anger pounds through my veins as his cruel, true genie form shows. "Wouldn't be the first time that's happened."

He blinks, taken aback. "You've been cursed by a genie before?"

"Oh, genies and I go way back," I say bitterly. "All the way back to when one killed my parents."

He blinks again, his hold on me loosening.

Seizing the distraction, I yank my arm away and shove him back. He stumbles only an inch, but it's enough to give me time to launch myself over the sofa and bolt toward the door. But then Arrow zips to the side at an inhuman speed and barricades my path.

I slam to a halt and let out a string of curses. I'm trapped. There's no running away from this. Time for my backup plan, one I was really hoping I didn't have to use.

"Fine, you want to know why I broke in here?" I stick my hand into my pocket and pull out the lamp. "To steal this."

Asher stiffens. "You made it into my trunk?"

I raise my green hand. "Obviously."

Fury flashes in his smoky eyes. "You know that's death poison, right? You're going to die."

"I know." I lower my hand to my side. "But I'm going to get out of here before I do."

Asher glares at me. "You're not leaving with my lamp."

I take a step back then wince as my back crashes into

Arrow's metal chest. "You can't take this lamp away from me. I know the rules. I hold all the power here. And if I want to, I can wish myself away."

"You're not going to, though." Asher winds around the sofa toward me, taking lazy, measured steps. "Because if you were, you would've already done it." He stops in front of me, his eyes no longer smoky, but smoldering in a way that makes my stomach do strange things. "You're not like most humans. You understand that, with every wish you make, there will be a consequence, which leaves me wondering why you went through so much trouble to steal the lamp."

My heart lodges in my throat as he extends his hand toward my head. I wince as his fingers brush my hair and start to step to back, but end up crashing back into Arrow.

Asher smirks as he ravels a strand of my hair around his finger. "Now, the question is: how are we going to punish you?"

I snap out of my fear-induced stupor and slap his hand away. "You're going to let me go. If you don't, I'll make the wish. And considering what I heard you say to East earlier, I'm pretty sure you don't like granting wishes." The frown that forms on his face makes me grin. "So, how about we do this the easy way?"

The muscles in Asher's jaw spasm. "I know you won't

make the wish. You don't want to deal with the consequences."

I arch my brows. "You think I care about the consequences? I probably have like, what, a couple hours to live? Who gives a shit about the consequences when I'm going to die anyway?"

As Asher assesses me closely, I try to appear neutral and mildly bored, examining my currently green fingernails.

"Well, if that's the case, then I guess you don't care if you have my lamp or not." He nods at East. "Take it from her. I mean, clearly, she doesn't care."

East rounds the sofa toward us. "Then what will we do with her?"

Asher tilts his head to the side as he studies me. "I haven't decided yet."

I hug the lamp to my chest. "No, I won't let you take it."

"You won't let me take it?" East glances at Asher with an amused smile. "Did you hear that, Ash? I think she wants to play a little game of cat and mouse. Or, well, faerie and human."

Asher's lips twist into an almost smile, his challenging gaze remaining fused on me. "I believe she does. Perhaps you should give her a head start. I know how much you love the chase."

East brushes his finger along the side of my neck

where my pulse races. "Not as much as after I catch them."

I fight to remain indifferent. "You say that like you're actually going to catch me."

"You're human, of course I'll catch you," East purrs, his fluttering wings brushing against the curve of my shoulder.

"You act like I'm incompetent and helpless." I meet his gaze. "But tell me this, if I'm so incompetent and helpless, then how did I make it past your magic seal?"

East's lips spread into a devious grin. "That is an excellent question. Maybe after I catch you, I'll make you tell me."

I raise my chin with false confidence. "*If* you catch me."

His grin broadens as his gaze roams back to Asher. "Can we please keep her? Just for a little while?"

"You can't keep me," I huff. "I'm not a pet. I'm a person."

Asher and East ignore me.

"I'm not taking a human on tour with us, East." Asher sighs, stuffing his hands into his pockets. "Not only would we be breaking a ton of laws by taking her out of this world, but taking care of a human is a lot of work. They're a lot of trouble, too."

East scrubs his hand across his jawline. "What if I

promised to keep an eye on her and keep her out of trouble?"

Asher snorts a laugh. "Yeah, I can only imagine how that would go down."

East dramatically presses his hand to his chest. "Hey, I know how to keep out of trouble."

Arrow chuckles from behind me. "Sure you do."

"You two together would be twice as much trouble than it's worth. And, like I said, we'd be breaking a shit-ton of laws by keeping her." Asher shakes his head. "It's not worth it."

East pouts. "Come on, Ash; I'm sure we could find a way to make her useful."

"Um, hello." I wave a hand in front of me. "No one's keeping me, so this stupid, little argument is pointless."

East's wicked gaze lands on me. "Don't pretend like you don't want to stay with us."

I roll my eyes. "Why the hell would I?"

East nonchalantly shrugs, though an impish smirk plays at his lips. "A lot of humans would love to be in your position right now—stuck on a world jumper vehicle with three very charming, very sexy paranormals who want to play with her. Not to mention we're fucking rock stars."

Cocky much?

"Well, then maybe you should go find one of those humans." I dodge to the side, but Asher sidesteps in my way again and I smack right into his bare chest.

He smells lovely, like cupcakes and frosting, neither of which I've tasted in years.

I'm so hungry I could almost bite him ...

I shake the thought from my head. *Where the hell did that come from?*

"You're not going anywhere." Asher's eyes illuminate fiercely. "Not with my lamp."

"Wanna bet?" Mustering a deep breath, I part my lips. "I wish that I—"

Asher covers his hand over my mouth. "Don't," he hisses. "It's more dangerous than you realize."

I glower at him, mumbling through his hand, "Let me go, and I won't do it."

He lowers his hand. "I'm not letting you out of here with my lamp."

I cradle the lamp tighter to my chest. "Sucks for you since I'm leaving here with your lamp."

Asher grinds his teeth. "Why?"

My brows furrow. "Why what?"

"Why is keeping my lamp so important to you?" He gives a pressing glance at my poisoned hand. The green, icky color has taken over half my arm now. "If you're going to die anyway, why does it matter if you have it?"

I give a small shrug. "Maybe I'm going to wish my death away."

"You can try, but it won't work. Not if I don't want it to," Asher says tightly. "That's the thing about genies and wishes—we always have all the control, even when someone has our lamp."

I know he's right, but admitting that won't help me get out of here.

"Maybe I found a way around that?" I challenge with an arched brow.

"There is no way around it; trust me." His relentless gaze makes me squirm. "So, tell me the truth. Why do you want my lamp so badly?"

I smash my lips together, my heart slamming against my chest. I could make the wish and cross my fingers that it works out in my benefit. More than likely, though, it'll end in disaster. Or, I could tell him the truth and maybe, just maybe, find a way to strike a bargain. I hate the thought of doing so—bargaining with a genie—but it might be the only way to save Jason.

"I made a deal with the underground mafia," I say, loathing how my voice slightly trembles. "If I don't bring them this lamp, they'll kill my best friend."

Asher's expression is blank as his gaze briefly flicks in East's direction before landing back on me. "How did your friend get in trouble with the underground mafia?"

"He became addicted to faerie euphoric dust and started stealing it from them," I explain. "He's a good guy. He just messed up."

Asher's gaze travels to my hand. "And yet, you're the one who's going to end up dying."

I raise my chin. "Yeah, so? I'd rather die than let another person I care about die."

"Another person?" he questions, a pierced brow curving upward. "You mean your parents?"

I press my lips together, refusing to answer. I've already told him too much about me.

The three of them remain silent, exchanging indecipherable looks. I hide my unease and tuck it away with my fear. The last thing I want is for them to know how nervous I am.

Finally, Asher tears his gaze away from Arrow and East and focuses on me. "So, were you the one who started the everlasting fire?" When I make no effort to answer him, not wanting to divulge my secrets, a half-smile appears on his lips. "And you got past our sealed door." It's not a question. "Seems like you've done this sort of thing before."

"What? Steal a genie lamp?" I laugh hollowly. "Yeah, no. I try to stay away from genies as much as possible."

The smile on his lips fades ever so slightly. "You said one killed your parents. What did you mean by that, exactly?"

I grind my teeth until my jaw aches. "I mean exactly that—one killed my parents."

"How, though?" he inquires carefully.

I shake my head. "I'm not going to talk about this with you."

His jaw muscles spasm again, a hint of internal agony flashing in his eyes. "Fair enough. I won't make you talk about something that upsets you this much."

I can't conceal my surprise at his easiness to let the subject drop. "How very un-genie-like of you."

"Asher isn't like most genies," East chimes in. "You'll soon learn that."

"No, I won't," I say, partly relieved by that fact and partly sad, but only because … "I'm going to be dead soon, remember?"

Asher trades a quick look with Arrow and East. "Maybe you won't."

Confusion swirls inside me. "Are you saying the poison isn't deadly?"

Asher shakes his head. "No, it is. But I could use magic to kill off the poison and let you live."

I open and flex my hand, trying to keep my anxiousness under control. "And what would I have to do in return?"

His eyes glint with vibrant blue flames. "Who says I'm not going to do this out of the kindness of my heart?"

I fight back a laugh. "I really doubt you are."

The flames in his eyes dim as he heaves a sigh. "All right, I'm not. But only because we need your help."

My gaze skims across the faerie, the cyborg, then

lands back on the genie. "The three of you need help from *me*?"

Asher nods. "With stealing a few items."

"That's it?" I question. "That's all you want from me in exchange for my life?"

Asher nods again. "That's it."

I shiver as East's wing tickles the side of my arm.

"And to let me play with you occasionally," he adds, earning him a glare from Asher.

"We'll have to bind the deal in magic," Asher tells me. "It will make sure that, if I give you your life back, you will retrieve the items we need. If you don't, you'll die."

I inch away from East as his wing continues to stroke my arm. "That still doesn't help me save my friend from the underground mafia."

Asher rubs his jawline, seeming to consider something. "I'm not going to give my lamp to the underground mafia leader. But I can add your friend's freedom to the binding spell, which means, if you break our deal, not only will you die, so will your friend."

I swallow hard, feeling less sure about this deal. I mean, I don't plan on trying to double-cross Asher or anything, but ...

"These objects you want me to steal, what are they? And why can't you steal them your—" Pain abruptly sears up my arm as the poison rises to my shoulder and neck, making me dizzy. I bite down on my tongue to stop myself from crying out, not wanting to look weak in front of them.

East must notice, though, because his wing begins soothingly stroking my arm. "Just make the deal with him … Wait. You never told us your name."

"And I'm not going to." The quiver in my voice reveals my discomfort and vulnerability.

"Make that part of the deal, too," East tells Asher. "I want to know this lovely human's name."

I put my green hand on my hip and twist to face him. "What's your fascination with me? You know I'm just like every other human, right?"

East's petal-thin wings glint against the chandelier's lighting. "No, you're not. You're a human who started an everlasting fire, turned my advances down, got past my seal, and broke into Asher's trunk. If I didn't know any better, I'd assume you were a very clever elf, but you're way too pretty."

I resist an eye roll. "You know, I've heard rumors that faeries were flirts. Those rumors didn't do the truth justice."

He winks at me. "We can be quite charming when we want to be. You'll see."

"I haven't agreed to the bargain yet," I remind him, turning back to a now frowning and confused-looking Asher. "And I'm not going to until you tell me what objects you want me to steal and why you can't steal them yourself."

"I can't tell you what the objects are yet," Asher replies. When I open my mouth to argue, he adds, "Not because I don't want to. I just can't while we're here in this world."

My brows knit. "Wait … Are you saying I have to leave this world to do this?"

Asher nods. "This is our last day on tour in this world, and the objects aren't here."

Both nervousness and excitement rush through me. I've always dreamt of seeing other places, of getting away from the rulers and the poverty that plagues every inch of this hellhole of a sphere I live on. Before, there was never a possibility of it being possible.

Wait.

"Humans aren't allowed outside this world," I inform them. "It's against the law."

"We'll just have to make sure we don't get caught smuggling you out." Asher steps toward me, invading my personal space.

I start to step to the side, but my arm bumps into East's chest. With Arrow standing right behind me, I'm left wedged between the three of them with barely any breathing room. Their scents overwhelm me, all sugary, strawberry cupcakes and frosting mixed with Arrow's cinnamon and vanilla. The scent is mouthwatering and kind of making me hungry.

I swallow down the urge to breathe in deeper. "And what happens if we get caught?"

"We won't," Asher assures me, raveling a strand of my hair around his finger. "We promise we won't."

"I don't trust genies." A shiver courses through me as East's velvety soft wing strokes the arch of my neck.

"Trust me, then," East whispers in my ear.

I want to push them all away, but my arms remain frozen at my sides.

While I'm usually a badass, the combination of their yummy scents, soft touches, the magic most paranormals emit, along with the poison in my body is making me lightheaded and weak.

"I don't trust faeries, either," I manage to get out.

"Then trust me." Arrow places his hands on my shoulders, his metal fingers cool against my overly warm, poisoned skin. "Cyborgs don't lie."

"I know." I let out a frustrated sigh. "Look, I want to make the deal. Or, well, want might be a strong word. More like, I'm considering. But I need to at least know a little bit about why I'm going to be your own little personal thief. I mean, why can't you just steal these objects on your own? You're paranormals who I'm sure are very powerful."

"These objects are protected with all sorts of curses

and spells to keep paranormals away." Asher lightly tugs on a strand of my hair, drawing my attention to him. "They aren't protected against humans. And since you clearly know your way around thievery, you should be able to get the objects we need."

"Oh." My lips part to fire more questions when the pain of the poison suddenly amplifies.

A cry rips from my throat as I collapse to the floor, tears stinging my eyes. As I claw at the hardwood flooring, I realize both my hands and arms are now green. Further observation reveals my legs are, too.

Has my time come to an end? Is this death I taste in my mouth?

"Make the bargain," Asher says as he crouches beside me, stroking his fingers up and down my back. "Make the bargain, and the pain will go away and your friend will be free."

Gasping breaths rip from my chest as I look into his eyes.

While most genies' gazes carry coldness, Asher's conveys a drop of remorse mixed with guilt. Does he feel bad about what he's doing to me? Would he save me anyway, if I didn't make the bargain?

I'll probably never know the answers because, as the stabbing pain beneath my flesh begins to increase, I surrender to the inevitable and nod.

"Fine," I grit out. "Let's make a bargain."

CHAPTER 5

As soon as I utter the words, Asher scoops me up into
his arms, carries me across the room, and lays me on the
sofa. Then he sinks down onto the edge of the cushion
and rests his hands beside my head.

"I'm going to verbalize the terms of our deal." He
stares into my eyes. "If you have any objections, let me
know, okay?"

With great effort, I nod.

*I can't believe I'm about to do this. I can't believe I'm about
to make a deal with a genie. One day, this is going to come
back and bite me in the ass.*

"Good." His chest rises and crashes as he takes a deep
breath. For a flicker of a moment, he seems nervous, but
the look promptly fizzles as he cups my face between his
hands. "I vow to free your body from the poison and let

you live a long life, just as long as you're able to retrieve three stolen objects of my choosing. I will also free your friend …" He pauses. "What's your friend's name?"

"Jason," I croak out as my veins scorch with agonizing heat.

He nods with a curious look on his face. "And yours?"

I consider lying, but worry that might ruin the bargain. "Harlynn."

He rubs his pale blue lips together. "That's an … interesting name."

"Are you insulting my name?"

"No, I just said it was interesting." Confusion floods his eyes.

"Not a top-quality shelf-worthy name, right?" Why the hell am I arguing with him when I'm on the brink of death? Usually, I'm not this stupid. He just seems to bring the stupidity out of me.

"Hmmm …" is all he says. "What's your last name?"

"Why does it matter?"

"Because it does."

I sigh, too tired to argue with him anymore. "Merringten."

When he swallows audibly, I whisper, "What's wrong?"

"Nothing." Blinking away his puzzlement, he leans closer and wets his lips with his tongue. "I will also free your friend Jason from the underground mafia and remove his debt to them. Your debt will be removed, as well. But, if you do not retrieve the objects by the end of the month, or if you try to break the bargain, all will be erased and yours and Jason's lives will return to how they are at this precise moment." He traces his tongue along his lip piercing. "Do we have a bargain?"

I blow out a deafening breath. My heart rate's insanely fast, and not just because of the poison. No, I'm more freaked out about making a bargain with a genie than anything else. But, as death continues to chew up my insides, I have no choice but to nod and utter, "Yes, we have a bargain."

Hesitancy flickers in his eyes, then he nods and crashes his lips against mine. Heat courses through my body before I have time to react. A heartbeat of an instant later, though, I return to my senses and place my hands on his chest to shove him away. He only presses closer, delving his tongue into my mouth. I gasp as effervescent magic spills from his lips and pours down my throat.

The longer he kisses me, the more the warm, tingly sensation spreads, starting at my lips and working down my chest, all the way to my thighs. As my toes curl, I start to worry that perhaps my reaction isn't solely from the magic.

I like this way too much.

Inhaling through my nose, I wedge my hands between us and shove him back.

"What the hell was that?" I ask as I gasp for air.

Asher blinks dazedly. "That was …" He blinks again, his heated gaze slowly turning cold. "I had to do that to make the bargain." He rises to his feet without looking at me. "We're done here," he tells East then strides past him. "Make sure no one else knows she's in our vehicle." He storms down the hallway and slams a door.

Uncomfortable silence stretches between East, Arrow, and me.

Seriously, what the hell is Asher's problem? He's the one who kissed me, yet he acts like it was *my* fault? Besides, it had to be done to make the bargain, right? I mean, why else would he do it?

"Okay, then." East breaks the silence with a clap of his hands as he turns toward me. "Let's go get you set up in a room, shall we?" He winks. "Preferably next to mine, right?"

I shrug, too confused to care. "Sounds good."

East's expression plummets. "Aw, come on now, sweetheart. There's no need to get all upset over Asher's mood swings."

"I'm not upset," I lie, pushing to my feet. A quick assessment of my arms and legs causes me to sigh in relief. *Well, at least the poison's gone.* "I'm confused as to why he freaked out. I mean, I know he thinks I'm repulsive, but—"

East snorts a laugh. "He doesn't think you're repulsive. That's not what that was about at all."

"Oh, trust me; he does. He made that perfectly clear when I knocked on you guys' door." I frown, more at myself. No, I'm not going to worry about Asher and his genie tizzy tantrums. I couldn't care less if he hates me or not. "That doesn't even matter. None of this does. He can be pissed off all he wants. I just want to know if Jason's okay."

East eyes me over before turning toward Arrow. "Get the Eyes All Mirror, would you?"

Arrow nods, his gaze skimming over me before he vanishes down the hallway.

"What's the Eyes All Mirror?" I lift my hand to fiddle with my earpiece, only to realize it's gone.

So weird. Does that mean the bargain worked?

"It'll show you what you need to see." He plops down on the leather sofa then pats the cushion beside him. "Have a seat. We need to talk."

I keep my feet planted to the floor. "We can talk with me standing right here."

"Yes, but I can't smell your lovely scent from way over there, or stroke your soft skin with my wings." He pats the cushion again with a smile full of trickery. "Now come, have a seat … unless you're too afraid." A dare gleams in his glittering eyes.

I cross my arms. "I'm not afraid of you."

He elevates his brows. "You sure about that?"

"Yes."

"I think you're lying."

"Good for you."

"Yes, good for me. Now come sit down by me. If you don't, I'll talk in circles all night. It's what faeries are best at." He sucks on his bottom lip. "Well, that and making passionate, magical love."

"Oh, for the love of all gods." Shaking my head, I sink down onto the sofa. "Making passionate, magical love? Seriously?"

His lips quirk in mild amusement. "Would you rather me call it fucking?"

Warmth floods my cheeks, one of the worst things a human can do in front of a flirting faerie. East more than notices, too, a grin taking over his face.

"Wait a second." He scoots closer to me. "Is the feisty little Harlynn still a virgin?"

I force myself to meet his gaze. "That's none of your business. And don't call me Harlynn."

"Then what do you propose I call you?" He sweeps my hair away from my shoulder. "Blushing princess? Virgin cheeks? A tasty, little p—"

"Harlynn is fine," I cut him off, holding up my hand, my cheeks on fire. "Look, faerie dude, I'm not here to flirt with you."

"You may not be, but I am," he teases, his wing sliding behind me.

"Can't you just tone it down for a bit?"

"I wish I could, but it's in my nature. Sometimes I don't even realize I'm doing it."

I heave an exasperated sigh. "Well, just know it'll never be reciprocated. I'm not into paranormals."

He radiates glittering amusement and an impish smile. "We'll see." When I frown, his grin widens. "Run away all you want. Eventually, I'll catch you."

Good gods, what the hell was I thinking, making a deal to stay with three paranormals? I should know better. I should've thought of another way. Shouldn't have let the fear of death cloud my judgment.

My remorse in my decision dissipates when Arrow returns to the room with a silver, oval mirror. Black, metal roses frame around the edge, and a magical mist radiates from the reflective glass.

"Just tell it to show you your friend." Arrow carefully hands me the mirror.

I glance at the mirror, shocked by the lack of a reflection. "How do I know this is real?"

"You'll feel the truth." Arrow takes a seat across from me and props his foot onto his knee, watching me with mild interest.

I trace my finger along one of the roses on the mirror,

thinking of my parents. "Will it show me anything I ask for?"

Arrow shakes his head. "It won't show you many things, like the future. Or someone who's dead. But your friend is alive, and as long as you ask to see him in the now, it'll show it to you."

I hide my deflation by peering into the mirror. "Show me my friend Jason—where he is, what he's doing, and if he's okay."

The surface of the mirror ripples, transforming into a scene that makes me smile. Jason is shopping at a bakery we used to always steal from, only he has a basket full of pastries in his hand, along with a wad of money to pay for the items.

"How does he have money to buy pastries?" I glance up at East. "Jason's usually broke."

East smiles musingly. "Asher must have a soft spot for you, if he gave the boy a better life than he had."

"Asher barely knows me." I watch Jason move about the bakery. "And from the whole whopping hour we've spent with each other, he made it pretty clear he doesn't like me, so why would he do this?"

"Perhaps he's trying to make up for what happened to your parents," East utters quietly. "If it's true what you said, that a genie killed them."

"Why would it matter to him? He's not the one who killed them." My gaze stays fixed on the mirror, a longing building in my chest as Jason laughs at something the cashier says.

She's pretty, with long, blonde hair, and big blue eyes. I wish I was with him. Laughing with him. Buying cupcakes with him. I wonder where he thinks I am. I wonder if he misses me. I wonder if he knows about the bargain.

East kicks his feet up on the coffee table and leans back into the sofa. "Here's a word of advice that's going to help you out during your lovely and very wanted time with us." He dazzles me with a grin. "Asher isn't what he seems. And if you're lucky, you'll get to know the real him."

I want to argue, tell him he's wrong, that genies aren't good. But the images reflecting back at me in the mirror complicate my argument.

"Does he remember me?" I change the subject. "Jason, I mean."

East shrugs. "You'll have to ask Asher. I'm not the one who cast the magical bargain."

My heart clenches and a bit of jealousy simmers under my skin as Jason gives the cashier girl a lopsided grin. I'm happy he's happy, I really am, but I've always secretly dreamed of him smiling at me like that. Of me being able to *let him* smile at me like that. However, the curse the genie put on me all those years ago makes it impossible for me to go down that road with anyone. If I do, I'm giving them a death sentence. It means I'll lose them, just like I lost my parents. That they'll end up however my parents did.

"I know you said the mirror won't show me those who are dead, but can I try to ask it about my parents? I've never been quite sure if they are … really gone," I whisper, clutching the handle of the mirror.

A drop of sympathy rises in Arrow's eyes. Again, his human-like mannerisms throw me off. "You can. Just know that, if they are dead, you won't be able to see them."

Nodding, my gaze falls to the mirror. I'm almost afraid to utter the words. If I do, then I'll know for sure they're really gone. And a tiny part of me has always hoped that perhaps the genie just sent them away somewhere.

But the need to know becomes too great.

"Show me my parents," I whisper to the mirror.

The ripples reappear, the images of Jason, the cashier girl, and the bakery fading. I wait for another scene to appear. Wait for the mirror to show me my parents. I wait. And wait. And wait until all I can see is the tears in my eyes.

"Harlynn," East says as a few tears drip onto the empty mirror. He reaches out to place a hand on my arm, but I hurriedly rise to my feet.

"Can you show me to my room now?" I wipe the tears

with the back of my hand, passing Arrow the mirror. "I'd really like to lie down. It's been a long day."

East's eyes are soft, full of pity and concern. "Of course."

He gets to his feet, leading me down the hallway, past all the shut doors. "I'd give you a tour, but I'm pretty sure you know where everything is, right?" He tosses a teasing smile at me from over his shoulder, but his eyes still carry pity.

When I only nod, he sighs.

We make the remainder of the journey to my room silently until we come to a stop at the last shut door.

"What are your favorite colors?" he asks, gripping the doorknob.

"Purple and black … Why?"

His lips move as he murmurs something under his breath. Then he twists the knob and shoves the door open.

The bedroom is almost as big as Asher's. The walls are a deep purple that contrast well with the black hardwood floor that matches the massive bed, dressers, and nightstands. The dome ceiling is painted with glittering silver and violet stars, and along the far back wall is a hologram view of a shimmering field of glowing violets and trees.

"It's Shimmerland," East says when he notes me staring at the hologram image. "It's where I was born."

"It's very pretty," I comment. "Are most faeries from there?"

He shakes his head. "And as pretty as the place is, it's just as dangerous." His flirty demeanor has fizzled into sadness, his eyes layered with fear. "Even more dangerous than your world."

"Then, why did you want me to see it?"

"Because it's where we're going first. I want you to get a head start on what you're getting into." With a snap of his fingers, the scene alters into a foggy forest crammed with creatures with glowing yellow eyes. "Also a part of Shimmerland and where you'll be heading."

I shudder at the sight.

"What're the eyes?"

He opens and flexes his hands. "The Banished."

"The what?"

"I'll explain in the morning and give you more details about that world. For now, get some rest." An ominous look crosses his face. "You're going to need it." He leaves the room, shutting the door behind him.

I swear I heard him whisper, "I'm sorry," before he shut the door completely.

I wonder what he could be sorry for. For forcing me to make the bargain, or for having to go to Shimmerland, a place that, if what I'm seeing on the hologram is correct, appears to be haunted by thousands of beastly creatures with the longest fangs I've ever seen?

CHAPTER 6

I TRY to get some sleep, I really do, but I'm wired. Not to mention it feels strange lying in a comfy bed. I can't even remember the last time I slept in a bed, let alone one that feels as though it was created out of clouds.

After tossing and turning for what feels like hours, I give up and climb out of bed. As I pass by a mirror, I notice a streak of glitter across my cheek. Fey magic, but what kind? I'm not sure.

Just what is that faerie up to?

I wipe the glitter off with my sleeve then wander around the room. To my surprise, the dressers and the closet are filled with clothes exactly my size and match my grungy style, except for a few fancy dresses I'll never wear.

After searching almost every nook and cranny and

not finding anything interesting, I leave the room to see if I can get anything to eat, because I'm starving. Plus, the view on the hologram is psyching me out for what lies ahead.

When I reach the end of the hallway and hear voices, though, I come to a screeching halt.

"She's asleep, then?" Asher asks from the living room.

"She should be," East replies. "I left her in the room and put a little bit of sleeping glitter on her pillow."

That's what the glitter was? Then, why didn't it make me feel tired?

I press my back against the wall to eavesdrop, curious as to why they want me asleep.

"Good. She's going to need a lot of rest," Asher replies in a quiet tone.

"You sound like you feel a bit guilty, Ash," Arrow says. "Do you feel bad for her?"

"Perhaps a little bit." Asher's answer is shocking.

"You have a soft spot for her already," East teases. "In all the years I've known you, I've never seen you warm up to anyone so quickly, let alone a human."

"There's something different about her," Asher mumbles. "I noticed it the moment I opened the door and saw her."

"You think she's not human?" Arrow wonders. "Because, my sensors say she is."

"I'm not sure if that's it," Asher says. "She's definitely different from other humans."

"She's very pretty," East states. "Perhaps she's one of those artificially-created humans."

What? Someone is creating humans?

"She's gorgeous," Asher agrees. "But I think she's real. Just has above-average looks."

Huh?

East snorts a laugh. "I knew you liked her the minute you told her she wasn't top-shelf. You're so fucked up sometimes."

"I panicked," Asher bites out. "She took me off guard, and I don't like surprises."

"I know you don't," East muses. "Except for maybe this one, right? That's why you kissed her for no reason at all?"

I shake my head. *So, he lied about the kiss being part of the bargain.*

Asher doesn't answer him. Instead, he says, "I feel like I know her from somewhere."

"Really?" Arrow wonders. "From where?"

"I'm not sure ... But those eyes of hers ... and her name ... I swear I've met her before. Maybe even talked to her once." Asher gives a brief pause. "I just can't place from where."

The air gets ripped from my chest. Afraid I'll start

gasping, I tiptoe back to my room and lock the door. Then I slide to the floor and hug my knees to my chest.

I've only notably crossed paths with two genies before, besides Asher. Once when my parents were taken away from me, and the other incident was when I thought I was seeking revenge for my parents' death, only to be wrong and get blasted by jinn magic. If Asher is right—if we've met before—then it was during one of those two times. Only, he doesn't resemble either of those genies, so perhaps he's thinking I'm someone else.

What if he's right, though? What if he is connected to one of those genies? What if he's changed his looks since then? Paranormals can use magic to alter their appearances, like the fey and their glamour.

I swallow the lump wedged in my throat. I have no idea what's going on, but I need to get to the bottom of it. And if it turns out he had anything to do with my parents' disappearances, I'll make him pay somehow.

CHAPTER 7

AFTER OVERHEARING ASHER, East, and Arrow's conversation about me, falling to sleep seems impossible. My body is coursing with way too much adrenaline, and my brain is crammed with worried thoughts of why Asher thinks he knows me. Plus, while I hate to admit it, fear is another reason dreamland isn't beckoning me. Yet, somehow between freaking out and bursting with frustration, I must've dozed off because I'm suddenly being shaken awake.

I jolt awake as a cold, steel hand touches my arm. Then I bolt upright with my fists raised, my reaction borne out of instinct. After living on the streets for years, sleeping wherever I can, like behind dumpsters, I've learned that being woken up by someone usually isn't a good sign.

It takes me several blinks to process my surroundings. I'm in the bedroom East created for me, sitting on the floor, and Arrow is standing in front of me with his hands in front of him.

Jeez. After years of dreaming about what it would feel like to sleep in a bed again, I ended up dozing off on the floor.

"I was just trying to wake you up." Arrow eyeballs my raised fists. "I promise I'm not going to hurt you." Despite his mechanical features, his eyes radiate a stream of warmth.

I gradually lower my hands to my lap. "Sorry. You just startled me."

The wheels in his arms turn as he lowers his hands. "That's completely understandable. You're in a strange place with a bunch of strangers. No one can blame you for being on guard."

"You're very understanding for a cyborg." I sweep tangled strands of hair out of my eyes. "Sorry. That was probably rude."

He shakes his head. "Not at all. You've actually been very nice to me."

I start to laugh, then falter at the sight of his serious expression. "You're joking, right?"

"No, I'm not. You've been very nice to me compared to most humans and paranormals. Neither are fans of cyborgs. I think it's because we don't reveal our feelings very well, so we come off as harsh and cold, which in turn, makes others harsh and cold toward us."

I discreetly eye him over. He's dressed in all black, from the leather necklace around his neck to the clunky boots on his feet. He's also wearing a shirt today, so all the gadgets and bronzed metal in his lean arms aren't on full display. I'll admit, he's very attractive for a cyborg. Maybe even good-looking in general.

"You don't look harsh or cold." I stretch my arms above my head and yawn. "And you actually seem pretty emotional to me."

He offers me a small smile. "That's because I'm not an average cyborg."

My brows pull together. "What are you, then?"

Gadgets hum as he winks at me. "A rock star cyborg."

I smile. I can't help it. With Asher's mood swings and Easton's shameless flirting, Arrow seems like the calmest of the three, which makes me feel more at ease.

Rising to my feet, I stretch out my stiff muscles. "You play the drums, right?"

He nods, stuffing his hands into his pockets. "I do."

"Is it fun?"

"Yeah. And relaxing. It's probably the only time I'm ever really relaxed."

"How good are you?" I wave off my question. "Never mind. You wouldn't be in a band if you weren't awesome."

His lips start to spread into a smile, then curve downward as I massage the back of my neck. "Did you not like the bed?" he asks. "If so, East can make you a new one."

I shake my head. "The bed's nice. I'm just not used to having one."

He blinks, looking lost. "A bed?"

I lift a shoulder. "I've lived on the streets for quite a few years, and beds are pretty rare out there."

He slants his head to the side. "Is that normal in your world?"

"For humans, it is." I pause. "Wait. My world? Are you not from here?"

He shakes his head. "Many cyborgs come from the planet Steel." He marches past me and toward the hologram window. The screen is displaying a lavender pool of water stretching between mountains. The scene would be lovely except for the monstrous, fanged beasts looming at the shore. "And we're not in your world anymore. We're in Shimmerland." He lines his palm to the screen. "Show me outside."

The hologram fades and a window pops up on the wall. Beyond the glass, stretching as far as my eyes can see, is a frost-kissed sky. Silver sunlight reflects along a field of shimmering violets and trees. Fortunately, no glowing eyes are peering from the distance, yet I can't help wondering…

"Those fanged beasts on the hologram … are they in those trees?"

"They are. They only come out at night."

I inch toward him. "What do they do, exactly?"

"I … I don't think I should tell you. It may frighten you."

"Am I going into the forest to steal an object for you guys?" As afraid as I am, I've always thought it's better to know what I'm getting into. "Because, if so, I need to know about those beasts so I can at least try to be prepared."

Arrow rubs his lips together, contemplating. "I think maybe I should take you to Asher."

"Can't you just answer me?" I plead.

Wariness creeps into his expression. "I can, but I think it'd be better if Asher tells you."

I frown. "And I think it'd be better if *you* told me. You're much easier to talk to."

A trace of a smile graces his highlighted bronze lips, a startling yet beautiful sight. "As true as that might be, I think you should give Asher a chance."

I elevate my brows. "And why's that?"

"Because, while he may come off intense sometimes, he's actually a really good paranormal. In fact, he's pretty much the only reason I'm standing here and can function."

"What do you mean by that?" I inquire, curious about Arrow, but also about Asher.

He starts back across the room, and then opens the door. "Another story for another time, okay? Right now, we need to get you ready for your first mission, which does require Asher's help."

I suppress a grimace. "Fine, let's go talk to the genie."

He chuckles, as if I'm hilarious, but I'm not trying to be funny. My enthusiasm about talking to Asher is hovering at about a negative one hundred right now. Plus, talking to him means I'm one step closer to endeavoring on my first mission, into the woods filled with creepy beasts. My only hope is that the mission will take place in daylight. Considering the ideal time to steal something is well into the hours of nightfall, though, I'm probably going to see those beasts whether I want to or not.

CHAPTER 8

WE FIND Asher in the kitchen, leaning over the counter and munching on some bacon, eggs, and toast while reading an article on a handheld hologram. East is nowhere to be seen, and Arrow appears eager to leave, shifting his weight as he and Asher stare silently at each other, exchanging a cryptic look.

"I have some stuff to do to prepare for the mission," Arrow announces as he backs toward the door. "When you guys are ready to go, let me know."

I eyeball the two of them. "Can you two speak tele-pathically or something? Is that what all the silent looks are about?"

"No," Asher says at the same time Arrow tells me, "We can actually—"

Asher cuts him off with a sharp look.

Arrow presses his lips together. "See you guys later." He exits the vehicle in a hurry, the door banging closed behind him.

"What was that about?" I ask, plopping down onto a stool at the kitchen island and discreetly eyeballing Asher over.

He's dressed in all black today, with chains embellishing his jeans, and cuffs adorning his wrists. The metal piercings in his face glint in the low lighting and tattoos peek out from his shirt sleeves. He looks like a rock star. That's all there is to it. A sexy, ridiculously beautiful rock star.

"What do you mean?" Asher stares down at the handheld hologram while popping a piece of bacon into his mouth.

My mouth salivates as I inhale the aroma of freshly cooked eggs. I can't remember the last time I've seen bacon and cooked eggs, let alone tasted them.

"I mean, what's up with you guys and those cryptic looks you keep giving each other? And why did you cut Arrow off when I asked about it?" I rest my elbows on the counter filled with sleeping mini water fey and try not to stare at his plate of yummy food.

"Because I don't want you knowing too much about us." He taps the screen of the handheld hologram.

I crinkle my nose. "Well, that's sort of rude."

His gaze flicks to me. "Why would I want you to

know anything about us? You're a thief who already tried to steal from me once." He returns his attention back to the handheld hologram. "The less you know about me and my band, the better."

"That's not really fair. Not when you know …" I sink my teeth into my bottom lip.

I was about to divulge that I overheard him talking about me last night. How he thinks he knows me. But I want to hold on to that secret for now, poke around a bit and gather more information. Announcing that I was eavesdropping on him will only make him put his guard up more.

His curious gaze elevates to me. "When I know what?"

I give a nonchalant shrug. "I don't know. I'm sure you know a lot of things."

He eyes me over dubiously. "You're keeping something from me."

"I'm keeping a lot of things from you."

He sets the handheld hologram down, picks up a fork, and scoops up some eggs, his gaze fixed on me. "You know, I could get every secret out of you if I wanted to."

My back stiffens, yet my voice is smooth and even when I say, "And I'm sure you will at one point or another. You are a genie, after all."

Smoke swirls in his pupils as he sets the fork down and leans forward, his expression as cold as an ice storm. "Are you hungry?"

My lips part to fire a comeback before I realize what he said. "Huh?"

The smoke in his eyes evaporates into sparkling dew. "You've been staring at my food like you're a vampire who hasn't fed in a decade. I'm assuming that means you're hungry."

"No," I lie, my stomach churning in protest. Despite that, I'm not about to take food from a paranormal who already poisoned me once. Or, well, his trunk did. Not to mention I don't want to need anything from him. "I'm not hungry at all."

"Really?" he taunts, bringing a piece of bacon up to his mouth. "That's too bad. It's *really* good." He slowly licks his lips then takes a bite.

I practically drool all over the countertop, for two very different reasons, one of which really pisses me off.

Stop drooling over him! He's a genie, for crying out loud!

"I'm sure it is, but like I said, I'm not hungry."

"Suit yourself." He stuffs the piece of bacon into his mouth.

My stomach growls as a whimper leaves my lips. So much for lying. It's been too long since I've eaten a real meal.

His lips kick up into a smirk, then he devours another piece of bacon. I watch his jaw work as he chews slowly.

"Mmmm …" He presses his lips together and closes his eyes. "It's so damn good."

All my willpower goes right out the hologram window.

"Fine, I might be a little hungry," I pathetically choke out.

His smirk returns as he lifts his eyelids open. "Well, I might be able to get you some breakfast ... if you ask nicely."

I grind my teeth from side to side. "May I please have some breakfast?"

"Well, since you asked so nicely ..." He snaps his fingers and *poof*, a plate stacked with pancakes, eggs, and bacon materializes in front of me.

Surprise flickers inside me. Honestly, I expected him to give me something gross, like oatmeal.

I slant forward and sniff the pancakes. "Blueberry. Holy fuck! I haven't had blueberry pancakes since ..." I trail off as I notice Asher watching me with a crease between his brow. "What?"

He gives a dismissive shrug. "It's nothing. I swear you just remind me of someone. That's all."

"A human?" Maybe he hasn't met me before and is getting me confused with another human.

He shrugs, avoiding my gaze. "Maybe. I'm not really sure."

I pick up a fork and cut into my pancakes. "Have you met many humans?"

"A few."

"How long ago?"

"The meetings were spread out over the years."

"Just how old are you?"

"Older than you."

I roll my eyes. "Thanks for the vague answer. That only leaves, like, a million different ages you could be."

A trace of a smirk plays at his lips as he glances up at me. "I'm pretty sure the oldest genie still living is only five hundred and thirty-three years old, so that only leaves five hundred and thirty-two different ages."

Smartass.

"Well, based on your looks, I'm betting you're somewhere toward the older end." I smile innocently as his eyes narrow into slits.

"You think I look *old*?"

Not really. Okay, not at all. But it's too fun messing with him.

I thrum my fingers against the counter. "I don't know. Maybe. I mean, it's really hard to tell with paranormals, but you have a little bit of crow's feet right here"—I point at the corner of my eye—"so I'm guessing you have to be older. But hey, I'm sure older paranormals can still be considered top-shelf quality."

He smashes his lips together as vibrant flames ignite in his eyes. "I'm seriously starting to wonder how in the worlds you're still alive."

My smile fizzles. "Is that a threat?"

"No, not at all." He slants toward me. "I'm was just trying to say that, with as much as you smart off, I'm surprised no paranormal has ever tried to kill you. Most don't tolerate smart-mouthed humans very well."

I raise a brow. "But you do?"

He gestures at me. "You're here, aren't you?"

My lips twitch as I recall our bargain. "For now."

"I'm not going to kill you, Harlynn. I want you to be safe." His soft tone and firm gaze shocks me speechless. "Now, please eat your breakfast so we can go. The last thing we want is to go into that forest at nightfall."

"Wait. I'm not going at night? Because, from my experience, that's the best time to steal. It makes it less likely that I'll be seen."

"You don't want to be in that forest at nightfall; trust me. And as long as you do exactly what I tell you, you shouldn't get caught." He nudges the plate of food closer to me. "You need to eat up. You're going to need your strength for where we're going."

"I thought the whole point of the deal we made was because you needed me to steal these objects for you, so why would you go with me?"

"I'm not going the entire way with you. I can't. I am going to escort you as far as I can, though."

I stuff a bite of pancake into my mouth. *Oh, my gods, I forgot how good food was.*

"Are East and Arrow going with us, too?"

"Nope. It's just going to be you and me." He surveys my reaction. I'm not sure what sort of face I pull, but a smile graces his lips. "Don't look so scared, little thief. I promise not to bite you while we're in that forest." He turns toward the fridge and opens the door. "All bets are off, though, when we get out."

I flip him the middle finger. His back may be turned to me, but he chuckles as if he has eyes in the back of his head.

"You're blushing," he teases while digging around in the fridge.

"I am not," I lie. The truth is, my skin is flooded with warmth.

Stupid, traitor body.

He chuckles again as he grabs a small, velvet bag from the fridge then bumps the door shut.

"What is that?" I wonder, desperate for a subject change.

He pats the bag. "It's how we're going to break into the forest."

I start to stuff a bite of eggs into my mouth, then freeze. "We're breaking into the forest? You can't just walk in?"

He tucks the velvet bag into the pocket of his black jeans. "Nope. Shimmerland forest is off-limits to all paranormals who haven't been invited in. Since the fey usually only invite their kind inside, Arrow and I can't get in, and East was banished a long time ago."

"So, how am I supposed to get in? I'm not fey, either."

"But you're human."

"Aw, thanks for reminding me. I almost forgot for a second."

He shoots me a playful, dirty look. "You're such a smartass."

"Yeah, so?" I shrug then take a bite of bacon. "Since you already declared you're not going to kill me, I'm going to keep being one."

"Good."

"Huh …? Wait. What?"

He grins. "Because of our band's popularity, most paranormals and humans kiss our asses all the damn time. Everyone acts so fake, and honestly, we've gotten to the point where we don't trust anyone. But with you …" He reclines back against the fridge with his arms crossed. "I've never met anyone more blunt and real."

"Hey, I lied to you, remember?"

"Yeah, so? You also told me the truth … eventually."

The way he's looking at me, as if I'm the most fascinating creature in all the worlds, it makes me squirm.

"I also told you off a ton of times."

"I know." He rounds the island and stops in front of me. His nearness causes me to nearly choke on the bacon in my mouth. "Why do you think East invited you back to our vehicle when we were at the arena?"

I smack my chest as I cough. "Because I'm a smartass?"

He tucks a strand of my hair behind my ear, a bit of confusion flickering across his face. "Because your truthfulness is a breath of fresh air."

I gulp as he pulls away, tracing his fingers along my jawline.

"So, East wanted me here because I'm a truth-telling smartass?"

He nods. "That and he wanted to play with you a bit."

My fingers tighten around my fork. "I'm not a toy. I've already told you guys that."

He cocks his head to the side, his gaze scrolling over me. "Perhaps not, but you'd definitely be fun to play with."

I work to remain neutral as I shovel a bite of eggs into my mouth. "You're very hot and cold."

He shrugs. "Genies aren't known for their calm demeanor."

"No, they're not." Bitterness creeps into my tone.

The flames in his eyes evaporate. "I'm sorry ... about your parents."

"Why would *you* be sorry? You didn't do it, right?" I measure his reaction, but he closes down, a portrait of indifference.

"No, I didn't. But a genie did, and all genies are

connected in one way or another." Before I can even attempt to ask him what that means, he turns on his heels, calling over his shoulder, "Eat your breakfast, then get dressed in something silver and meet me out front."

He disappears down the hallway, leaving me with a dozen questions. Like, why are all genies connected? Why do I have to wear silver? And, what on earth am I stealing?

Mostly importantly, how in the worlds am I going to get into the forest if I'm not fey?

CHAPTER 9

AFTER I WOLF down my breakfast, I head back to my temporary room to change into something silver. After ransacking the closet and dresser, I manage to find a total of one outfit.

"You have got to be kidding me. *This* is what Asher wants me to wear into a forest full of beasts? Jeez. He may say he's not trying to kill me, but this dress completely contradicts that. Or maybe he wants a good laugh, because I'm going to look pretty damn stupid in this." I slip the short, velvet, silver dress off the hanger and pull a face at it.

The straps are thin, and the hem reaches me mid-thigh and has a slit up the side. How in the hell does Asher expect me to steal anything in this? I'll stand out from a mile away. Not to mention running in it is going to be practically impossible.

"Wear it with boots."

I whirl around, pressing my hand to my chest.

East is standing in the doorway, leaning against the doorjamb, with his arms crossed and a tricky smile tugging at his lips. His blond hair hangs in his eyes, a pair of worn jeans hang low on his hips, and he has on a shirt, yet his wings somehow poke out from over his shoulders.

"How long have you been standing there?" I ask, lowering my hand to my side.

He straightens and crosses the room toward me. "Not too long." He stops in front of me, his paper-thin, glittery wings spanning out wider. "Asher isn't trying to kill you. The dress will help you blend in."

"In a forest full of beasts?" I doubt.

"In a faerie forest full of beasts," he stresses. "Every fey, even ones wandering through a forest, usually wear extravagant outfits." He fiddles with the hem of the dress I'm holding. "And we're known for loving and collecting sparkly, pretty things." His gaze lifts to mine, his lips quirking. "So, you better be extra careful. If you cross paths with a faerie, they just might try to keep you."

"You mean, like *you* tried?"

"Not try. *Did*."

I target him with a nasty look that only makes him grin.

For some dumb reason, I almost grin, too.

Dammit, the faerie is wearing on me.

"I'm not here under my own free will," I remind him. "And once I've gotten you guys your objects, I'll be gone and you'll never see me again."

He smirks. "We'll see."

My insides constrict. "We had a bargain. If I get the objects, then I get to leave."

"Yes, but get and want are two different things."

"I'm going to want to leave; trust me."

"We'll see," he repeats, seeming so sure. "I have a feeling you might just end up falling in love with us, and then you're not going to want to leave."

My stomach clenches at the mention of love. "Not likely."

He twirls a strand of my hair around his finger. "Many humans have, you know—fallen in love with paranormals. They have this fascination with how powerful we are, and it makes us nearly irresistible."

Bitterness stirs inside me. Not toward him, but toward the genie who cursed me.

"Well, for your sake, I hope that doesn't happen."

His forehead creases. "Why would you say that?"

I shrug, grinding my teeth. "Let's just say I've been cursed when it comes to love."

He rubs his free hand across his jawline. "That sounds like a lyric from a cheesy love song."

I latch on to the subject change. "Please don't tell me you're going to put it into one of your songs."

He busts up laughing, his fingers falling from my hair.

"What's so funny?" I ask.

He shakes his head, tears of laughter glimmering in his eyes. "It's nothing. I'm just wondering if you've ever heard any of our music."

"No, but why does that matter?"

He presses his palm to his chest, feigning hurt. "Aw, sweetheart, how you wound my heart."

I stare at him blankly, a smile threatening to turn my lips upward.

I don't want to like him. He's a paranormal. He can't be trusted. Plus, he's the biggest flirt I've ever met. Yet, I'm starting to find him amusing. I don't know how to feel about that.

He grins as he notes the look on my face. "If you listen to our songs, you'd realize we're not really cheesy love songs kind of musicians."

I shrug, trying to pretend like I'm not as curious as I am. "Whatever you say."

"Don't pretend like you're not intrigued." His eyes glitter as he snaps his fingers.

Music begins to filter through the room, a low bass mixed with strums of guitar and passionate drumbeats.

"Enjoy," he singsongs as he backs across the room. "And make sure to wear the thigh-high lace-up boots with that dress. You'll be able to walk easier. Plus, it'll show off those killer legs of yours." He winks at me before stepping out of the doorway, pulling the door closed behind him.

As the door clicks shut, Asher's voice rises into the song, mixing with the instruments. His tone is a mixture of low, sultry, and raspy. The lyrics are anything but cheesy, all pain and darkness, and internal and worldly agony. He sings about torture. He sings about loss. He sings about a world painted in shadows. He sings about a world I know.

It makes me wonder if he understands me.

How could he? He's a genie. Isn't he part of what brought the shadows into the human world to begin with?

As much as I don't want to, I find myself getting lost in the music as I peel off my clothes and slip into the dress. The soft material conforms to my body, almost making me feel naked. Adding the thigh-high boots does make me feel more like myself. I also strap on some leather bracelets to feel more comfortable and leave my hair down in an untamed mess of waves. Still, when I look in the mirror, I hardly recognize myself. Probably because I haven't worn a dress in at least a decade. But … I don't know. There's something else, something about the way my face looks, like my eyes seem a bit bigger and sparkly, my lips fuller, my skin smoother.

Maybe East did something to me? Like sprinkled faerie magic on me or something?

I grimace at the thought then head out of the room, scooping up my trusty lock pick on the way. I never do a job without it.

When I reach the living room, instead of walking outside, I crack the door open and listen for any exchange of words that Asher, East, and Arrow might be having. I need something that will help me figure out why Asher thinks he knows me, and why my eyes are sparkling like fireflies right now.

"I'm not so sure about this," East mutters lowly. "Something's not right."

"If we don't send her in, then we won't have the rock, and then we'll never be able to take them down," Asher replies with a sigh. "Is that what you want? For them to continue carrying on with their lives after what they did to our families?"

"No," East utters softly. "But I don't want to put her in danger, either. I mean, what if she's not what we think she is? Then the moment she steps into the forest, chaos is going to break loose."

"She is one," Asher assures him. "It's all she could be."

"Not necessarily. She could be something rare and Arrow's sensors just can't recognize her, so they just associate her with something she resembles."

"That seems like a really big stretch."

"But a possibility." East pauses. "You said you thought you knew her?"

"I don't know …" he murmurs. "Sometimes it feels like I do, but not all the time."

"She said something strange to me while we were in her bedroom," East says. "When I suggested that she could end up falling in love with all of us."

Asher lets out a low laugh. "I really doubt that's going to happen."

"We'll see," East quips. "We're getting off the point. My point is that, when I suggested her imminent falling in love with us, she told me that, for my sake, she hopes that doesn't happen."

"Perhaps she's not amused with your flirting."

"No, it wasn't like that. It was more like a warning."

"A warning for what?"

"I'm not sure. She was pretty vague."

A murmuring breeze fills up the silence that stretches between them.

"Perhaps you should …" Asher starts.

"You think I should?" Hesitancy laces East's voice.

"I don't want you to," Asher mumbles quietly, "but I think it's for the best."

My fingers curl around the door handle. Just what are they up to?

I wait for them to continue, but they grow strangely quiet.

After about five minutes of maddening silence, I give up, push out the door, and step outside into Shimmerland, the first world I've ever been to besides Endlessland.

The pale light glistening from the sky is alarmingly bright, and I instantly squeeze my eyes shut.

"Ow," I gripe.

"Good faerie gods," East mumbles from close by. "That's just ridiculous."

"I'm not used to this brightness, okay?" I defend my reaction. "The sunlight here isn't like in my world."

East chuckles. "That's not what I meant."

I crack an eyelid open and find him standing in front of me with a look of pure wonderment on his face.

"Why are you looking at me like that?"

He shrugs, his eyes sparkling like the sky. "Because you're glowing."

I squint down at my hands, and my jaw nearly smacks the iridescent ground.

"Why is my skin shimmering?"

"Because we're in Shimmerland where everything shimmers," he teases, his gaze sweeping up and down my body. "The look suits you, sweetheart."

I rotate my arms over, examining the glassy appearance of my skin. "I'm not sure I agree with you."

Asher moves up beside me, lightly wrapping his fingers around my wrist. He skims his finger along the inside, watching as my flesh swishes like floating glitter. "Pulchra mirantibus."

"What does that mean?" I ask, fighting back a shiver brought on by his touch.

"Yeah, Ash, what does that mean?" East mocks with a smirk.

Asher blasts him with a fiery death glare, his fingers leaving my wrist. "We should get going." He begins hiking away from us and across the flowery field toward the trees.

"Man, genies are moody." Sighing, I start after him, when East captures my elbow.

"Just a second. You're missing one thing." Lifting his hand to his mouth, his cheeks puff as he blows a breath. Glitter appears out of nowhere, sprinkling all over my face and shoulders.

I cough, wiping my cheeks with the back of my hand. "What? I wasn't sparkling enough already?"

His lips twitch as he shrugs. "Just thought I'd make you extra sparkly and delicious."

I dust the glitter off my hands. "Are you trying to get The Banished to eat me or something?"

Frowning, he shakes his head. "I'd never wish such a treacherous death on anyone, let alone my new toy." He grins as my eyes narrow. "Don't worry; I can be your toy, too."

"Oh, for the love of faeries." I walk toward Asher, who

came to a stop in the middle of the field and is watching us.

"Why did you say that, for my sake, you hope you don't fall in love with me?" East calls out after me.

I smash my lips together as it clicks into place. The glitter must've been some sort of truth magic. That's what Asher and he are up to. They're using magic to force me to tell them the truth.

I mentally curse all paranormals as my lips part. "Who knows? Sometimes I just say stuff. Honestly, you really shouldn't pay much attention to anything I say."

East's brows knit. "Are you sure that's the reason?"

I nod. *Huh. Maybe I was wrong about what the glitter was.*

When East trades a perplexed look with Asher, I question if the glitter was exactly what I thought it was and it just didn't work on me. Just like the sleeping glitter Easton put on my pillow.

Why isn't his magic working on me? Magic has worked on me before. What's different about me now?

"Can I go now?" I ask East. "Or do you want to blow more glitter in my face?"

"I don't know …" He nibbles on his bottom lip, his worried gaze straying to Ash. "Maybe she shouldn't go."

With a sigh, Asher backtracks toward us, his boots crushing the glassy flowers. "We already talked about this." His gaze bores into East. "We need that rock."

I dust some glitter off my neck. "This seems like a lot of trouble to get a simple rock."

Asher glances at me. "It's not just a rock. It's the Rock of Forthcoming Magic. And once we get it working, it'll warn us of any magic coming our way."

I adjust the bottom of my dress. "Do you expect a lot of magic to come your way?"

He nods. "We have a plan to take on—"

"What are you doing?" East hisses, glancing around the field nervously. "Don't discuss that shit out here."

"I didn't mean to …" Asher rakes his hand through his hair. "I have no clue why I said that."

East breathes loudly as he scans the trees. "I can't believe you just did that. You're usually so careful."

"I know. I swear it was like my tongue was being controlled or something. Like I had to answer her question …" His gaze zeroes in on me.

So do East's.

I step back. "Why are you guys looking at me? I didn't do anything."

Asher glances at East, who nods with his jaw set tight.

Asher strides toward me, taking long, determined steps. I turn to run, although I'm unsure of where I'm going since I'm in an unfamiliar world full of faeries that East insists are going to want to eat me up.

I make it a whole two steps before Asher loops his arm around my waist.

"Let me go!" I shout as he picks me up and slings me over his shoulder. The cool breeze hits my butt as my dress rides up. My eyes widen as I reach back and tug the hem down.

"No." Asher marches toward the world jumper vehicle. "Not until we talk."

"We can talk without you carrying me," I gripe, smacking his back with my free hand.

"No, we can't." He throws open the door to the vehicle and storms inside.

East trails at our heels with his head angled to the side. "What are you, sweetheart?" he whispers so lowly I barely hear him.

"I'm *human*," I annunciate. "Have been since the day I was born."

East's eyes enlarge. "You shouldn't have been able to hear me while I was speaking in that frequency."

I sweep my hair out of my face. "You sounded like you were talking normally to me."

Worry creases his perfect features. "Asher?"

"I heard." Asher sets me down on the sofa then puts his hands on his hips and stares down at me. "Who are you, little thief?"

"I'm Harlynn." My voice drips with sarcasm as I rearrange my dress into place. "We already went over this, remember? While we were doing the bargain."

East plops down on the armrest, his eyes sparkling with fascination. "Is it one of your tricks?"

"Is what one of my tricks?" I literally have no clue what's going on, other than I did something that apparently implied I'm not human. Whatever it was has them spooked.

"You reflected my magic," East tells me, measuring my reaction closely.

"Um, no, I didn't," I deny. "I didn't even know you could do that."

"Most can't." He places his hand on the back of the sofa as he leans in, his wings cocooning around me. "But certain paranormal species can. Most of them are rare and unheard of. But the question is: which one are you?"

I try to recline away from him, but his wings secure me in place. "I'm human. I swear I am."

Asher shakes his head. "There's no way you can be. Humans can't reflect fey magic on other paranormal creatures like you just did to me. It's why I was about to tell you …"

"Tell me what? The truth? Like how you tried to use magic to get me to tell you the truth?" I cross my arms and stare him down.

"Yes," he answers with a drop of shame. "But instead, *I* almost ended up telling *you* the truth." He moves closer to me, his eyes darkening. "What did you do to me?"

My mind drifts back to the day I lost my parents and the genie cursed me. My body was so hot I thought I was going to start on fire. Then the genie ignited into flames himself instead and asked me what I'd done, just like Asher is now.

"What is it?" Asher presses, his gaze never wavering from mine.

I shake my head. "It's nothing."

He momentarily searches my eyes then sinks down on the sofa beside me. "If you know something, you can tell us. We won't hurt you."

A hollow laugh escapes my lips. "You guys tried to use magic to trick me into telling you my secret. How the hell does that scream *trust me?*"

"That was a bad decision on our part," Asher agrees with a nod. "But I promise you, you can trust us. In fact, I'll even make a bargain with you."

"To let me go?" I ask with hope. "I mean, if you guys don't think I'm human, then what's the point of keeping me, right?"

Asher shakes his head. "Whatever you are, you're rare enough that you still come off as human, so you should be able to steal the objects we need." He scoots closer to me, and so does East, sliding off the armrest and onto the cushion. "I'll make you a bargain. Whatever you tell us will stay between us. We won't use anything you say against you. We won't get upset. And we won't hurt you in any way."

While I'm human and have virtually nothing important to tell them, making the bargain is enticing. After all, it'd give me security that none of them could hurt me. Although, I'm unsure they would. Well, I'm pretty sure East and Arrow wouldn't. Asher's still a bit iffy.

"I really don't know much," I tell Asher. "But I'll tell you what I do know if you make the bargain."

He nods, wetting his lips with his tongue. "Okay."

"And you have to tell me one of your secrets, too," I add. "A secret of my choosing."

Wariness floods his expression. "What do you want to know?"

I lift a shoulder. "I'll let you know after we strike the bargain."

He deliberates. "All right, in exchange for you telling us what you know about your strange abilities, I'll reveal one secret about me of your choosing. We won't use anything you say against you, we won't get upset, and no harm will come to you. Do we have a bargain, Harlynn?"

I replay his words then nod. "We have a deal."

He nods, too, and then his mouth crashes against mine. He parts my lips with his tongue as I clutch his shoulders, my heart racing like a cracked-out hummingbird. For a moment, I get lost. For a moment, I let him kiss me deeply. For a moment, I like the feel of his warm lips against mine and the way he slides his hand around my back. Then I remember what I overheard. How kissing isn't really part of making a genie bargain.

I shove him away, panting for air, my lips tingling. "Why do you keep doing that?"

His eyelids flutter open, his eyes glazed over. "Doing what?"

"Keep kissing me." I swallow hard, ignoring the fluttering in my chest brought on from the kiss. "I know it isn't part of the deal. I heard East say so."

Asher's lips sink into a frown. "When?"

I take a few measured breaths, my heart continuing to soar like a lunatic. "Last night while you guys thought I was sleeping."

"But my magic …" East stares at me in astonishment. "Fuck, it didn't put you to sleep, did it?"

I shake my head. "No. And I don't appreciate you trying to dope me up."

"I wasn't trying to dope you up, sweetheart," East insists. "I was trying to help you rest. You looked exhausted."

"Well, thanks, I guess." Confusion dances through me. I'm not sure whether to be angry or touched by his gesture. And that uncertainty is even more puzzling. "For the record, I'm not a fan of drugs."

"Because of your friend?" East asks, and I nod. "All right."

I return my attention back to Asher, only to find him

staring at my lips as if he wants to devour them. It makes it hard to breathe, and my voice sounds a bit wobbly as I say, "How do you know me? Because I also overheard you say that you thought you did."

He tears his gaze off my lips and focuses on my eyes. "Is that the secret you want to know?"

I nod. "Yes."

His throat muscles work as he swallows hard. "I'm not exactly sure yet, but perhaps, if you tell me what you are, it might strike my memory."

"I don't know what I am," I answer truthfully. Then words start pouring out of my mouth, under no control of my own. Damn genie bargain magic. "There was this one time, right after that genie killed my parents, that something strange happened. He had just cursed me. It was an awful curse, too."

"What was the curse?" Asher asks, looking a bit pale.

"That when I truly fall in love with someone, they're going to end up like my parents, which means they're going to turn into dust and blow away to who knows where." Tears sting my eyes, yet the magic of the bargain keeps me talking. "Anyway, after he cursed me, I felt like I was going to combust. I was so hot, but then I suddenly wasn't. Then the genie burst into flames and asked me what I'd done." I release a deafening breath as I slump back in the sofa. "Holy shit, I've never told anyone about that. Not even Jason."

"What did this genie look like?" Asher asks, placing a hand on my knee.

"He was tall, with heavily tattooed arms and raven black hair," I reply automatically. "And he had these weird bluish-purple tinted eyes, like the color at the bottom of a flame."

Asher squeezes his eyes shuts, now gripping my knee.

"Fuck," East mutters, rubbing his hand across his forehead.

I glance back and forth between them. "What is it?"

Asher presses his fingers to the brim of his nose. "The genie who cursed you and took away your parents … he was—is—my father."

CHAPTER 10

IF IT WEREN'T for the bargain, I'd run. But, since the bargain protects me from any harm, I stay on the sofa, needing answers.

"How do you know that for sure?" I ask, my voice strained.

His father killed my parents? His father cursed me? His father was the genie who ruined my life?

"Because my father is the only genie with that color eyes." Asher lowers his hand from his nose and stares out the window, avoiding my gaze. "And it explains how I know you."

"How does that explain how you know me?" My voice trembles with rage.

His father killed my parents. Oh gods, I feel sick.

Asher's chest rises and crashes as he releases a

stressed breath. "About seven or eight years ago, my father put a curse on me."

"I was cursed about eight years ago, too," I say absentmindedly.

He meets my gaze. "I know."

My anger morphs into confusion. "How?"

I see flames rise in Asher's eyes then he looks away, the muscles in his jaw ticking. "Because he cursed me with the same curse."

"You've never been in love before?" I question skeptically.

"Who really knows?" He shrugs, staring at the floor.

"You should know if you have," I say, feeling a twinge of pity for him, knowing what it's like to never have been in love. To know that I never will be without awful repercussions. "From what my parents told me, love isn't the sort of thing you're not sure you've ever felt before."

"Well, then I guess I've never felt it before," he snaps. Then his voice softens. "I'm sorry. I shouldn't be taking this out on you. This is in no way your fault."

"It's fine." I place a hand on his knee, feeling even more sorry for him. Who would've thought me, the girl who despises genies, would pity a genie? I guess there's a first time and right circumstance for everything. "I get it. That curse has haunted me for eight years. I have to worry about every person I get close to and worry if I'm going to end up killing them."

He stares down at my hand on his knee, then his gaze drags up to my face. "So, my father didn't tell you who you'd fall in love with?"

"No, just that I would." I pause. "Did he tell you?"

Shaking his head, he looks away and rubs his hand across his face. "This is so fucking unbelievable. I mean, I knew my father was fucked up, but this ..." He shakes his head again, his gaze welding with mine. "I'm sorry about your parents. I really am. I know that doesn't make it better, but I promise that one day my father will pay for all the wrongs he's done. It's part of the reason we need that rock."

"To get rid of your father?" I like the idea probably way too much. I've wanted to do it myself since the day he took my family away and cursed me with a loveless future.

Asher nods, resting his hand on my knee. "Well, him and a handful of other powerful and corrupt paranormals."

Suddenly, journeying into that forest with the beasts sounds appealing.

"I want to help."

Asher eyes me over. "With killing my father?"

I nod. "I made a vow the day he took my parents away that, if I ever have the chance, I'd make him pay." I push to my feet. "So, how about we get going on stealing that rock thingy?"

East snatches ahold of my hand as I start to walk toward the door, his lips tugging into an amused smile. "As much as I love your enthusiasm to slay Asher's father, we need to find out what you are before we send you out into those trees."

"Why? You said I registered as a human." I try to wiggle my arm from his grip, but he tows me back down onto the sofa. I heave a dramatic sigh. "Come on; quit wasting time."

East chuckles, glancing at Asher. "You're lucky."

"Not if we can't fix it," Asher mutters, staring at the window again.

"We'll fix it," East reassures him, tangling his fingers through mine. "Until then, I'm still going to play."

Asher glares at East. "You seriously love pushing my buttons sometimes."

East's smile is all sorts of wickedness. "Of course I do. But, I'll tell you what, if you just say it aloud, I'll stop."

I attempt to tug my hand from his, to no avail. "Will someone please tell me what in the worlds you two are talking about?"

East smiles at Asher. In return, Asher glares back.

"We're talking about nothing," Asher replies, I think to me, but it's hard to say for sure since he's glaring at East. "Now, can we please talk about how we're going to figure out what Harlynn is?"

"I might know a way." Arrow walks in from outside. "But it'll take a few days."

"Were you standing out there the entire time?" East asks Arrow with his brow curved up.

Arrow shrugs, stuffing his hands into the back pockets of his jeans. "I didn't want to interrupt, so I just listened. Figured I'd save you guys some time filling me in."

East muses over something. "You cyborgs, always thinking ahead."

"You should try it sometime," Arrow jokes with a ghost of a smile.

East dismisses him with a flick of his wrist. "Nah, that's way too boring for my taste." He leans back in the sofa, still holding my hand and pulling me with him.

"So, what's your plan?" Asher asks Arrow, his breath tickling my shoulder.

I turn my head toward him, finding him so close our lips nearly touch. I slant back automatically, only to bump into East. Seriously, these guys have issues with personal space.

"The steel books," Arrow replies with a hint of hesitancy.

Asher quickly shakes his head. "It's too dangerous."

"It might be the only way to find out what she is." Arrow crosses the room and sinks down into a chair across from us.

"And who's supposed to go get it?" Asher asks, sliding his arm across the back of the sofa behind me. "From what I understand, they're nearly impossible to get."

"I'll go get them," Arrow replies, the wheels in his arms craning as he shrugs. "I know some cyborgs who live inside the city. They might be able to get me in."

"What are these steel books?" I interrupt. "And where are they exactly?"

"The steel books contain all the knowledge and history of our worlds, including all the various types of paranormals," Asher explains. "They're also locked up in Planet Steel and, like I said, nearly impossible to get to."

"Nearly, but not impossible," Arrow insists, propping his boot onto his knee.

"It's too dangerous," Asher insists. "Remember the last time you were in your world."

For a flash of an instant, fear sparks in Arrow's eyes.

My heart constricts in my chest. Out of the three of them, Arrow has been the kindest to me.

"If it's dangerous, maybe he shouldn't go," I chime in. "Maybe there's a better, less dangerous way to find out what I am." Although, I'm still not even sure I believe this whole idea that I'm not human. I've never shown any signs of magic. And other than my ability to steal, and apparently, occasionally reflect fey magic, I've never been extraordinary at anything.

"You're worried about him?" Asher asks me, brushing strands of my hair away from my shoulder.

I shrug. "Why wouldn't I be? He seems nice, and I don't want him to die just so we can figure out if I'm some strange creature."

Asher's lips quirk. "The little smartass thief has a kind heart."

"So, I'm kind, a smartass, a thief, and blunt. Good to know you're keeping track of all my lovely traits." I dazzle him with a smirk. "I must be super fascinating."

"Perhaps." He absentmindedly plays with my hair.

I want to duck away from him but, since East is hovering close to my other side, there's nowhere to go. And Arrow is sitting right in front of me. I'm surrounded by them again. Surrounded by paranormals. Yet, for some crazy reason, fear isn't spiking through me.

"I won't die." Arrow holds my gaze. "It takes a lot to kill a cyborg."

I open my mouth to protest, but East talks over me.

"I'll go with him," he says. "Between the two of us, we should be able to pull it off. Although, we're going to be late for our next tour stop."

"You guys are still on tour?" I shiver as Asher's fingers graze my shoulder. *Why in the weirdo genies does he keep touching me?*

"We're almost always on tour." East winks at me. "If

you're lucky, maybe we'll let you come see us play. I know how much you love our music."

He doesn't give me a chance to protest, jumping right into planning how they're going to steal the steel books. It doesn't really matter anyway, since the truth is I do like their music. May even like *them* a little bit, too. But my feelings are conflicted.

Is it wrong to like paranormals? Especially paranormals who know the genie who took my parents away from me? I don't know the answer. Maybe I never will. All I can hope for is that I'll at least get revenge for my parents' deaths.

CHAPTER 11

It's not until I've wandered back to my room that a random thought occurs to me.

Asher never explained how he knew me.

Sure, he told me that his father cursed him with the same curse he put on me, but that still doesn't explain why he thought I looked familiar.

Damn evasive genies.

Needing the answer, I abandon changing and head back to the living room to demand some answers. Again, the sound of voices makes me pause before I reach the end of the hallway.

"So, she's the girl your father showed you?" East asks. A pause drifts by, and then he says, "I can't believe it."

I press my back to the wall and listen, surprised

they're talking about me since they're aware of my little eavesdropping habit.

"Actually, I can believe it," East continues over the lovely sound of guitar strings being plucked. "She's sort of perfect for you, in a weird, twisted way."

"My father always did love fucking with me," Asher replies tightly as music flows through the air.

"Aw, don't pout, Ash," East teases. "Deep down, you know you're not disappointed. I saw that look in your eyes. You like our little questionable human."

"No, I don't," he snaps as the guitar strumming stops. "And even if I did, I couldn't admit it. She'll die if I do."

"Only if you fall in love with her."

"According to the curse my father showed me, I will. And then I'll have to hold her in my arms while I watch her die." Asher hastily clears his throat as he starts to choke up. "Just like I watched my mother die."

A wave of pain, sadness, and anger tears through me, nearly ripping the air from my lungs.

Asher's father didn't just curse him? He showed him how the curse was going to play out? That he'd fall in love with me then watch me die? Like he watched his mother die?

"We're going to change the outcome," East promises. "I swear we will."

"I just don't want … to see her die." Asher's voice wavers. "I already feel … different about her."

"But different isn't love, so we still have time," East reminds him. "Although, we should probably be more careful about what we say. She can hear different pitch frequencies. Just another thing that makes me question if she's human."

Silence briefly stretches between them, and then the music begins playing again.

"So, I think we should start working on some new songs," Asher says, and then they jump into a conversation about the band.

I tiptoe back to my room, my legs shaking as I shut the door. My mind races a million-faerie wing flutters a second as I sink to the floor and process what I heard.

Asher is going to fall in love with me, and then I'm going to die.

I'm going to die.

I'm going to fall in love.

I gulp, unsure which one frightens me more.

I can't let that happen. Can't fall in love, with anyone, let alone a genie.

I'll find a way to stop this, I vow to myself. *Somehow.*

Deep down, I understand I may not have any control over the outcome. Love isn't always controllable. I may not want to fall in love, and I can fight it with every breath I take, but in the end, I could lose. And then I'll lose everything.

CHAPTER 12

GENIES ARE SO ANNOYING. Huge pains in the asses. Faeries aren't that fabulous either, at least not as much as they seem to think they are. Cyborgs are cool, but they do like to participate in dirty, little lies that could hurt someone.

I know I sound like a straight-up bitch, but I'm going through some stuff, okay? Like how I just discovered I may not be human. Or a normal human anyway. And that the genie who made my parents vanish and cursed me to never be able to fall in love also cursed his own son with a similar curse. Only, he gave Asher the great pleasure of seeing who his demised lover will be, and apparently, the lucky dead girl walking is moi.

Le sigh. I don't understand how me, hater of all genies and most paranormal creatures, is supposedly going to fall in love with a genie then die in his arms.

Sure, Asher isn't as awful as his father or other genies I've crossed paths with, and I feel terrible for what his father has done to him, but he still has a way of working underneath my skin. Like, for instance, right now.

I already woke up in a really bad mood. Then the moment I stepped foot into the kitchen, my irritation grew the instant Asher opened his mouth.

"Are you going to make me do this every time I want to eat?" I huff an exasperated breath. "If so, you seriously have control issues."

He's standing on the opposite side of the kitchen island, wearing a pair of black jeans that hang low on his hips, with chains dangling from the pockets. He may be completely irritating, but I have to admit he's sexy.

Dammit, why do genies have to be so sexy? It'd make my despising him so much easier if I wasn't attracted to him.

Asher slants forward, resting his arms on the glass countertop filled with mini water fey blowing glittery bubbles. "All you have to do is say please. I don't see what the big deal is."

"It's not a big deal. I just wanted to point out that you're a control freak, just in case you weren't aware."

"Oh, I'm well aware." He plucks up a piece of sausage from the plate in front of him, sticks it into his mouth, then licks his lips clean.

My mouth salivates, but I refuse to say please. I refuse to let him win.

Yesterday when he did the same thing to me, I quickly caved. Today, though, I'm feeling pretty stubborn, mostly because of what I found out last night about Asher's curse. Between his curse and mine, I highly doubt I'm going to fall in love anytime soon, which makes me feel super sulky.

Sure, I already knew I couldn't fall in love, but now it seems even more impossible.

"You seem particularly moody this morning." Asher glances down at his handheld device. "Any particular reason?"

"Um, yeah, because an *old*, douchebag genie refuses to let me eat breakfast."

When his gaze snaps up to mine, I offer him a sugary sweet smile.

His eyes darken as he sets the handheld device down. "You know, that's twice you've called me old. Most genies would've gotten rid of you by now."

"It's a good thing you need me then, isn't it?" I casually slide my arm across the countertop toward his plate in a lame attempt to steal a piece of sausage.

As my fingers graze the edge of the plate, he moves it out of my reach.

"Say the magic words, little thief, and I'll give you the

best breakfast that's ever passed across those pretty lips of yours."

I mentally roll my eyes at his cheesiness. Between him and East, I'm on cheesy overload.

"The best breakfast I've ever had?" I draw my hand back to my lap. "That bar isn't too high since most of my breakfasts came from dumpster diving."

Curiosity sparkles in his eyes. "What's dumpster diving?"

"Digging food out of a dumpster."

His face twists in disgust. "You've eaten food out of a trash can before?"

My jaw ticks, but not necessarily because of him. "Starvation sometimes leads to having to take drastic measures. like digging food out of a trash can."

"I'm sorry you had to go through that." He *almost* sounds genuine.

"Why? It wasn't your fault." I eyeball his food again, on the verge of giving in and begging.

I'm so hungry.

"Perhaps." He wavers his head from side to side. "Maybe it is, though. I mean, my father took your parents away from you, which led to you living on the streets, right?"

My chest constricts at the reminder. "I was dumpster diving when my parents were still around. Not that much, but ... Starvation is—was pretty unavoidable. And

I'm sure it'll still be after I steal these objects for you and my life goes back to normal." I wait to see if he'll divulge why he's said more than a handful of times that he feels like he knows me. See if he'll admit he's cursed to fall in love with me, only to watch me die.

I doubt it. No, the only way to get the truth around here is to listen in on conversations. And with East and Arrow about to endeavor to the planet Steel, Asher will have no one to chat with, so my resource for getting information will be long gone. Probably doesn't matter anyway. Ever since they discovered I have the ability to hear other pitch frequencies, they've started being careful about what they say.

"When your life goes back to normal, huh?" A pucker forms between his brows.

"What? Is it not going to?" I challenge. "Because we made a deal that after I stole these objects for you, you'll set me free, remember?"

"Of course I remember. In fact, I'm counting down the days until our bargain is completed." He smirks when I glare at him. "However, I wouldn't be surprised if you got so attached to us that you wanted to stay. Humans can be rather clingy."

"Well, according to you guys, I may not be human." I grin haughtily. "So, I guess that doesn't apply to me. It's probably why I had such an easy time turning down you guys' offer to come back to your world jumper vehicle when we were back at the arena."

"Doubtful. I think you just wanted to make sure the vehicle was empty so you could try to steal my lamp." His pierced, pale blue lips kick up into a smirk. "And other creatures can be clingy, too. I'm betting you're one of them." He reclines against the counter behind him, crossing his arms and grinning as I flip him the middle finger. "What? It's true. I can't tell you how many times a groupie has fallen in love with the band and wanted to come on tour with us. It's pretty pathetic, if you ask me."

"I'm not a groupie or a fan of paranormals, so I doubt that's going to be a problem," I quip, sneaking a glance at his plate of food. "Plus, I find you guys super annoying."

He's far enough away that I might be able to snatch the plate and run, if I'm sneaky enough. Well, unless he blasts me with a curse. But from what I've seen, Asher doesn't possess normal genie cruelty. And as far as I can tell, he loathes using his magic.

"If you say so." Doubt twinkles in his smoky eyes. "You've only been with us for a couple days, though."

"Yeah, so?" I arch my brow, carrying his gaze in an attempt to distract him as I discreetly slide my arm across the countertop.

"So, you'll more than likely be with us for at least a couple months, which leaves a lot of time for your feelings to change."

"Ha, I highly doubt that's going to happen. And why the hell would you even want my feelings to change after what you found out about me …" My eyes suddenly pop wide. "Wait. Back the hell up. A couple *months*?" I shake my head, pulling my arm back. "No, no, no, no, no. There's no way I can be stuck on this world jumper vehicle with you guys for a couple months. I'll lose my mind! We have to find a faster way to do this. Like, how can we shave off some time?"

He searches my eyes for worlds knows what. "With all the stops we have to make, including the planet Water, which takes over three weeks of traveling to get there, a couple months will be pushing it already."

My expression sinks. "Isn't there a shortcut?"

"That traveling estimate *is* with taking shortcuts. The only other way to get through this quicker would be to teleport, and since none of us are witches, that's impossible."

My lips tug into an even deeper frown. "Don't you know any witches?"

He stares at me for an unnerving amount of time before pushing away from the counter. Then he strolls around the kitchen island and comes to a stop unsettlingly close to me. "We do know a few witches, but no one can know what we're up to, Harlynn. Asking for outside help means dealing with questions and leaving tracks behind, which could lead to us getting caught."

I tilt my head up to meet his gaze, my hair cascading down my back. "But you told me about your plan. Well, some of it."

He leans in, his eyes darkening with smoke. "Yes, little thief, but I swore you to secrecy with magic. Plus, you have a lot riding on us succeeding."

True. If I don't succeed, or if I try to double-cross these guys, not only will I die, but so will Jason.

"You know, I really wish you'd just tell me exactly what you guys are up to, instead of feeding me bits and pieces."

He lowers his head, his lips dangerously close to mine. "If I told you, then I'd have to keep you. And from what you just told me, you don't want that … right?"

My heart thunders in my chest, for various reasons. One reason has a lot to do with how delicious he smells, like cupcakes and frosting.

Dammit, I'm getting so hungry I just might bite him.

A low chuckle reverberates from his chest. "Go ahead."

I blink. "Huh?"

A cocky grin tugs at his lips. "Take a bite out of me. I won't mind."

Oh, my ditzy unicorns, did I say that aloud?

"I didn't mean that in, like, a sexual way," I say in an attempt to salvage some dignity. "I meant, bite you aggressively so you'll go away and I can eat."

Rubbing his lips together, he nudges my legs open with his knee.

"Hey, what the hell—"

In the snap of a magical wish, he's positioned himself between my legs and has an arm on each side of me, his lips dipping close to mine. "Has anyone ever told you that you're a terrible liar?"

"No, because I'm not." Like a boss, my voice comes out even. "In fact, back on the streets, my nickname was Miss Perfect Liar."

He cocks a brow, tucking a strand of hair behind my ear. "Is that true?"

I steadily hold his gaze, ignoring the flutters going mad crazy inside my chest.

Stupid flutters. They need to chill the eff out and stop getting all excited over stupid genie touches.

"If I'm such a terrible liar, like you implied," I say evenly, "then you should already know the answer to that."

He presses his lips together, struggling not to smile. "I guess so." His gaze descends to my mouth and, holy crazy troll babies, I think he is considering kissing me.

If he does, I'm for sure going to slap him.

I think so anyway …

Okay, okay, I don't know what I'll do, and I never get to find out, because East and Arrow stroll into the room and ruin the moment.

"Well, well, well, this looks interesting." East scans over the distance—or lack of—between Asher and me. His glittery wings are spanned out, and he's dressed in black pants and a matching shirt, his blond hair a perfectly styled mess.

Asher's gaze flicks to mine, and then he pushes away from me and turns to East. "Harlynn and I were just arguing about breakfast."

"Sure you were." East gives Asher a knowing smile.

Shaking his head, Asher wanders back to the other side of the kitchen and collects his handheld device. "When are you guys taking off?"

East gives me a look that I don't bother trying to decipher, then he strolls over to the fridge. "Pretty soon. We just need to grab some supplies."

"Don't forget to grab some extra faerie dust," Arrow says as he takes a seat on the barstool beside mine. His arms that are spun of flesh and bronzed gadgets flex as he crosses his arms on top of the counter. "Are you hungry?" he whispers lowly to me.

How did he know?

I nod. "Starving actually."

"What are you two whispering about?" East asks us as he turns away from the fridge with two small velvet bags in his hand. "And why the hell can't I hear you?"

A small smile pulls at Arrow's lips. "Because we're

speaking in a frequency only cyborgs can hear and speak."

Asher's gaze zeroes in on Arrow. "So, not only can she hear other frequencies, she can speak them, too?"

Arrow shrugs. "Apparently."

Asher sets the handheld device down, his gaze flicking between me and Arrow. "How did you know she could do that?"

Arrow gets to his feet, the gadgets covering his body gearing up as he lifts his arms above his head and stretches. "I had a hunch and decided to test out the theory." He rounds to the other side of the island, opens a cupboard, and pulls out a tall, bronzed box.

Asher frowns. "I was going to take care of that. We were just working up a deal first."

"There's no room for deals. She needs to eat about twice as much until her body adjusts to world traveling." Arrow sets the box down in front of me, earning a nasty look from Asher.

Whatever's in this box has got Asher's panties all twisted up in a bunch.

That makes me smile.

East rests his arms against the countertop as he grins at me amusedly. "What's causing those beautiful lips to smile, sweetheart?"

See, cheesy overload again.

"Oh, nothing." My smile grows as Asher's annoyance

doubles. Then I turn to Arrow. "So, what's in the weird metal box?"

With a trace of a smile, Arrow twists the knob on top of the box and a ray of light illuminates from inside. "Since I don't possess a lot of magical abilities, I can't just snap my fingers and make food appear, so I use this." He taps the box. "All you have to do is say what you want and it'll make it for you."

"Wow, that's pretty cool." Although, I didn't realize until now that cyborgs ate food. I slant forward in the stool, the light reflecting against my pupils. "I can say anything I want?"

Arrow nods, watching me with intrigue. "Anything at all."

"What do you usually ask for?" I've never had the option of having whatever I want for breakfast, and all the possibilities ... it's almost overwhelming. Everything sounds so delicious. My belly grumbles with possibilities.

"French toast is one of my favorites," he tells me with a tiny smile.

"French toast sounds awesome," I tell the box. "With sausage and bacon, and biscuits. Oh, and waffles and eggs and real maple syrup and cupcakes with lots and lots of frosting." I cringe, feeling Asher's gaze boring into me, as if he thinks my request for cupcakes has to do with his scent, which I guess it sort of does. He doesn't need to know that.

"And hot chocolate with marshmallows," I continue with my ordering, my appetite growing by the second. "And coffeecake. And …" I trail off as I note the three of them staring at me with wide eyes. "What?"

East's tongue slips out to wet his lips, then he trades a look with Asher and Arrow. Arrow's lips pull into a smile, and East lets out a chuckle. Even Asher, the grump, looks amused.

"What's so funny?" I demand, crossing my arms.

East simply shakes his head. "You're absolutely adorable. You really are."

"That she is," Asher mumbles, his gaze relentlessly welded to mine.

Since I'm fairly sure they're making fun of me, I shoot East and Asher a glare. "You know what? I think I've decided who my favorite band member is." I lean toward Arrow with my eyes narrowed on East and Asher. "From now on, I only like Arrow, and you two can suck it."

"Suck what exactly?" East muses, his gaze drifting to my chest. As his lips part, I hold up a hand.

"Whatever you're about to say, don't. Just don't." I shake my head as his glinting gaze meets mine.

"You're the one who told me to suck it," he says. "I was just going to tell you what I'd like to suck on."

Asher whacks him in the back of the head. "All right, that's enough. Harlynn needs to eat breakfast, and I'd like to keep mine down."

"Like you didn't think the same thing," East mumbles, rubbing his head.

Asher's gaze strays from East to my chest then to my face. The hue of desire in his eyes makes my skin flush.

I casually scratch my neck, trying to hide the bit of cleavage popping out of my tank top.

When I wandered into the kitchen after barely sleeping, I hadn't bothered to change out of my pajamas. At the time, I didn't care, but now … my tank top seems too thin, the shorts too short, too much of my skin showing so they can see just how flushed I am.

And the longer Asher and East openly check me out, the deeper my blush gets.

"Would you guys stop looking at me like that?" I demand. "In fact, don't look at me at all."

"Are we making you uncomfortable?" Asher asks, sounding strangely concerned.

I waver. "Sort of." Not necessarily in a bad way, though.

No, I sort of like their attention. I'm just not a fan of how obvious it is that I'm blushing because of it.

"We're sorry." Asher collects his handheld device and motions for East to follow him as he heads out of the kitchen. "I need to talk to you privately before you leave."

East offers me an apologetic look then follows Asher down the hallway.

I watch them go, confused as a leprechaun who was

cursed with two left feet. "Why did East look at me like that? Like he was sorry for something."

"Because he was." Arrow sits down beside me again. "Asher was, too."

"For what?" I twist on the stool to face him, our knees touching.

"For staring at you like they were, and for making you feel uncomfortable." Arrow reaches for the knob on the top of the box. "I think they're worried they crossed a line."

"They didn't. I just didn't like how they could tell I was blushing," I admit. Talking to Arrow has been easy from the start. I think it's because his gentle demeanor makes him less intimidating. "But I appreciate them backing off."

I'm surprised, though, that a moody, brooding genie, and a flirty, perverted faerie respect me enough to back off when I ask. Too bad all paranormals and humans can't be the same.

"None of us ever want you to feel uncomfortable," Arrow tells me with such genuineness that, if I didn't know any better, I'd wonder if he was human.

But then the gadgets in his fingers crank as he moves to open the top of the box, reminding me that he's part machine. Still, I'm more than certain his heart has to be real, along with his soul.

"Are you ready for the best breakfast you've ever

had?" he asks, and I eagerly nod. Smiling, he lifts the top off.

A bright light flashes, and I flinch, lifting my arms to shield my eyes.

"That's so bright."

A beat of silence goes by, and then Arrow utters, "You can look now."

Slowly, I lower my hands. Then excitement bursts through me.

Covering the countertop is every single drop of food I ordered, from the fluffiest French toast I've ever seen to cupcakes covered with mounds and mounds of glittery purple frosting.

I quickly reach for a fork and dive into the French toast. "Oh, my gods, I'm seriously having a foodgasm right now," I moan as I lick a droplet of syrup from my lips.

Arrow's brows knit. "What's a foodgasm?"

"Um …" I mentally curse my big mouth. "It's an expression used when you practically have an … orgasm over food."

"Oh."

Dead silence stretches between us.

That silence gives me too much time to think. About orgasms. And food. And foodgasms. About if cyborgs can have foodgasms. And orgasms …

My gaze unintentionally drifts toward Arrow's crotch area. Wait. Do cyborgs have mechanical penises?

Someone clears their throat, and I jolt, nearly spitting out a mouthful of French toast. Warmth floods my cheeks as East enters the kitchen, a wicked grin curving across his face.

"So, I'm not allowed to stare at the mouthwatering parts of your body, but you can stare at Arrow's junk?" he asks wickedly.

"I wasn't staring at his junk," I hiss, then glance at Arrow. "I wasn't. I swear."

"It's fine." He nervously rubs his hand over his head. "I didn't think you were." Sucking in a breath, his gaze skates to East. "I'm going to send for a world jumper vehicle to pick us up so we can get this mission over with." His gaze fleetingly flicks to mine before he high-tails the hell out of the kitchen.

Can't really blame him for acting so skittish after I stared at his man parts, wondering if they were mechanical.

I shake my head at myself. What in the stupid pixies is wrong with me? I swear being with these guys is messing with my ability to think rationally.

"Don't worry. He's probably as embarrassed as you are," Easton says with a lazy smile.

I narrow my eyes at him as I stuff my mouth full of

bacon. "I don't know why he'd be embarrassed. I wasn't staring at his guy parts like you implied."

"Sure you weren't. Just like I wasn't staring at your girl parts before Asher made me leave the kitchen so he could lecture me on not ogling your goodies." He slants forward and rests his arms on the counter, his wings shimmering in the light. "You know, it's the first time I've ever seen a female get upset with me for checking her out."

"That you know of."

He laughs, his eyes crinkling around the corners. "Oh, Harlynn, how you amuse me."

"What? You think there's never been a time when you've checked out a female and she felt uncomfortable yet pretended to be fine because she didn't feel comfortable enough showing her vulnerability?" I cock a brow at him as I pop a few chunks of coffee cake into my mouth.

A frown forms on his face. "I've never thought of it that way. It's always been so natural for me to flirt. I guess it might come off as too much to those who aren't my kind."

"Are all faeries as flirty as you?" I ask curiously as I peel the wrapper off a cupcake.

He nods, wisps of his hair falling into his glittery eyes. "Worse even."

I crinkle my nose. "Well, hopefully I don't cross paths with any more faeries."

"Considering we're in Shimmerland, I wouldn't hold your breath." A crooked grin pulls at his lips. "And I highly doubt fey are the only creatures you have to worry about."

I pause mid-bite with frosting on my lips and my mouth glazed with sugary sweetness. "What's that supposed to mean?"

His smile broadens as he ambles around the counter toward me. "It means you're delectably delicious, just like that cupcake."

"What is your—" My eyes widen as the floor begins to quake. "What the hell is that?"

A crinkle forms between Easton's brows as his gaze drops to the floor then zips to the hologram window. "Shit." He rushes over to the farthest wall, lines his palm to the hologram, and whispers, "Show me the outside, but keep the blinds up."

The forest and lake currently on the screen morph into the flowery field, lofty trees, and shimmering, iridescent sky that make up the outside. Only, unlike when I was out there yesterday, a clusterfuck of paranormals dressed in black cargo pants and matching boots and shirts fill up the space around the vehicle. In the distance behind them, dogs the size of giants drool on the ground.

"Holy crap, are those, like, super-sized werewolves?" I ask in horror.

"Worse." The fear in Easton's tone causes my fear to soar. "Hellhounds."

My jaw drops. "Like the Devil's dogs?"

Shaking his head, he glances at me. "Any creature can own a hellhound. It's just a pain in the ass to catch and train them. But if you manage, then you can pretty much start a war."

I swallow the bite of eggs I was chewing on. "Why are they outside your vehicle?"

"I think because we broke a law."

I startle at the sound of Asher's voice.

I turn around, then instantly lean back at his nearness. "How did you get in here so quietly?"

"It's a secret." He winks at me, but the playfulness doesn't reach his eyes. Then he strides across the room and peers at the scene outside. A deep frown etches into his face. "We should've assumed that, once we figured out she was different, this would happen."

"But we were careful sneaking her out." East frowns. "How did they find out?"

"My bet is because of whatever she is, she registered on their radar," Asher mutters. "We should've thought of this sooner."

"But she registers as a human to Arrow," East reminds him. "Which means she shouldn't register on their radar."

"You know as well as I do that their radars are far

better than any magical creatures' sensors," Asher says with his gaze fixed on the outside.

"Yeah, only because they slaughter paranormals to build their magical supply," East practically spits out.

He seems so irritated, so pissed off. Honestly, up until now, I thought he had only one level and that was super flirty and happy. Guess I was wrong.

Doesn't explain who the hell is outside, though.

I snatch up a cupcake then slide off the stool and pad across the room to them. "So, who are the dudes in the combat uniforms that have you guys all worked up?"

"The Worlds Patrol," Asher tells me with reluctance. "They're in charge of making sure paranormals don't leave their worlds without the proper passes and paperwork."

"I know what the Worlds Patrol is." I nibble on the cupcake, licking off a mouthful of frosting. "But, why are they here?"

Asher and East exchange a wary look, then Asher's smoky eyes settle on me. "They're here for you."

A BEAT TICKS by as I process what he said. The Worlds Patrol is here for me? No. I must have heard Asher wrong. The longer the silence ticks by, though, the more painfully aware I become that I heard him as clearly as I see the crazy iridescent sky outside.

"But I'm not a paranormal," I gripe. "I thought they were only allowed to arrest paranormals."

"They are. But only because paranormals are usually the ones jumping around in worlds. Plus, we're easier to track because we leave magical traces behind." East crosses his arms and keeps his gaze trained on the outside. "I hate to break this to you, sweetheart; we may not know what you are, but you're definitely not just a regular human. And I think the patrol may have caught on to that. How, though, I'm not sure."

"So, does that mean they can arrest me for leaving my world?" I put my hand on my hip, fuming mad. "Because the only reason I left to begin with is because you guys made me."

Asher's gaze glides to mine. "You didn't have to make the deal."

My fingers twitch with the urge to smack him, but I take a deep breath, refusing to allow him to get me riled up. "No, I did, or Jason would've died and I wouldn't have been able to live with myself." A shaky breath eases from my lips as I think about Jason. *Man, I miss him.* Part of me really wants to go back to my world, if for nothing else than to see him. "And maybe it's better if the patrol takes me. It'll get me out of this deal and away from the two of you."

"Two?" Asher arches a brow. "There're three of us."

"Yeah, but I like Arrow," I say with a smirk.

Asher's eyes swirl with smoke. "Did you hear that, East? Arrow is Harlynn's favorite."

"I never said favorite," I correct. "I said he's the only one I like."

Asher looks at Easton, who grins slyly in return.

Grinning like the devil himself, Asher returns his attention to me. "After we take care of this little problem, East and I are going to punish you for that."

"You can't do that. We made a deal you wouldn't harm me, remember?" My heart tremors in my chest.

Genies can be tricky little buggers, twisting words around and casting bargains with underlying meanings. What if I messed up when we made the deal that none of them could harm me?

"I said *punish*," Asher clarifies with a dark smile that sends shivers across my flesh. He takes a step toward me. "Not harm."

I instinctively step back, only to bump into East's chest.

What the hell? When did he move behind me?

I start to skitter to the side to get out from between them, but East folds his fingers around my upper arms, securing me in place.

"What are you two doing?" I cringe at the breathiness of my voice. "Trying to scare me or something?"

The tip of East's wing tickles a path down my arm. "Quite the opposite actually."

I resist the urge to shudder, but faeries, oh faeries, do I want to. "If that's the case, you're going about it all wrong."

Asher reaches out, I think to tuck a strand of my hair behind my ear, but instead he drops his hand to my side. I flinch as his fingers brush against mine then wrap around my wrist.

"What're you …?" I trail off as he guides my hand holding the half-eaten cupcake up to his lips. When the treat reaches his mouth, he takes a slow bite.

"Mmm … That is fucking good …" He licks frosting off his lips with his gaze melded to mine.

Between all of Easton's touching and the way Asher keeps licking his lips, I momentarily get lost and forget who I am, my past—I forget everything. Then my gaze travels to the hologram and I pull my head out of my ass.

Stupid, sexy genie and faerie! They're messing with my head.

"Okay. I don't even want to know what you guys are up to, but the Worlds Patrol is closing in on us, so we should probably take care of that problem." I loathe the shakiness in my voice. "That is, unless you guys want to lose your thief."

With another skim of his tongue along his lips, Asher tears his gaze off me and fixes his smoky eyes on East. "What do you think? Plan A or Plan S?"

"Plan A or Plan S?" I stare at them in confusion. "Okay, first of all, you guys never discussed a plan. And second, you skipped about twenty letters."

"We always have plans on hand. And the letters, they stand for something." Asher's gaze sweeps up and down my body, then he nibbles on his bottom lip. "I'm not sure Plan S will work, no matter how much I want to try it."

Don't do it. Don't ask.

"What does the S stand for?" Why, oh why, can't I keep my mouth shut?

Asher sucks on his lip ring. "As much as I'd love to tell you, I don't think you're ready to hear the answer."

Warmth floods my skin as words that begin with *S* invade my thoughts. *Sexy, sweltering, suck, scream, sex, sex, sex.*

Asher chuckles. "You're ridiculously cute when you blush."

I narrow my eyes at him. "I'm not blushing. I'm pissed off."

"Liar," he starts to tease, but then sighs, his gaze shifting to the hologram window again. "So, Plan A?"

"Unfortunately, I think so," Easton replies with his gaze on me. "She's definitely not ready for Plan S yet." He strokes my upper arm with his wing. "No matter how much I want her to be."

"You guys are so annoying," I scoff, crossing my arms.

"If you say so," Easton whispers in my ear.

Before my body can work up a shiver, Asher claps his hands. "Let's get started then." Wrapping his fingers around my wrist, he guides me toward him with what looks like a hint of jealousy in his eyes. "East, go get Arrow and fill him in."

East salutes Asher then whisks off toward the hallway, laughing to himself.

What he thinks is so funny is beyond me.

"Now, for your part in the plan …" Asher leaves the anticipation hanging as he tugs me toward the hallway.

"Can you please tell me what I'm going to be doing," I plead as I stumble after him, "so I can try to mentally prepare myself?"

"You, little thief, are going to be doing what you do best," he explains as he steers me into my temporary bedroom.

"Which is what? Stealing? Smarting off? Being a pain in your ass?" I grin when he shoots me an unimpressed look. "What? I'm good at all those things."

"That might be true"—he leans toward me, smoke swirling in his eyes—"but as of right now, all I need you to do is sneak around."

"In the vehicle or outside? And where's the end point?"

"Outside. And the end point is …" Hesitancy crosses his features. "I need you to make it to the forest."

I slant away from him, blinking in shock. "The forest? But I thought you guys said I couldn't go in there until we found out what I am?"

"That's the tricky part about this plan. You need to go far enough into the forest to wait for us, but under no circumstances are you to actually cross into the borders of faerie territory. The distance between the edge of the forest and the border into fey territory is very small. So small you won't be able to squeeze in there." He pulls me toward the hologram window that's in my room, which is currently displaying a waterfall cascading into a river. "However, I know of a place on the far east side where there should be enough room for you to hang out for a bit. The problem is, you're going to have to cross a river."

"I can do that. It doesn't actually sound too bad. Although, I don't get why you guys don't just transport away from here."

"The patrol has our vehicle on lockdown right now. We could override it, but that would be part of Plan S, which we already agreed you aren't ready for." Wariness shines in his eyes. "And don't be so relaxed about the river. It's full of sirens."

Chills break out across my skin. "As in, those winged creatures that lure men to wreck their ships?"

"That's more of a myth than truth. The truth is way worse." He presses a few buttons on the hologram and the waterfall scene fades into a massively wide, flowing river that weaves between the towering trees of the Shimmerland forest. Moving up behind me, he reaches over my shoulder and traces his finger along a faint silver line on the hologram. "See that line right there?" he asks, and I nod. "Well, that lines marks where the faerie territory starts, which means, if you cross that line and another creature registers that you're not human, you could be in some serious trouble, depending on what the creature is. It's not nightfall yet, so you shouldn't have to worry about the Banished, but that doesn't mean the forest isn't less dangerous—"

The vehicle suddenly jerks harshly to the right, sending me slamming into the wall. Asher stumbles, too, his body pressing against mine, and my head ends up pinned between his arms.

"Holy shit," he breathes into my hair.

"What the hell was that?" I whisper, moving to push back, but he doesn't budge and my ass ends up grinding against his genie goodies.

He groans into my hair, his hand lowering from the wall to my hip. "Gods, it's been too long." His fingers delve into my waist. "Way, way too long."

My heart thunders in my chest, and those crazy-ass butterflies in my stomach get stupidly excited again. I want to tell them to calm the hell down, but holy freakin' what-the-shit-is-happening right now? Because I can't seem to do anything other than pant. Loudly.

"Are you okay?" Asher whispers, his grip on me tightening.

I'm not even sure what he means. If I'm okay because I was thrown into a wall or because I'm breathing as loudly as an elf participating in a tap dancing competition.

"Yeah," I manage to croak out.

"Harlynn," he groans, sounding pained.

I feel the same way. Pain. An aching deep inside me. A longing perhaps?

I'm not sure.

I'm not sure about anything anymore. Whether these … butterfly feelings are from the magic of the curse his father cast on us, or if the last eighteen years of not getting any has finally caught up with me.

Get your hormones in check, Harlynn. Right now!

"Asher." It takes a lot of effort, but my voice comes out steady. "What the hell just shook the vehicle?"

A drop of silence goes by, then …

"Fuck." He pushes away from me, and I turn around, my heart still a mess in my chest.

Our gazes connect for a faltering, breath-stealing moment before the door swings open and the moment poofs away like genie smoke.

"They put a shield around our vehicle," East announces as he rushes into my room with Arrow trailing behind him. "So, it looks like we're going to have to do Plan S."

Asher gives me a strange look that makes my heart rate quicken while East grins, seeming pretty happy. Arrow, on the other hand, offers me a remorseful look.

I sink my teeth into my bottom lip. "All right, will you guys cut the shit and tell me what the hell Plan S is? Your weird, contradicting looks are starting to freak me the crazy genies out."

"Crazy genies?" Asher cocks a brow at me then quickly shakes his head and points a finger at me. "All right, you need to stop talking."

My lips part in surprise. "What the heck did I do?"

"You're distracting," East explains as he rolls up the sleeves of his shirt. "Every time those gorgeous lips of yours part, we end up forgetting our vehicle is surrounded, and we need to deal with the problem."

"I'm not doing it on purpose," I sulk, wrapping my arms around myself.

"I know." East steps toward me. "But you have this way about you. An allure. I'm starting to wonder if perhaps it may have to do with whatever you are."

"You make me sound like I'm a siren." My gaze skates to the hologram. "Like the ones in the river. Which FYI, do I still have to go there?"

East shakes his head. "Nope."

I'd be ecstatic about that, except for the fact that we're about to do Plan S and I still have no clue what the *S* stands for.

"Don't look so frightened, little mouse." East moves to stand in front of me, crowding my personal space. "No one here is going to hurt you. In fact, what we're about to do ..." A grin curls at his lips. "I have a feeling you're going to like it."

I shake my head. "I really doubt that."

East eyes me over. "I guess we'll see then." Then his

hands come down against the wall, trapping me between his arms.

I glance worriedly at Arrow, since he's the only one I really trust. Remorse remains in his eyes, but he offers me a tentative smile.

"He's not going to hurt you, I promise." Arrow rubs his lips together. "None of us are."

While I believe him, his words do nothing to alleviate my nerves. It doesn't help that a voice suddenly blares from outside.

"This is the Worlds Patrol," they declare. "Our radar has registered an illegal and potentially dangerous paranormal on your vehicle. You need to turn it over immediately. If you refuse to do so, you will be detained. And don't even think about trying to escape. We have you surrounded, there are hellhounds nearby, and we've put a restriction shield around your vehicle."

"Wow, that's a lot of work they're putting into this," East teases, but nervousness resides in his eyes. "Whatever you are, sweetheart, you must be important."

"Or dangerous," I whisper. "Did you hear what they said?"

East shrugs. "They're just trying to get us worried so we'll toss you out."

Then why does he look a bit uneasy?

I glance in Asher's direction. He appears edgy, as well. Are they afraid of me? Should I be afraid of myself?

"No one's afraid of you," Asher insists, either because he read what I was thinking all over my face, or I accidentally said my thoughts aloud again. "We're just concerned over what's about to happen."

I can't tell if he's being truthful or not, but I guess it doesn't really matter at the moment.

I may have said before that perhaps it'd be better if the Worlds Patrol arrested me, but after what the announcer just said … yeah, I'm thinking it might be better to stay with the cocky genie, flirty faerie, and sweet cyborg.

"What's about to happen?" I dare ask aloud.

East's eyes twinkle with excited glee. "Our lips are about to get reacquainted."

"Reacquainted?" Asher growls at the same time I say, "No freakin' way."

"What do you mean *reacquainted*?" Asher asks more calmly this time.

East pulls a *whoopsie* face. "I may have licked some frosting off her lips earlier, but only because I was hungry."

"For what exactly?" Asher snaps with raised brows.

"You two are getting off the subject again," Arrow intervenes, giving a pressing glance at the hologram. "And we're running out of time."

I start to turn to see what's happening on the hologram when East's lips come down on mine. I suck in a sharp breath through my nose and just as quickly as it started, it's over.

But then in the snap of a wish, Asher is in front of me and crashing his lips against mine with so much force I swear I'm going to have a bruise. But it feels so good, like heat and sparks and fire. Scorching. Blazing. Powerful.

When I gasp, he slides his tongue into my mouth. The taste of warmth and cupcakes flood my senses, and a groan escapes my lips, embarrassingly loud. I clutch the bottom of his shirt, while he finds my waist, skimming his fingers along my sides as he tugs me closer, devouring me with his mouth.

I have no clue what in the hell of all orgies is going on, but I let him keep kissing me and even bite his lip a few times, basking in the taste of him, basking in the way he touches me, basking in—

He jerks back, smoke funneling in his eyes. Then he spins me around and straight into Arrow's lean, mechanical arms. I gasp as our chests collide, still struggling to catch my breath, as he kisses me quickly.

"I'm sorry," Arrow says apologetically.

"Why did you guys do that?" I direct my question at Arrow.

His lips part, but Asher speaks first.

"We need you to be able to confuse the patrol's radar so you can sneak out and access the lockdown override in the chamber of the vehicle. The only way to confuse their radar so they don't register you immediately is to put a little taste of all our magic inside you. But since you block most of our magic, we had to put it directly inside." He steps toward me, his eyes drifting to Arrow's hands on my waist.

Arrow swiftly pulls away, causing me to frown.

They kissed me to put their magic in me?

I wrap my arms around myself, feeling a bit used.

"It's not like we didn't want to kiss you," East says when he notes my offish behavior.

"That's not why I'm upset." I stare down at my hand, half-expecting my skin to be glowing. Everything appears normal. "You guys put magic in me without my permission."

"I'm sorry," Arrow apologizes again, raking his fingers through his hair. "If there was another way, we would've done it."

"Yeah, I wouldn't go that far." East gives me a look that makes my pulse speed up. "But maybe we should've asked for your permission first. We just figured you'd say no."

"Yes, you should have," I agree, lowering my hands to my sides. "And if it was necessary … I wouldn't have said no."

"Well then, I'm sorry for kissing you without your permission." East takes my hand and lifts it toward his mouth, kissing my knuckles.

I sigh with exhaustion, struggling not to smile. "Oh, whatever." I slip my hand from his. "Can we just get Plan S over with so I don't have to go with the patrol and their big-ass hellhounds? Although, I'm still a bit confused why I'm the one who has to override the lockdown. And what about the shield?"

"East, Arrow, and I are going to take care of the shield while you override the lockdown." Asher steps closer to me. "The trapdoor that you have to use to get to the chamber is extremely small, and you're the only one who can fit in it. And the only way to get into the chamber is to go through a door on the front right side of the vehicle. And you're going to have to do that without being seen."

I tuck a strand of hair behind my ear, my brows pulling together. "How am I supposed to do that when the entire vehicle is surrounded?"

"You're going to do one of the things you do best." Asher leans closer, his eyes darkening with smoky magic. "Be sneaky."

I wish I could tell him I got this, but this is entirely new territory for me. Usually when I break in somewhere, I spend weeks planning and scoping out the area. My main rule: never go in blind.

I guess I don't have much of a choice in this matter. Either I succeed at this and stay with Asher, East, and Arrow, or I get arrested and hauled off to who knows where with a bunch of paranormals who think I'm some dangerous creature.

When faced with the two choices …

Yeah, I'm going to override the lockdown no matter what it takes.

CHAPTER 14

So, in order for me to get to the chamber to override the lockdown, I'll use a trapdoor that's in the floor of the living room and shimmy my way down a narrow tunnel that will take me outside. Then I'm supposed to crawl underneath the vehicle until I reach the back end. There, on the far right side, is a small chamber that I have to somehow make it into without being seen. Once I'm inside that, if all goes smoothly, the guys should be able to get the shield down and take off the moment I hit the override button.

A lot could go wrong. Plus, I'm going to be stuck in the compartment until they can find a safe place to land.

Awesome, right?

Yeah, not so much. But I've been in worse scenarios before.

Still, I can't help wondering …

"Can't you guys just use your magic to get us out of this?" I ask as I sit down on the floor and lower my legs into the trapdoor.

I've changed into a pair of black pants and a T-shirt made of a stretchy material that will allow me to blend easily, because apparently, the tunnel is going to be a tight fit, even for me.

"One use of magic directed at them, and they'll attack us." Asher crouches in front of me with worry in his eyes. "And if we hurt or kill any of them, we're going to be chased and have a bounty put on our heads."

"But you won't if we just take off?" I question with skepticism.

Asher and East are digging through the fridge for magical supplies, but every so often, they throw a concerned look in my direction.

What I'm about to do is dangerous. I get that, which is why I can't help wondering if there's another way.

"There's less likely of a chance," Asher says, adjusting his cuffs. "Plus, we'll have an easier time ditching them if we just take off."

"Oh. All right then. I guess the trapdoor plan it is." I take a deep breath and start to lower myself in, when Asher wraps his fingers around my wrist, stopping me.

"Be careful, Harlynn," he whispers. "Don't let them see you. And don't get caught."

"I won't." I wink at him. It's all bravado, but I've got to fake it, or else I'm going to lose my shit. "I'm good at this sort of stuff."

"I know." He brushes his knuckles across my cheek, the worry in his eyes increasing. "Still, be careful."

My nod is a bit shakier this time, yet I toss my nervousness aside and drop into the trapdoor before I can chicken out.

The moment I land, I have to lie down flat on my stomach just to fit in the dark tunnel. "All right, here goes nothing." With another inhale and exhale, I army crawl inside.

I immediately tense as darkness encases me, but then my skin illuminates, the light cascading against the walls. From the magic the guys put in me, I assume.

"Holy crap, I look like a glow bug," I mutter as I continue dragging myself down the tunnel.

The journey feels endless, knowing that the moment I reach the end, I'm going to be outside with the patrol and their hellhounds. I still haven't come up with a way not to be seen, but I'll assess the situation when I reach that part of the plan.

A few sprinkles of magic later, I reach the end of the tunnel. Again, I don't give myself time to overthink what I'm about to do; instead, I hurriedly open the door and stick my head out, practically hanging upside down as I scope out the surroundings.

Below me is a strip of glassy grass and about a foot above it is the bottom of the vehicle.

Crap, it's going to be a tight fit.

Sucking in an exhale, I wiggle out of the tunnel. The glassy grass feels bizarre underneath me as I lie flat on the ground, peering around at all the paranormals just outside the vehicle. None of them appear to be moving toward me, so I take that as a sign that I haven't been spotted ...

Yet.

No negative thoughts. You got this.

Like I did in the tunnel, I army crawl toward the back of the vehicle, stopping at the far right side. Lowering my head, I scan the area then mentally curse myself for not coming up with a plan beforehand.

There're so many of them. And they're so close.

Shit.

I roll behind the wheel to avoid being seen then rack my brain for all the information I've ever read about the Worlds Patrol.

Made up of various kinds of paranormals, they're extremely powerful. Knowing that doesn't help me one bit. In fact, it makes me feel even more hopeless.

Don't give up. You can do this. Think outside the box. You're good at that.

Outside the box. What's outside of the box, though? I mean, I really don't know much about the Worlds

Patrol. Hell, I didn't even realize they could own hellhounds.

Dammit.

I pound my hand against the ground in frustration and the glassy grass shatters, the dirt cracking apart.

What the hell?

I pat my palm against the ground again with a bit more force, and the same thing happens, only the cracks in the dirt are a bit bigger. Lifting my hand, I stare at my palm, searching for … well, I'm not sure what. First the glowing and now this? This has to be because of the magic the guys put in me, right?

Gods, I hope so.

Part of me wonders if these wonky gifts have something to do with the Worlds Patrol being here to arrest me. Doesn't really matter right now, though. All that matters is escaping them. And this little gift … curse—whatever the heck it is—could help me.

Lying flat on the ground again, I crawl back toward the front of the bus. My fingers tremble as I prepare to do what I'm about to do. One wrong move, and I'll get caught. Or worse, create a hole in the ground that I'll fall into.

You've got this. You've got this. You've got this, I mentally chant to myself as I smack my palm down on the ground hard.

The glassy grass ripples and tips over like shattering

dominos, and the ground begins to splinter, a giant crack zipping out and across the field in front of the bus.

"What in the worlds?" a patrol officer mutters from nearby. Then his voice grows louder. "We have a situation over here."

And … that's my cue.

Twisting around, I hightail it back to the rear end of the bus and peer out at the field. The patrol officers have migrated to where the shattering grass and dirt are carving a path toward the field. A smile starts to break across my face until I realize the dirt and grass have begun shattering in the opposite direction, as well, making a giant path—or should I say massive crack in the ground—straight underneath the vehicle.

The vehicle starts to wobble as the ground crumbles underneath it.

Shit. I so did not think this through all the way.

Seeing no other option, I hurry out from under the vehicle, crossing my fingers no one is looking my way. Once I straighten, I yank open the compartment, dive inside, and lock myself in. Darkness smothers me, but again, light glitters from my skin, revealing the override box just in front of me. It consists of a series of buttons, and on the bottom row in the farthest corner is a button labeled *lockdown override*. I push it then sit back and wait for … well, I'm not really sure. The guys never explained what would happen after I pushed the button.

"Come on, come on. Please work," I mutter as the vehicle rocks and sways, sending me bouncing against the walls.

I hug my legs to my chest, breathing loudly, waiting for either the ground to collapse or for the patrol to yank open the compartment door. Neither of those things happen, though. Instead, the vehicle suddenly grows still.

Does that mean it worked? Did the guys get the shield down and transport us away from Shimmerland?

I almost reach over and push open the compartment door to see, but exhaustion suddenly overtakes me and my eyelids lower shut.

CHAPTER 15

THE SOFTEST SURFACE presses against my cheek. My entire body is so relaxed. I feel so comfortable, so content, so at peace. I feel better than I have for a long, long time. Someone is stroking my cheek, the movement almost sending me back to dreamland. Then reality slaps me across the face.

Someone is stroking my cheek!

My eyes pop open, and I suck in a sharp inhale as I sit up. It takes several blinks to process the scene around me. The deep purple walls, a black hardwood floor, and a dome ceiling painted with glittering silver and violet stars. I'm in the bedroom East created for me. And not only that, I'm in the bed. A bed I just slept in.

"Oh, my worlds, I actually slept in a bed," I mumble as I rub the sleepiness from my eyes. "Gods, I feel so good."

"Thank gods you're awake. We were getting worried about you."

I startle, whirling around, and find Asher sitting in a chair beside the bed. He still has on the same outfit as he did earlier, but his hair is a mess, strands sticking up everywhere, and dark circles reside under his eyes.

"Hey," he greets me with a nervous smile, his eyes drinking me in. "How are you feeling?"

"Good, I guess." I sweep my hair out of my eyes then lift my hand to my cheek. My skin is warmer than usual. "Were you touching my face while I was asleep?"

"Maybe." He assesses me closely. "Would it bother you if I was?"

"Yes." I'm not even sure if I'm lying or not; my brain is such a confused mess. "Wait. How did I get here, in this bed? The last thing I remember is being in the chamber and the ground cracking apart, and then I fell asleep. Which seems sort of odd, I guess. I mean, I've never fallen asleep on a job before."

"You weren't really working for us." Asher's gaze never wavers from me, as if he's searching for something. "But the reason you fell asleep probably has to do with the fact that you used your power for what I'm guessing is the first time. Unless you were lying to us about not knowing what you are. My guess is you're just as clueless as us."

I start to nod when his words really hit me. "Wait. I

used *magic*?" I shake my head. "No, I don't have magical abilities. That stuff I did—the glowing and the ground cracking—that was from the magic you guys put in me."

Asher cautiously shakes his head as he shifts from the chair to the edge of the bed. "The magic we put in you was simply to confuse the patrol's radar. There's no way you could actually have used it. It was your magic that broke the ground and apparently caused some glowing. Although, I didn't know about that until you just said it." He starts to reach for me, but then he pulls away, swallowing hard.

The move spikes fear through my veins.

Is he afraid of me now? Do I care?

I do. I don't even know why.

"Are you afraid of me?" I whisper. "Because of what I am?"

"We still don't know what you are," he clarifies. With a shaky inhale, he scoots closer to me. "And no, I'm not afraid of you. East and Arrow aren't either." He trails his fingers down my cheek, my jawline, the arch of my neck. "We do need to find out what you are, though."

"But with ..." I sigh, leaning away as he presses his fingers to my throbbing pulse. Despite how much my body seems to enjoy him touching me, I need some space, need to keep a clear head, need to remember why I've always avoided getting close to anyone. Need to remember he's a genie.

Although, the latter doesn't seem as important anymore. Sure, Asher can annoy the shit out of me, but I'm not certain I hate him as much as I did when we first met. Okay, maybe I don't even hate him at all. Not even a little.

Like. Yes, that's what this is. I like Asher like I like Jason. Like I like Easton and Arrow. That's not a big deal. Like is fine. Love is what's dangerous.

Asher's brows furrow. "What's wrong?"

I waver, wanting to keep my question to myself. But I've never been good at keeping my trap shut.

"It's just that, with all the problems I'm causing you guys, why are you even bothering to find out what I am?" I hug my legs to my chest and rest my chin on my knees. "Wouldn't it be easier to just find a different—real—human to be your thief?"

Asher cocks a brow. "You don't want to be in the bargain anymore?"

I shake my head. "No, I want Jason to stay alive and I want to stay alive, too … It's just that I don't see how I can help you if I have the Worlds Patrol after me."

"The Worlds Patrol isn't going to find you anytime soon—we made sure of that. And you could still help us, depending on what you are."

"But what if I can't? What if I'm useless?" Will he cancel the bargain and strike Jason and me dead?

He drags his teeth along his bottom lip, a smirk

playing at his lips. "Well, even if you can't, you're still not completely useless to us."

The wicked gleam in his eyes should make me want to keep my lips zipped, but again, I stress, I'm not very good at that.

"Why?"

His smile breaks through. "Because we could always use a fun little toy to play with while we're traveling for the tour and collecting those objects."

Glad to see we're back to that. Honestly, I'm kind of relieved. The serious demeanor he had when I woke up was sort of throwing me off balance.

"Good to know you're still a mean, *old* genie." I bat my eyelashes innocently at him.

He leans toward me, his eyes a thunderstorm of smoke. "And it's good to know you're still a smartass." Then he picks me up and flings me over his shoulder as he strides out of the room.

"Hey, I thought we already talked about you not carrying me," I whine. "Put me down."

"And I thought I already made it pretty clear I'll carry you if I want to." He storms down the hallway, taking long, determined strides.

I growl in frustration. "Where are you even taking me?"

"To the living room."

"Then, is it really necessary for you to carry me?"

"Yes."

"Why?"

"Because I said so."

"Oh, for the love of gods, you're so annoying."

"So are you." He sets me down on the sofa then steps back, crossing his arms. "I think deep down, though, you like it."

I roll my eyes, but he only grins.

"You know what? You're—" I squeak as a pair of arms loop around me from behind.

I relax a smidgeon—and let me stress the smidgeon part—when East's faerie scent touches my nostrils.

"I'm so glad you're all right." He hops over the back of the sofa, landing on the cushion beside me, sitting so close he's practically sitting on my lap.

"You were worried I wasn't going to be okay?" I raise my brows at East.

"We weren't sure. You were pretty out of it when we found you. And to make the ground break like that ... it had to have taken a lot of power." He stares at me in awe. "How did you do it, sweetheart?"

"I hit the ground with my palm. The first time was by accident, but when I realized what I could do, I thought it could be a good distraction." I shrug, pretending to be all calm on the outside when really, uneasiness stirs inside my chest.

I have power. I'm not human. I cracked the ground

apart with my hand. The Worlds Patrol is after me. And just a few days ago, I thought I was only a human.

How am I supposed to deal with this?

"You'll learn to accept it. It'll just take some time." Asher takes a seat on the other side of me. Like Easton, he's sitting way too close.

I grimace. "Did I say my thoughts aloud again?"

Asher grins. "You have a habit of doing that."

"Apparently." I sigh heavily, sinking back into the sofa. "So, what am I supposed to do now until we find out what I am? And where are we even?"

"On my old planet." Arrow wanders out from the hallway with his hands stuffed in his pockets. He offers me a shy smile before lowering himself onto the edge of the coffee table across from me, his knees pressing against mine.

Trapped. That's the first word that comes to mind when I take in the situation. With Arrow in front of me, and Asher and East at my sides, it feels like I should be flipping out. Instead, I feel strangely content, as if maybe their issues with invading my personal space have finally started to not bother me so much.

"We're on Steel?" I ask, shock ringing in my tone. "Like, right now?"

"Yes. Or, well, hovering above it." Arrow nods at the hologram.

I turn around and my jaw about smacks my knees at

the sight of a giant orb made of gadgets, steel, and liquid bronzed rotating amongst the seemingly endless stars outside.

"It's pretty," I whisper honestly.

"Pretty things can be dangerous," Asher says, slipping an arm behind me. "Don't let the flashy gadgets of Steel give you the false illusion that you're safe, because you're not."

"You say that like I'm going there." I cast a glance at the three of them. "Wait. Am I?"

They trade a wary look at each other, then Asher fixes his gaze on me while twisting a strand of my hair around his finger.

"After what happened in Shimmerland, we decided that it might be best if we stick together until we can figure out if the patrol is going to continue chasing us or put a bounty on us."

"What if they do?" I question. "Won't that ruin you guys' mission to take down Asher's father and those other corrupt paranormals you're going after? And what about Shimmerland? We were supposed to get that rock thingy while we were there."

"If the patrol comes after us, we'll just have to be more careful. We'll worry about that, though, after we find out if they are. For now, we need to get the steel books so we can find out what you are and what you can do. Then we'll loop back to Shimmerland when we're ready. While we're here, the patrol will have a harder time tracking us down because the cyborgs make their radars a bit wonky."

"And," Asher adds, "after seeing you in action, we decided you might be useful if we need to sneak into any small spaces to get the steel books."

"You'll be safe with us." Arrow's bronzed lips tilt upward into a reassuring smile. "We won't let anything happen to you."

"I'll go, but on one condition," I say.

Asher cocks a brow. "Which is?"

"You guys need to stop with all the touching." Even though my body gripes in protest, I slant forward away from him and Easton. That only puts me closer to Arrow. But he seems like the safest bet right now, appearing more nervous about the touching than I am.

Asher and East exchange an amused look while Arrow heaves a tired sigh.

"Fine, that's doable." The smirk on East's face doesn't match his words.

I soon find out why when Asher adds, "For now. But I have a feeling you're going to change your mind about it."

Then the three of them rise to their feet.

"Okay, who's ready to steal some steel books?" East asks, rubbing his hands together as his gaze lands on me.

The question makes me feel more in my element. Stealing. Thievery. I'm good with that sort of stuff. It's all this emotional, touching, confusion that I can't figure out how to deal with. Stealing will offer me a good distraction from that. Plus, with my newfound powers, I might even be a better thief than I was before.

See? A silver lining to this whole being a freak of nature thing.

Pushing to my feet, I crack my knuckles. "All right, let's do this." I throw them a sassy smile.

Asher studies me with his brows creased. "You know what? I have a feeling you might be our salvation or our downfall. I can't figure out which." Then he strides toward the door, leaving me to wonder what he meant.

Leaving me to wonder a lot of things.

Instead of wondering about the answers, I focus on what I'm about to do, because that's much easier.

After Asher pushes a few buttons and the vehicle descends into the planet, Easton takes my hand and guides me to the door.

"Are you ready for this?" he asks me as we reach the door.

I nod with confidence. "Yep."

Sure, I've never been to Steel before, and I've heard rumors of how dangerous it is, but if there's one thing I'm certain of in these worlds, it's that I never fail when it comes to stealing. Except for maybe when I tried to steal Asher's lamp. But I'm starting to wonder if that wasn't necessarily me failing. After all, Jason got to live and I found out I'm not human. Who knows what would've happened if I'd been alone when I made that discovery? I'm not sure what I would've done. I guess that means that, technically, I'm grateful I got stuck on a world jumper vehicle with a genie, a faerie, and a cyborg.

That thought's a little unsettling, but oh well, I guess there's no turning back now.

Yep, there's definitely no turning back now, I think to myself as I follow the guys off the vehicle.

CHAPTER 16

I'M NOT GOING to try to be tough and lie about how I feel right now—that I'm a little bit freaked out about going to the planet Steel. I want to hold on to my badass image, so I'm pretending to be calm. Really, though, I'm a cluster-fuck of nervous pixies.

I can't believe I'm about to step out onto another planet.

That thought repeatedly crosses my mind as I step off Asher, East, and Arrow's transporting vehicle. I'm unsure what I'm about to walk into. Yeah, I saw planet Steel while we were floating above it; saw the giant orb made of gadgets, steel, and liquid bronzed rotating amongst the seemingly endless stars outside. But to actually step foot onto the planet is an entirely different experience.

Not only is the ground shiny, smooth, and metallic brown, the atmosphere gives off a brownish aura, making everything appear shimmering bronze, including the sunlight glaring down from the liquid-like sky. And don't even get me started on the gadgets. They cover every-thing—the lofty, metal trees; the grassless ground; and even the clouds.

"This place is …" I turn in a circle, taking everything in. "Crazy weird," I decide. "Not in a bad way. Just in a … weird way."

"Planet Steel is one of the more stranger planets," Arrow says as he jumps out of the vehicle.

Half-man, half-machine, his arms and neck are spun of flesh and bronzed gadgets, and his fingers are mechanical. And while he may be wearing a shirt right now, I've seen him shirtless and know his abdomen is inked with small pieces of steel. But his face is human-like, with bronzed, full lips; short, black hair; and the most beautiful silver eyes.

He's changed his clothes since we landed and is now rocking a shirt and vest, black pants with pockets, and heavy boots. The look is topped off with a worn leather jacket covered in bronzed buckles and fingerless, leather gloves. His outfit is way fancier than what I'm wearing.

Should I have changed?

I have no idea and wonder if Asher and East are going to change, too. They haven't gotten off the vehicle yet, so I don't know. But if the creatures on this planet are dressed like Arrow, I may stand out in my black pants and T-shirt. Since we're supposed to be stealing the Steel books, I should try to blend in, especially since the worlds patrol might be after me.

"It's not the strangest, though," Arrow adds, staring at the fields enclosing the area with his arms crossed and his jaw set tight.

The guys have mentioned a couple of times that planet Steel is dangerous. Asher also implied that Arrow was once locked up here. They've said a couple of things that make me think Arrow doesn't have a good past, but they've never given any details, so I don't know his story. I'm curious, though, about the sweet, quiet drummer of the band Ash East Arrow.

Who is he? What makes him seem more emotional than the other cyborgs I've crossed paths with?

"What's the strangest planet?" I ask, shielding my eyes with my hand.

Arrow rubs his jawline. "Probably planet Ivory."

"I've never heard of that planet." I squint at him. "What's it like?"

"Very soft." He faces me, his lips lifting upward. "I have a book that shows all the different planets. When we have extra time, you can borrow it, if you want."

I nod eagerly. "Thanks. I've always been interested in other planets, but I haven't had much access to books since my parents ... Well, you know."

He smiles understandingly. "I have a whole collection of books in my bedroom that you can borrow anytime."

"Thanks," I say again, offering him a genuine smile.

"You're welcome." His smile fades as his gaze drifts toward a city in the distance, just beyond the forest that surrounds us.

"What's the city like?" I ask, fiddling with the hem of my T-shirt.

"Dangerous," he mutters, his gaze sweeping the land.

"Yeah, I got that from some of the stuff you guys have said. But, why is it dangerous? And why is there no one out here?"

"We parked on the outskirts of the city to avoid our landing being seen."

"Because it's so dangerous?"

"That and our band's pretty popular. If anyone recognizes our transporting vehicle, we might get mobbed by fans."

"Oh." My brows dip. "Cyborgs are fans of your band?"

"No, not really. Most don't even listen to music." The wheels in his arms turn as he scratches the back of his neck. "But other creatures on this planet do."

"If cyborgs aren't into music, then how did you end up a drummer in a band?"

His throat muscles work as he swallows hard, glancing at the city. "I'm not like other cyborgs, Harlynn."

"I already caught on to that." I deliberate whether or

not to ask the question burning on the tip of my tongue since he appears so uneasy with the subject. But I feel like, if I ever want to be comfortable around them, especially since I'll be around for the next couple of months, I need to learn more about them. "Why, though? I mean … what makes you different?"

He sighs. "You really want to know?"

"I do, but you don't have to tell me if you don't want to …" I trail off as he encloses his mechanical fingers around my wrist. While Asher and East frequently touch me, Arrow has only done it a couple of times.

His metal fingers are startling cold against my skin, but not necessarily in a bad way.

My heart beat speeds up as he guides my hand toward him and lines my palm over his chest, right above where most creatures' hearts are. Cyborgs aren't supposed to have beating hearts, though, just a mechanical device that sends energy through their bodies. So, when I feel a heart beating inside his chest, my eyes widen.

"You have a heart?" I peer up at him and find him staring down at me with nervousness all over his features. His fingers are shaking slightly, too.

He's anxious, but why? Perhaps he isn't supposed to be sharing this information with me?

"Cyborgs usually have a machine in their chest, but I was created with a heart," he says quietly. "I don't know why or how, since I can't remember a lot of my life."

I flatten my palm against his solid chest. "It's beating really fast. Is that normal?"

Squirming, he shakes his head. "I'm just nervous about … about being back on this planet."

"Oh." No wonder he's been acting so squirmy.

"Are we feeling each other up before we head to the city?" East's amused voice sails over my shoulder. "Because, if so, I call next."

I roll my eyes, and a trace of a smile rises on Arrow's lips.

Sighing, I step back, lowering my hand from his chest and twisting around to face East.

"Arrow and I already did it, so I guess that leaves you and Asher to do it to each other." I smirk, but then my smile falters as I note East has also changed his clothes and is now wearing a pinstriped jacket; black pants; and thick, buckled, steel boots. His blond hair is swept out of his sparkling eyes, and his wings are hidden beneath his jacket. "Dude, did you squish your wings underneath your jacket?"

Amusement dances in East's eyes. "My wings are retractable." He steps toward me, his boots squeaking against the metal ground. "When we get back from the city, I'll make sure to strip down and show you."

"And when you do, I'll make sure to show your balls what I do to guys who strip down in front of me." I throw him a snarky grin.

He throws it right back at me. "I'm going to hold you to that. My balls love getting fondle—"

"That's not what I meant," I say loudly, my cheeks flushing with embarrassment, an emotion only he seems to bring out in me. It annoys the living pixies out of me, but the more I try to get him to stop, the more persistent he gets.

Damn faeries.

His smile broadens as he stalks toward me, his strawberry faerie scent engulfing my nostrils. I discreetly breathe it in, secretly loving it and secretly despising myself because I do.

"You know, when I first met you, I thought, with how sassy you are, that you might be a dominatrix," East tells me, his lips curling. "Now that I've been around you for a bit, I realize that, excluding your sassy mouth and attitude, you may be the most innocent creature I've ever met."

"Thieves are far from innocent," I point out, trying to mentally will my embarrassment away. "I've been in trouble with the law a ton of times. I've even spent time in the electric cells."

"I'm not referring to your criminal activities." An impish grin tugs at his lips. "I'm referring to your sexual ones."

Arrow lets out a strange cough, and then wanders away, pretending to scope out the trees.

"My sexual experiences are none of your business." I hold his gaze, despite the increasing warmth in my cheeks.

He rubs his jawline, considering something. "Is it because of the curse? Is that why you haven't done anything yet?"

I cock a brow. "Who says I haven't?"

His lips span into a wide grin. "You can't pretend your way out of this one, sweetheart. Faeries have a sixth sense about these things."

"About how sexually experienced creatures are?" I question in doubt.

"You think I'm lying?" he asks, highly amused. "Faeries are the flirtiest and most sexual creatures in existence. We even have festivals that celebrate sex."

"You're not the most sexual creatures," I quip. "Succubi and incubi are."

He dismisses me with a flick of his wrist. "That's a myth."

"Hmm ... I think you're wrong. In fact, I once crossed paths with a succubus that said faeries were lacking in the sexual department." I'm so full of shit, but I want to get the upper hand in this conversation before he makes me blush again.

His eyes glint as he leans closer to me. "How about we step back onto the vehicle and I'll show you how wrong that statement is?"

Do not blush. Don't you dare, Harlynn!

"If I really am as sexually inexperienced as you think, then how would that prove anything?" I question, giving myself a mental high-five for being so chill.

His eyes shimmer in delight. "I'm a fan of your innocent blushing, but I think I might like the sassy side of you, too. It's an alluring combination." He tucks a strand of my hair behind my ear, letting his fingers linger on my cheek as he stares at me in complete fascination.

I'm about to step away from him, even though his touch is sending wonderful tingles all over my skin—stupid, traitor body—when Asher exits the bus.

He takes one look at East and I, standing close enough to kiss, with East's hand on my face, and a frown pulls at his pale blue lips.

I wonder if his irritation has anything to do with the curse his father put on him? You know, the one where he's supposed to fall in love with me, only to watch me die in his arms. None of the guys are aware that I know this little tidbit of information, since I only learned about it while eavesdropping on one of their conversations.

While Asher's father may have cursed him, I'm not sure if I believe in the possibility of me ever falling in love with anyone, let alone a genie. Sure, Asher doesn't seem as cruel—or even cruel at all—like the other genies I've crossed paths with. But, just because I don't entirely despise him, that doesn't mean I can envision myself falling in love with him. Love is more complicated than that. At least, from what I've seen.

I've spent most of my life shutting down any possibility of falling in love, which means closing myself off from almost everyone and only watching others fall in and out of love. I even closed myself off with Jason, my friend, especially after he kissed me.

It happened one time and lasted about a second—an amazing, better than melted chocolate second—before I had to pull away and suggest we just be friends. He seemed cool with it. Later, I discovered he was high when he kissed me, so I'm not even sure he ever really wanted to.

Being so closed off sucks and can get lonely. Never kissing, hugging, touching. For the most part, though, no one's ever tried to get intimate with me, except now. But I think the only reason East continues to flirt with me is because faeries flirt with anything.

As Asher continues to frown, East drapes an arm around me and tugs me against his side.

"I was just telling beautiful Harlynn that she should let me prove to her that faeries are amazing at fucking," East tells Asher with a wicked grin. "And I think she was about to say yes."

My cheeks flame with heat. "I was not."

East chuckles, stroking my cheek with his fingertips. "She's so cute when she blushes, isn't she?"

Asher gives him a hard look, but then his gaze blazes when it glides to me. He gradually scrolls over my body, and his frown deepens.

"You should change," he mutters.

I suddenly become aware that, like Arrow and East, he's also changed his clothes. He's now dressed in a pair of striped pants, a black shirt, and a black overcoat covered with buckles and chains. Fingerless gloves cover his hands, his trademark genie cuffs are visible, and buckled boots run all the way up to his knees. His short, cropped, brown hair is styled, and his crazy blue eyes are framed with eyeliner, which yes, I'll secretly admit is extremely sexy.

Honestly, all three of them are sexy, but I'm never going to tell them that.

"Are you done mentally undressing me?" Asher questions, arching his brow.

"That's not what I was doing." A partial lie, but whatever. "I was just wondering what was up with all the buckles and metal on all you guys' clothes."

"Sure you were." Asher smirks, but then his lips sink back down as he sighs. "Planet Steel has a very distinct look, which is why you need to change. You already stand out too much."

"I do not. Well ... unless there isn't a lot of human-looking creatures here. Then maybe I do."

Asher trades a look with East before looking back at

me and shaking his head. "You really have no idea, do you?"

"Nope, I'm completely clueless," I reply, irritated because it feels like he thinks I'm an idiot, which I'm not.

Sure, I don't know much about world traveling and other planets, but I took care of myself since the day my parents were taken away from me. I learned how to get food and find shelter at a very young age. How to swindle, how to survive. A clueless person couldn't do that. Or, would at least be terrible at it.

"I wasn't trying to insult you, so stop sulking"—Asher sticks out his hand—"and let's go look through your closet and find a different outfit."

I don't want his help at the moment, so I swing around him and head back inside the vehicle.

When he follows me, I quicken my pace, striding down the hallway and hurrying into the room. Then I shut the door and lock him out.

Of course, two seconds later, he materializes in the center of my room, encompassed by a cloud of smoke.

Damn genie magic.

"You know, when someone locks the door, it usually means they want to be alone." Giving him a dirty look, I move to step around him.

He folds his fingers around my wrist, stopping me. "I'm sorry if I upset you," he says with a hint of sincerity. "I don't think you're clueless. In fact, East, Arrow, and I have had many conversations about how clever you are."

I raise my brows. "I highly doubt that."

"It's true," he promises. "If we thought you were clueless, we never would've tried to convince you to be *our* little thief."

"I'm not yours," I quip. "And you guys really need to stop trying to claim me."

His smoky eyes glint wickedly. "Hmm … If you say so."

"Think whatever you want, but I'm not yours. And I haven't and never will belong to anyone." I raise my chin as he continues to grin. "You know what? If you guys keep it up, I'm going to start referring to you as *mine*. How does that sound?"

His eyes cloud over, tiny sparks igniting in his pupils. "You can't claim a genie."

"We'll see. I mean, I did steal your lamp, so …" I smirk.

His eyes darken as he tugs me toward him. "You never would've stolen my lamp. I wouldn't have let you." He traces his lips with the tip of his tongue, his gaze flicking to my lips "And no genie in history has ever been claimed. But we've claimed a lot of creatures."

"There's always a first for everything." I grin, but I'm all bravado, my nerves bubbling the closer my body gets to his.

"Careful, little thief," he warns. "If you keep trying to

win this argument, I'm going to start wondering if you *want* me to belong to you."

For a mind-losing moment, I envision what it'd be like if Asher belonged to me. Then I quickly pull my head out of my ass.

I don't want him to be mine.

I don't want any creature to be mine.

If someone ever belonged to me, they'd probably die.

What I want is for things to go back to how they were.

Yeah, the last thought is a lie. The truth is, during my little journey with Asher, East, and Arrow, I've eaten better, slept better, and felt safer than I ever have. But I need to make sure I don't get used to this lavish lifestyle, because eventually, I'm returning home.

Like I even have a home ...

I heave a sigh. "Whatever. Will you get out so I can get dressed? I want to get this job done ASAP, so I can hopefully find out what I am."

He skims his finger along the inside of my wrist. "I understand your eagerness, but the city is full of cyborgs and other creatures, and it might take some time to get the Steel books."

I fight back a shiver stemming from his touch, but flustered magical creatures, does my body want to!

"How long?"

"I'm not sure."

"What about the tour? Don't you need to be somewhere soon?"

"We made a few changes to the schedule and moved our next stop to the end of our tour. Still, we'll be playing here tonight."

I gape at him "You're going to do a concert *tonight*? But what about the books?"

"We'll get them. I already said it'll take some time." He draws me closer until the tips of my boots touch his. "Doing this concert is a good excuse for us to be here and looks less suspicious."

"But Arrow said you guys parked all the way out here to avoid drawing fans' attentions? It doesn't make any sense." Unless they're lying to me about something.

"When it gets closer to showtime, we'll drive the vehicle to the arena and park there for the night." He's confusing the crap out of me, and it must show on my face, because he adds, "We always spend at least a day away from all the chaos of the tour."

"Really?" Cynicism drips from my tone. "Because it seems like you guys like the attention. Well, you and East seem like attention whores. Arrow … not so much."

His eyes narrow, but his lips tilt upward. "East loves the attention to an extent, but he gets tired of it. You're right about Arrow. He's always preferred being in the shadows rather than the spotlight. Unfortunately, he rarely gets the pleasure of the shadows. As for me"—he settles his hands on my waist—"I only like attention from creatures who don't annoy the fuck out of me. And so far, East and Arrow are on the only ones on that list. Although, East frequently bounces on and off it." He grows silent, observing me closely.

I think I know what he wants—for me to ask if I'm on his list, too—but I'm not about to give him the satisfaction.

"I guess I'll find out tonight if that's even remotely true." I give him a pat on the arm. "I'd really appreciate it, though, if you guys tied a scarf on the door or something so I know when aftershow women are in the vehicle. Well, unless I'm just going to stay on the vehicle. Then I'll just lock myself in my room and wear some headphones or something."

"You can come to the show." He momentarily searches my eyes. "And we're not going to sign up for an after-show party this performance."

"Don't do it on my account. I'm totally okay with going to my room and putting some headphones on or wandering around the city for a while." Am I, though? Who the hell knows anymore? "I just want to point out that I never have and never will be okay with the general idea of women having to whore themselves out ... Wait." A thought occurs to me. "Human women aren't on this planet, are they?" When Asher shakes his head, I ask, "Then, how is there even an aftershow?"

"Despite what you think, not every single person who signs up for the aftershow does it because they have to. And they aren't always human." His pale lips curl upward. "There're a lot of humans and creatures who have a fetish for getting fucked by rock stars."

I offer him a sugary-sweet smile. "How do you know? Maybe they just put on a show so they'll get good tips."

"I know the difference between wanting and having to do something," he assures me, his eyes smoldering. "And East, Arrow, and I always avoid hanging out with aftershow women who *have* to be with us."

I eye him over, wondering if he's telling the truth. In typical genie form, his face looks intense, his eyes flickering. What that means is beyond me.

"If that's true, then I guess you guys aren't as terrible as I thought. But I'd still appreciate a heads-up before you guys get some. The last thing I want is to accidentally walk in on *that*." I give an exaggerated shudder.

He rolls his eyes. "I already said we aren't signing up for the aftershow this time, so your little shuddering performance is pointless."

"It's not a performance." Sort of a lie. In reality, the idea of them being with aftershow women bugs the water fey out of me, but I'm not sure if I'm ready to confront why. "You can do whatever you want. I'm just saying, give me a heads-up."

His eyes shadow with smoke. "Has anyone ever told you how stubborn you are?"

"All the time. But it's what's kept me alive."

His smile falters as he assesses me. "Your life back on your old world … it wasn't good, right?"

I shrug. "It wasn't great, but it wasn't entirely bad either. There were some good moments." A small smile tugs at my lips. "Like this one time when Jason and I snuck into a circus. We didn't have any money, so we couldn't buy tickets to see any of the shows, but we did manage to steal a whole cartful of cotton candy. I'd never had it before and ended up eating, like, five bags in a row. Totally puked my guts up later, but it was worth it."

Pity fills his eyes, the opposite of the reaction I was aiming for. "Arrow mentioned that you hadn't slept in a bed since your parents … vanished."

My chest tightens a bit. "It's pretty common for humans not to have beds."

"And you didn't eat very well." More pity shows in his eyes.

Beyond uncomfortable, I crack a joke. "Um, *hello*, did you not just hear my cotton candy story?"

His lips tug upward, but the pity remains in his eyes. "Tonight, you're going to come to the show. And afterward, we're taking you out."

"But I thought this city was dangerous? And what about the books?"

"I already told you it's going to take a couple of days to get the books." He sighs tiredly. "And while we're here, we need to act as normal as possible, which means performing and partying."

"That's you guys' normal?"

"No, but that's what everyone believes." He reaches up and ravels a strand of my hair around his finger. "And while we're in the city, you need to be careful. Trust no one, okay?"

"I rarely trust anyone," I point out. "Except myself. And Jason."

He untangles his finger from my hair, angling his head to the side. "You've mentioned Jason a lot. Have you known him for a long time?"

I nod, stepping away from him and sitting down on the bed. "We were really close up until he got addicted to faerie euphoric dust. We grew apart after that, but only because of his addiction. When I go back, I'm sure we'll be close again. Well, that is, if he knows who I am." I give Asher a questioning look. "When East had me look in that Eyes All Mirror thing, his life didn't seem the same as it was before I made the deal with you."

"Really?" He plays dumb, but tension ripples through his body.

"Yes, really." I arch my brows. "He could afford baked goods, and he's never been able to do that."

"Maybe he stumbled across some money after the underground mafia freed him?"

"Or maybe you gave him a better life when we made the bargain."

His lean muscles flex as he crosses his arms. "Now, why would I do that?"

"I have no idea," I answer honestly. "But you seem awfully uneasy, genie dude."

The corners of his lips kick up. Then he steps toward me and nudges my knees apart so he can step between them. My heart thumps wildly in my chest as he places his hands on the bed, trapping me between his arms, his gaze so intense I swear he's about to curse me.

As he dips his lips toward my ear, his cupcake scent surrounds me and makes my mouth salivate.

"And you, gorgeous creature, need to get changed," he whispers in my ear.

I shiver as he traces his fingers against the side of my leg then steps back, smirking.

I shoot him a dirty look, but I don't say anything, too worried I'll sound as breathless as I feel.

Giving me a cocky grin, he spins on his heels to leave.

The second he steps away from me, I let out a shaky exhale.

Get your shit together, Harlynn! You're better than this! Do not let some genie affect you so much that you forget who you are! And don't let him sidetrack you from the questions he still hasn't answered!

"He at least remembers me, right?" I call out before Asher exits the room. "Jason, I mean."

He doesn't look at me when he nods. "You may think I'm cruel, but I'd never take away someone you care about. Although, personally, I don't think he deserves you."

My fingers curl into fists. "You don't even know him."

"I know you almost died to save him."

"*I* chose to do that. He didn't force me to."

He remains silent for a beat or two before glancing over his shoulder at me. His eyes are flooded with smoke and pity. "If that's true, then how did the underground mafia know you're a thief?"

"I … I have a reputation around town." Not a total lie. Some people have heard of me and my thieving abilities, but not everyone. Still, the underground mafia could've easily found out.

"Jason cares about me—he always has." I loathe how my tone trembles. "And don't you dare try to take that away from me."

The smoke in his eyes dissolves. "You're right. I'm sorry." He offers me an apologetic look then walks out of the room, shutting the door behind him and leaving me to wonder why he brought Jason up. To hurt me? Maybe.

I don't know, though. It seemed like more than that, as if he knew something.

"No," I mutter, shaking my head. "I know Jason. He'd never do anything to intentionally hurt me."

It's Asher I barely know. I need to remember that.

Need to remember that, despite everything going on, I can trust no one but myself.

It's the first rule of surviving.

Picking out an outfit is a pain in the ass. Sure, I saw what Arrow, Asher, and East were wearing, but I'm struggling to pick out a girly outfit to wear. Finally, I give up on trying to solve the problem myself and wander out of the room to find Arrow and get his help. He seems like the best out of my three options, for several different reasons.

The three of them are in the living room when I enter, messing around with their instruments. East is tuning a guitar, Asher has his balanced on his lap and is plucking the strings, and Arrow is perched on a stool behind his drum set and near the hologram window revealing a view of outside.

"I'm not sure if that's the best one to start with," Asher says to East.

"It's fine." East rotates a knob on the guitar. "And it's better than the other choice."

"That's your opinion." Asher plucks a few more strings. "But we need to all agree."

Arrow sighs, spinning the drumsticks between his mechanical fingers. "You two have been arguing a lot lately."

Asher blasts him with a cold look. "Because we've been stressed out."

"You're always stressed out." Arrow stands up and slips his drumsticks into his back pocket. "I think your mood swings might have something to do with something else."

Asher gives Arrow a dirty look while East grins in amusement.

"I think he might be on to something." East leans his guitar against the sofa and sinks back in the chair.

Asher heaves an exhausted sigh. "Can we just pick a song? I want to be done with this by the time Harlynn comes out. We've already wasted too much time."

Since they seem too distracted to notice me, I clear my throat. "Actually, Harlynn needs some help before we can go."

The three of them startle, glancing at me, their eyes slightly wide.

Strands of East's blond hair fall into his eyes as he rises to his feet. "You walk more soundlessly than an elf."

"I'm not sure how soundlessly an elf walks, but I do know I can walk as soundlessly as a boss." I grin in pride. "If I couldn't, I wouldn't be a fantastic thief, now would I?"

East's lips curve into a grin. "Your cocky side turns me on so damn much."

I cross my arms. "Are you ever going to get tired of hitting on me?"

"Nope," he shamelessly divulges.

I sigh, my gaze skating to Arrow. "I need your help with something."

"Why not me?" East pouts at the same time Asher and Arrow ask, "With what?"

"With getting dressed." As soon as the words leave my lips, I realize my mistake and quickly try to recover. "I mean, with picking out an outfit."

It's too late. My slip-up has already caused Asher's eyes to funnel with smoke and East's pout to deepen.

"You're letting Arrow dress you?" East sulks. "That's not fair."

"It's not going to happen." Asher sets his guitar down and pushes to his feet.

"Will you guys chill out?" I gripe. "I said I want his help *picking* out an outfit, not helping me put it on."

"Actually, you didn't say that the first time," East points out. "And if he gets to dress you, then I want to next time."

"Oh, my gods," I groan, bobbing my head back. "No one gets to dress me." I gesture at their outfits. "You guys are just dressed so differently than what I'm used to, so I'm not sure what to wear. And since Arrow is from here, I figured he'd be able to help me." Not the entire truth, but they don't need to know everything that goes on inside my head.

Like how I don't want East to help me pick out clothes because his little flirty jokes are starting to make me smile and blush too much. Or how I refuse to let Asher help because, every time he touches me, my skin tingles and the air gets stolen from my lungs.

East visibly relaxes, but Asher remains wound up. Still, he doesn't argue when Arrow follows me back to my bedroom. Then we head to my closet, and he begins sorting through the selection.

"I can understand why you thought I'd be able to help you pick out an outfit," he tells me, "but I should've warned you that I know nothing about fashion."

"But you know how women … or female creatures here dress, right?" I lean against the closet doorframe with my arms crossed.

He stiffens. "Yeah, but I've never been a fan of how they dress … or of female creatures here," he nearly whispers the last part.

Sensing a sink in his attitude, I tread cautiously. "Can I ask …? Do you mind if I ask why?"

He avoids my gaze as he assesses a leather corset. "A lot of them wear these types of tops."

His avoidance makes me wonder what happened to him, but I'm not about to press. No, if anyone can understand not wanting to talk about their past, it's me.

"A leather corset?" I step farther into the closet, frowning at the top. "Isn't that going to be a little … I don't know, binding?"

He shrugs. "Probably. But if you don't want to stand out, this is probably your best choice."

I crinkle my nose. "I guess I can wear it if you think it'll help me blend in."

"Unfortunately, I think it will. Although, I'm sure not everyone will agree with me on the unfortunate part." His gaze quickly skims over me, and then he looks away, appearing embarrassed.

This isn't the first time I've seen him do this. The last time being when I accidentally stared at his crotch.

Okay, it wasn't an accident. My mind temporarily went in the gutter when I wondered if cyborgs have mechanical penises, a question I'm still waiting to hear the answer to. Not that I'm going to ask anyone on this vehicle.

"What do you think I should wear with it?" I decide to let him off the hook from his embarrassment, something East never does for me.

When his gaze slides to mine, a hint of gratitude flashes in his eyes.

"Let me see what I can find." He starts digging through the clothes again, finally pulling out a dark purple, velvet skirt that's long in the back and bunched up in the front with ribbons.

"This won't make me stand out?" I ask, fiddling with the ribbons and stitching on the front. "It looks pretty fancy."

"You'll be fine," he promises, reaching toward the top shelf and grabbing a pair of thigh-high, lace-up boots. "Wear these. And if you can find some fingerless gloves in your dresser, put those on, too." He waits for me to nod then steps out of the closet and opens the door to leave.

I glance down at the corset, at all the ribbons and clasps on the back.

Awesome. I'm never going to be able to get this on myself.

"Arrow, wait," I call out, glad I chose him to help me with this task. I don't even want to imagine how Asher or East would react over the question I'm about to ask.

He pauses with the door halfway open, glancing at me with his brows knit. "What's wrong?"

I hold up the corset. "I might need some help getting this on."

His throat muscles work as he swallows hard. "Maybe I should go get East or Asher."

"I'd rather you help me." When he frowns, I hurriedly add, "Never mind. I'll figure it out myself."

He remains standing in the doorway for a faerie kiss of a second before stepping back inside and shutting the door. "No, it's fine. I can help."

"Are you sure?" I ask, and he nods. "Okay, give me a second to slip it on. Then I'll have you do up all the ribbons and clasps on the back."

He stuffs his hands into his pockets. "Okay."

Offering him a thankful smile, I duck back into the closet. Then I peel my shirt off and start trying to figure out the best way to wiggle into the corset. Slipping it over my head seems too complicated, so I decide to step into it and slide it up over my hips.

"Do creatures dress differently on all the planets?" I ask as I pull the leather corset up my body.

"Yeah, everywhere has its own style," he replies with a hint of uneasiness. "Shimmerland is very shimmery. Here they dress more steampunk. Planet Water is probably the worst, though."

"Why's that?" I suck in as I slip the corset over my breasts. *Gods, these things are even more uncomfortable than they look.*

"Because at least half the creatures walk around naked."

"*What?* Please tell me you're joking. Or at least tell me we're not going there."

"Um … I'm joking, and we're not going there?" he says it more like a question.

"You're a terrible liar. Has anyone ever told you that?" And come to think of it, I can vaguely recall Asher mentioning that we're going to planet Water.

Lovely. I can imagine the sort of jokes East is going to come up with about following the dress code.

"Actually, yeah," Arrow replies. "I hear that a lot."

"It's okay, though. I kind of like it."

"Why's that?" he asks curiously.

I press my hands against my chest to hold the corset in place as I step out of the closet. "Because I've spent a lot of time around people who are excellent liars, and it gets tiring."

He smashes his lips together, his gaze scrolling up and down my body. If he were East or Asher, I'm sure he'd make some sort of dirty remark about the cleavage popping out of the top, but he remains silent as walks toward me, making a circular motion with his finger. "Turn around so I can do all the laces and clasps up."

I turn my back to him. "Try not to do it up too tightly. I can barely breathe right now as it is. But try not make it too loose, or else it might fall off and everyone will think I'm from planet Water."

He chuckles, his breath dusting the back of my neck as he brushes his fingers along my back.

I peek over my shoulder at him. "What's so funny?"

"It's nothing." He shakes his head, smiling.

I narrow my eyes at him playfully. "Obviously, it's something, or else you wouldn't be grinning."

"Maybe ..." He sighs, but the smile on his face remains as he laces up the ribbon on the bottom of the corset. "I was just thinking how irritated East and Asher probably are right now."

"Why? Because you're in here with me?" I wince as he moves to the next ribbon and tugs on it.

"Yeah ... They're probably losing their minds with wondering what we're doing." He yanks on the third ribbon, pulling the leather tighter against my chest.

I grin, facing forward again. "We should pretend like we're doing something wicked just to fuck with them."

"What should we pretend to do?" His fingers slightly tremble as he moves to the next ribbon and softly tugs on it. "Your skin's so soft," he murmurs, skimming his fingertips up the mid-section of my back.

"That might be a good place to start," I breathe out, feeling breathless. I'm going to blame that on this death grip of a top and not on the way his fingers are lightly tickling my skin. "Maybe say it a bit louder, though, so they can hear you."

He chuckles, sweeping my hair to the side and out of the way. Then his laughter fizzles. "What is this?" He sketches his fingers over the space of skin between my shoulder blades.

I peer over my shoulder at him. "What is what?"

He meets my gaze, a crinkle between his brows. "How long have you had this tattoo? Because it looks really fresh."

"What tattoo?" I honestly have no clue what he's talking about.

He briefly studies me before steering me across the room and into the bathroom connected to the bedroom. Then he positions me between two mirrors hanging on opposing walls so I can see my back.

Sure enough, between my shoulder blades is what appears to be a tattoo in the shape of a star, the dark purple ink contrasting with my pale skin.

Holding up the corset with one hand, I reach back and trace my fingertip along the star and across the strange shapes and symbols inside of it. "I've never seen this before."

"So, it's new and just appeared?" Arrow leans down to inspect it.

"Not necessarily. I mean, I can't remember the last time I've actually seen my back, if ever, so it might've been there for a while." I shift my weight as his breath tickles my skin. "Honestly, I can't remember the last time I looked at myself in a mirror."

He lifts his head in surprise. "You can't remember the last time you looked at your reflection?"

"No, just not looked at it in a mirror. I've seen it plenty of times in windows and in water."

A trace of pity masks his expression. Then he sets his hands on my shoulders and turns me toward the full-length mirror on the wall beside the sink. "Well, now's your chance."

I angle my head to the side, taking in my big eyes; my messy, long, brown hair; the freckles on my nose; and my extremely long legs.

"I don't think I've been missing out on much."

He shakes his head. "You have no idea just how uniquely gorgeous you are, do you?"

A sweet thing to say, but entirely inaccurate.

I offer him a small smile. "Thanks for saying that, but I look like every other human. And I'm okay with that. There are way more important things in life than being pretty. Besides, if I were gorgeous, then I probably would've been forced into prostitution by the underground mafia. Or worse, turned into a paranormal's plaything."

He rubs his lips together then captures my gaze in the mirror. "Do you know we thought you were an artificial human when we first met you?"

"I heard you guys talking about it, but I'm not sure what that is, so ..." I shrug, the movement awkward with his hands on my shoulders.

"There's a factory here on planet Steel where cyborgs

are created." He gives a short pause, sorrow masking his face. But, as quickly as the look arises, it erases. "There's been rumors that the manufacturers have been trying to come up with a way to create more realistic cyborgs, ones that are created completely of flesh, bone, blood, and organs so they resemble a human, but they have the strength and abilities of a cyborg."

"And you guys thought I might've been one them?" I ask, and he nods. "Why? Because your sensors register me as human, yet clearly, I'm not?"

"That was part of it. But it was also because of how you look." He nervously reaches around and brushes strands of my hair around. "You look human-ish, but if my sensors didn't register you as human, I'd have guessed you were a faerie."

I snort a laugh. "I'm nowhere near pretty enough to be a faerie."

"Yes, you are," he insists. "In fact, you sort of look like Lavender."

I give him a blank stare. "You think I look like a flower?"

He smiles, his eyes crinkling around the corners. "No, the Shimmerland princess." I start to shake my head when he says, "Take a look if you don't believe me." Reaching over, he places his palm on the small hologram window that's currently showing a view of a serene field lined with daisies. "Show me the Shimmerland princess."

The daisies and field shift into a magical area covered with trees and moss and vines blooming with glittering silver flowers that sparkle against the iridescent light shimmering down from the sky. Standing in the center of it all, next to a wooden throne carved from a tree trunk, is a faerie who looks around my age, although she's more than likely older. Her big eyes reflect the light that Shimmerland emits and her long, purple hair whips in the wind as she strides forward, her long, green dress trailing across the ground. Her pale skin sparkles, and her features are startling flawless.

"You think I look like her?" I give Arrow a are-you-crazy look.

He lightly brushes his fingers across the top of my head. "Aside from the purple hair, yes."

I shake my head as I glance back at the hologram. "Yeah, I don't see it. She's way too ..." I try to think of the right word to describe her. "Otherworldly-looking."

"If you had purple hair or shimmering skin, you would, too," he insists. "And even without that, you still look otherworldly sometimes. And I'm sure others have thought that. But, since you register as human and haven't shown any signs of having powers until the other day, I'm sure everyone just assumes you're a gorgeous human."

"You're overwhelming me with flattery," I joke, feeling extremely uncomfortable. Not just with how many times he's called me gorgeous, but because I'm starting to wonder if Arrow, Asher, and East may not have been the only ones to think this about me.

When the underground mafia called me in to strike a bargain to save Jason's life, Lead, the leader, asked me a strange question. At the time, I couldn't figure out why.

"Maybe we can strike a bargain to save your friend's life," he said, thrumming his fingers against his desk. *"Let me hear what your gifts are, and I'll see if you're of any use to me."*

"Well, I'm great at stealing stuff." I said the only thing I could think of.

"I already know that," he replied. "But, tell me how."

"Why I make such a great thief?" I was so confused.

He nodded, leaning forward and resting his arms on the desk. "Tell me about your gifts and how you manage to get into places without being seen. And tell me the truth. If you lie, your friend dies."

So, I proceeded to tell him about my awesome lock-picking skills, my soundless footsteps, and my ability to create a great distraction.

He seemed super unimpressed and questioned if I wasn't telling him everything. He spent over an hour making me answer question after question about my past, my current life, and why I could easily sneak into places most humans couldn't. Eventually, he struck the genie-lamp deal with me, but he seemed almost disappointed about it.

Thinking back, he threw the word *gifts* around a lot. I

thought he meant my ability to sneak around and stuff like that. Maybe, though, he knew I was different and that was why he accused me of lying to him several times.

Then again, he could've just been wary that I wouldn't be able to steal the lamp.

"What's wrong?" Arrow asks with a crease between his brows.

"It's nothing …" I yank my mind away from memory lane. "I was just remembering when I met Lead—the leader of the underground mafia. He was really interested in my gifts and was asking me all sorts of questions, but I think maybe he was just making sure I could hold up my end of the deal. He seemed super paranoid. He even made me sign a contract in blood."

His eyes widen. "He has some of your blood?"

"Well, some of my dried blood on a piece of paper …" I tense as I feel a wave of anxiety roll over him. "What's wrong? Why are you panicking?"

"It's nothing." He shakes his head, his posture stiff. "Let me do up the rest of the corset so you can get dressed." He starts lacing up the ribbons again.

I wince as the corset constricts around my chest, my breasts curving out of the top.

"Are you sure nothing's wrong? You seem upset."

"I'm fine. I just realized how late it is. We should probably get to the city soon, or else we won't have time to get things done before our concert tonight." He secures the last ribbon then steps away from me. "I'm going to go get a few things. Meet me in the living room when you're finished getting dressed, okay?" He hurries out of the bathroom without waiting for me to reply.

I watch him leave, more than aware that he's keeping something from me. But what?

My mention of the blood contract seemed to have set off his anxiety, but even before that, when he was staring at the star tattoo on my back, he appeared edgy. And what even caused the tattoo to suddenly appear? It's not like I ever got one. I'd remember if I did.

Turning around, I look at my back in the mirror again. The ink looks fresh, just like Arrow said. Reaching around, I run my finger along the tattoo. For the craziest moment, I swear I feel sparkly. But, as swiftly as the sensation emerged, it fizzles away, leaving me to wonder if I imagined it.

Then again, a lot of strange things have been happening, so who the hell really knows?

CHAPTER 18

After Arrow leaves the room, I quickly put on the skirt then rummage around for some fingerless gloves and knee-high tights to wear underneath the boots. I throw clothes out of the dresser and onto the floor, not bothering to pick it up. Why the rush? Because I'm hoping, if I can get dressed quickly enough, I may be able to do a bit of eavesdropping on the guys and figure out what had Arrow acting stiffer than a … well, a cyborg. But like it's been mentioned before, Arrow isn't like other cyborgs, so his rigidness seems out of character for him.

It takes me longer than I'd like to find the gloves and tights, but I eventually do. Then I hurriedly tug the gloves on, slip the tights over my legs, and then lace up the boots over them. I top the look off with a velvet choker, pin my hair up in a mess of waves and braids, and then dash toward the door, not bothering to glance at my reflection. Not just because I'm in a rush, but because I'm worried that, if I actually see myself, I'll want to change into an outfit that will cover up my legs and chest area.

Seriously, while the material of the skirt is soft, the hem is extremely high in the front, resting about mid-thigh. And the corset is worse, barely covering my chest. Not that I'm super modest or anything like that. I've just always been a holey jeans and T-shirt sort of girl. And this outfit is … well, it's sexy. And I'm not sexy. I'm a kickass thief who knows how to defend herself if she needs to. If I had to try to fight in this getup, I'd probably end up falling on my ass.

"This outfit better make me blend in," I mutter as I crack open the door and slip into the hallway.

I cringe as the heels of the boots softly *click* against the floor and the fabric of the dress swishes.

So much for sneaking up on the guys.

I really hope they don't expect me to steal the Steel books in this.

Despite my noisy outfit, I do my best to quietly creep down the hallway—

"Oh, Asher, how I've missed you!"

I freeze at the sound of a feminine voice. *What in the worlds?*

"Now, Darla, I know that's not true," East replies lightly. "No one ever misses Asher."

Arrow snorts a laugh. "I'll toast to that."

"Now, now," the woman scolds jokingly. "What have I told you about teasing my poor, grumpy Asher."

Her poor, grumpy Asher? *What the shit?*

"That we should do it as often as possible," East replies wickedly.

"And to make sure to hide his lamp while we do," Arrow adds, his upbeat tone almost unrecognizable.

Who the heck is in there with them? And why do they sound so happy?

Taking a deep breath, I peer around the corner and into the living room.

Arrow is sitting on a chair with his boot-clad feet kicked up on the coffee table; East is near the bar, filling a glass with a sparkling silver liquid; and Asher is lounging on the sofa with his arms stretched out across the back, a relaxed smile on his face.

A relaxed Asher? That actually exists?

My gaze travels to the fourth person in the room; a female-type creature standing near the kitchen. Tall, curvy, and wearing a pinstriped dress and thigh-high boots, she looks maybe a handful of years older than me, but it's hard to tell for sure. And she's definitely paranormal; her long hair like fire, her lips stained crimson, and her pale white eyes glow against the low lighting in the room.

What is she?

"You seem in an awfully good mood," she says to Asher as she raises a glass to her lips. "Any particular reason?"

He flashes her a grin. "Because you're here, of course."

She takes a sip of her drink then struts across the room and sits down on his lap. "I've missed you," she purrs, running her fingers through his hair. "We need to start seeing each other more often, especially if you're going to be this elated to see me."

Asher's lips pull into a grin as he slips his arms around her waist. "Oh, I'm beyond elated to see you, baby."

Baby? Gag me.

His gaze drops to her lips, flames blazing in his eyes. She wets her lips with her tongue and leans in, her lips nearing his ...

I should look away, especially since the closer her lips get to his, the more pissed off I feel. I have no idea why and know I have no right to be upset. Asher isn't mine, and I don't want him to be mine. And if he ever did become mine, either him or I would end up dead. So, yeah, I definitely shouldn't care that he's about to kiss some fire-haired creature, but holy jealous vampires, anger is bursting through me.

And the anger only erupts when she crooks a finger at East, who eagerly complies, striding across the room and sitting down on the sofa beside Asher. His lips instantly magnetize toward her neck, and he starts sucking on her skin.

She tips her head back and lets out a moan, reaching for Asher's hand. Then she laces her fingers with his and guides his palm toward the hem of her dress ...

I look away, my face bright red, and not entirely from embarrassment.

"Come on, Arrow," she begs. "Please join in. I want to know what it's like to have all three of you—"

A flash of energy ripples off me and waves through the air, shaking the floor and causing all the portraits and knickknacks on the shelves to topple over. Even Arrow's drum set topples to the side, the cymbals crashing loudly against the floor.

Whoops. I *so* didn't mean to do that.

East jerks back, his wide eyes matching Asher's and the creature's. Arrow is the only one who doesn't seem that surprised, but that's typical for him.

"What in the worlds?" She glances around at the broken picture frames and glass covering the floor. When her gaze lands on me, her nostrils flare as she jumps off Asher's lap and hisses, "Who is *she*?" Flames flare from her lips as scales ripple across her skin.

Fear spikes through me. While I've never seen one before, I think she might be a dragon-shifter, a very rare and very dangerous creature.

I slowly back away toward the hallway, a little bit

scared and a bit mortified. "Um … I'm the girl who's going to back up and let you guys finish your little … orgy." I start to turn when she lunges at me, smoke funneling from her nostrils.

Then her lips part, and she blows fire at my face.

I barely duck out of the way in time, and the flames graze my cheek.

Breathing wildly, I reel toward her and try to will my body to send out that wave of energy again, to no avail. So, I do the only thing I can do. I make fists and hope she doesn't have a super hard jaw.

Her lips curl in delight, and then her jaw unhinges—

East leaps to his feet and wraps his arm around the creature's waist, pulling her back against him. "Oh no, you don't, you evil wench."

Asher and Arrow jump to their feet, too, rushing toward … the bar?

What the hell? They're getting a drink? Right now?

"Let me go!" she snarls, smoke funneling from her lips as she tries to wiggle away from East. "You said you were alone, but clearly, you're not. You lied!"

East wraps his hand around her neck. "Yes, we did lie, didn't we?" he purrs. "I'm surprised you didn't figure it out sooner, since we turned you down the last time you showed up on our doorstep, looking for a good fuck."

She snaps her teeth, throwing her weight forward.

"Fuck you all! You have no idea who you're messing with."

"Actually, we do." Asher returns to the middle of the living room with a small glass bottle in his hand.

"It's the only reason we let you in," Arrow adds, positioning himself in front of her and crossing his arms.

I've seen them do this before—strategically placing themselves around someone so they can't escape. That time being when they caught me trying to steal Asher's lamp. While I was nervous when they did it to me, now it's kind of amusing watching it from the other end. But I'm not sure why they're trying to trap this creature or what they plan to do with her …

My mind briefly wanders back to how touchy they were getting with her on the sofa. While none of them actually did anything, except for East kissing her neck, anger still flickers through me again and the floor trembles.

"Sweetheart, could you tone that lovely magic of yours for just a minute?" East begs as he fights to keep the creature in a headlock.

"Sorry," I mutter, beyond confused on how my anger is making the floor shake.

East offers me a tense smile then tightens his grip on the creature's neck, her face turning as red as her hair. "Hurry up, please," he says to Asher and Arrow. "Her hair's burning the shit out of my chest."

Asher twists off the cap of the bottle then moves to dump the contents inside the creature's mouth, but she spits fire at him.

"Shit." Asher jumps back, cursing and shaking his hand.

"This'll be a lot easier if you just cooperate," East grits out as he lifts the creature up until her feet are no longer touching the floor.

Her lips twist into a pained grin, and then she sinks her fingernails into his arm. East winces, his grip loosening from her just enough that she manages to wiggle away.

Her pale eyes lock on me. "You're dead."

"What the hell did I do?" I gripe, skittering back.

She grins then lunges at me again, but Asher sets the bottle down and grabs her. Then him and Arrow wrestle her to the ground, pinning her onto her back and holding her arms and legs to the floor.

East kneels down beside her head then pries her mouth open with his hands. "Quick. Someone pour the sleep mist down her throat," he says as he positions his knees on her shoulders.

Asher removes his hand from her arm to reach for the bottle, but then flames immediately ignite across the creature's flesh.

"Dammit." Asher returns his hand to her arm. "It's taking all our power to keep her fire contained."

"Well, someone has to pour the mist down her throat," East growls, his anger startling the crap out of me.

As stupid as this might sound, I thought the only emotion he knew how to show was flirty, except a couple of brief times when he appeared pained.

"I'll do it," I offer, surprising myself and them. "Well, I will if you tell me what the mist will do to her."

"It'll knock her out," Asher explains, his features flowing with tension as he positions his knee on the writhing creature's arm.

Tendrils of smoke wisp from her nostrils. "Na uns unna ock e ow!" she shouts while East holds her mouth open.

Asher rolls his eyes, his gaze settling on me. "Hurry up, little thief." He winces as her skin sizzles. "Before she ends up burning the entire place down."

"Why do you want her knocked out?" I ask, scooping up the bottle he dropped—the sleep mist, I'm guessing.

The lid is off so some of it spilled out onto the floor, but there's still a little bit of wispy ribbon-like liquid inside.

"Because we need something from her." Arrow grasps the creature's wrist tightly as she tries to take a swing at him. "And we can only get it if she's asleep."

"You're not doing anything bad, are you?" I ask, rotating the bottle in my hand.

"Trust me; if we are, she deserves it." Asher flinches as

blisters sprout across the back of his hand. "She's an energy sucker."

My brows pull together. "I've never heard of those."

"It's the slang term." Asher's face bunches in pain as the creature huffs smoke into his face. "Look, I'll explain more after you've knocked her out."

I have a lurking feeling he may be avoiding telling me exactly what kind of creature she is, but I find myself stepping forward anyway. Then I move around toward her head and, gathering the bottom of my dress in one hand, kneel down beside East. I don't feel very guilty as I pour the mist down her throat, and that makes me worry that perhaps my time away from my world is taking away some of my compassion. Then again, she did try to set me on fire, so …

"Your eyes are really freaky," I tell her, stroking her head, mostly to fuck with her. "And your scales are super gross."

When she snaps her teeth at me, I grin.

"You know what? I think you should look into becoming a dominatrix." East winks at me. "In fact, I can give you some pointers." A glint twinkles in his eyes as he shakes his head. "No, pointers won't do. I think a demonstration is the best way to learn, don't you?"

I roll my eyes. "In your dreams, faerie dude."

He grins. "Is that you giving me permission to do anything to you in my dreams?"

I roll my eyes again. "Sure—"

Asher hastily covers my mouth with his hand.

"What the hell?" My voice is muffled against his hand.

Asher stares East down hard. "Did you seriously just try to get her to agree to that?"

East shrugs, a mischievous smile twitching at his lips. "Don't pretend like you wouldn't do the same if you could."

I pry Asher's hand off my mouth, relaxing a smidgeon as the energy sucker's body goes still, her eyelids drifting shut.

"Will someone tell me what's going on?" My gaze bounces between Asher and East. "Because, as far as I know, faeries don't have the power to enter dreams."

"Most don't." Asher's gaze never wavers from East. "But East has a rare gift." He glances at me. "A gift he can only use with permission."

"So, you're saying, because I told him he can go into my dreams, that he can now?" I gape at East.

"Relax. I'm not going to do it." East pushes to his feet and dusts off his hands. "Well, unless you ask me to."

I shrug. "Go ahead. I barely remember any of the dreams I have. In fact, sometimes I wonder if I dream at all."

"Everyone dreams." East strolls over to the bar and picks up a glass and a bottle of silvery liquid. "Even if you don't remember them." He pours himself a drink then takes a long swallow before turning back toward me. "My bet is, your lack of proper sleep ruins your cycle and makes your dreams hazy."

"Maybe." I glance at the creature to make sure she's completely passed out then push to my feet. "So, what's the deal with her?"

"We already told you. We need something from her." Asher gracefully stands then strolls over to the bar to pour a glass of the silvery liquid stuff for himself.

"Yeah, I know, but you never specified what that was or what she"—I gesture at the creature—"is."

Arrow's gadgets hum as he straightens to his feet and comes over to stand beside me. "She's a demon," he says, rubbing at a charred bronzed piece on his arm.

My eyes pop wide as I skitter away from the demon sprawled out on the floor. "She's a *demon*? I just leaned over a demon's mouth?" I put my hands on my hips, glaring at them. "You guys should've warned me."

Demons are probably the most dangerous creatures. At least, if you're a human. People on the streets run for miles if they even hear rumors of one being in the area. The main reason they instill so much fear in us—well, humans—is that demons have the capability of stealing souls by drinking them from human's mouths.

"Will you relax? You're not human, so your soul was always safe," Asher says then devours his drink in one, long gulp. Then he sets the glass down on the counter and steps toward me, his gaze deliberately scrolling from my boots to my thighs, along my chest, and all the way up to my face. "That's what you're wearing?"

I shift my weight, self-consciously adjusting the corset then fiddling with the ribbons on the front of the skirt. "Arrow said I'd blend in, in it."

Asher glances at Arrow with his brow cocked.

Arrow lifts his hand to massage the back of his neck. "She would've stood out in anything I put her in. Even jeans and a T-shirt. At least, this way, she looks in style."

Asher doesn't reply, continuing to stare Arrow down.

The gadgets in Arrow's arms hum louder as he grows more fidgety. "Don't blame this on me," he says, lowering his hand to his side. "If you want her to put on something else, then go ahead. But I think she looks … lovely."

"*Lovely?*" Asher questions with his brows arched. "Since when do you use the term *lovely?*"

East lets out a soft, amused laugh. "Well, this is fun." He takes another sip of his drink then leaves the glass on the counter and crosses the room. "I think everyone needs a time-out."

Asher glances at him. "*You're* telling us to take a time-out?"

East shrugs, his eyes glinting. "There's a first for everything."

They grow quiet, silently staring at each other, Asher

sporting a grumpy face, while East sparkles with amusement, and Arrow continuously shifts his weight.

Finally, I can't take the maddening silence anymore.

My dress swishes as I step forward, positioning myself in the center of them. "Will someone please explain why you guys needed to knock out a demon? And for how long is she going to be passed out? Because I sure as hell don't want to be around when she wakes up."

They stare at each other for a drumbeat of a second longer before tearing their gazes off each other and fixing their eyes on me.

"She'll be out for at least half a day," Asher says, stuffing his hands into his back pockets. "And she'll be far away from here by the time she wakes up."

"How? Are you going to drag her body into the woods or something? Because I'm betting she'll get back here pretty quickly. And I'm sure she'll be pissed off and wanting revenge. And while I'm not positive what demons do to get revenge, I'd rather not find out." I move my fingers to my cheek where her flame lightly grazed my skin and wince from the soft sting.

"She won't be getting back here anytime soon," Asher assures me. "Because she'll be in a prison."

"A prison?" I glance warily at the demon. "There's a prison for demons?"

"On this planet, there is," Arrow answers. "She'll probably escape eventually, but we'll be gone by then."

"I sure hope so," I mumble, touching the spot on my cheek again. "Because she didn't seem to like me, and that was before I poured sleep mist into her mouth."

"So what if she doesn't like you?" East says in amusement. "If she comes after you, you can just use your amazing little powers on her."

"Yeah, I don't think shaking the floor is going to protect me from a revenge-crazed demon." I fold my arms around myself. "And I'm not even sure how I unleashed my power."

East slowly wets his lips with his tongue. "You sure about that?"

I nod, feeling super twitchy inside. "One minute, I was standing there, watching you guys …" Fuck, did I seriously just about admit aloud that I was watching them get their orgy on? "And the next, the floor was shaking."

A slow grin carves across East's face. "You were watching us do what?"

"Nothing," I stress. "I didn't mean to say that."

"Liar," East says, circling me. "You were watching Asher and I touch Darla, weren't you?"

My shoulder involuntarily shudders upward, but my voice comes out even. "I didn't know you touched her."

"You lie well, sweetheart, but I can tell you're not being truthful."

In front of me, Asher watches me with fire-lit eyes, his arms crossed, his muscled tightly raveled.

"Why would I lie about this?" I turn my head and lock gazes with East. "It's not like I give a shit if you were touching some nasty-ass demon. That's your issue, not mine."

"Nasty-ass demon?" He smirks, leaning over my shoulder and setting his hands on my hips. "Is that jealousy I detect?"

"Nope." Another flawless lie. Inside, though, my pulse is quickening.

Calm down and win this argument. Don't let the faerie win or let him discover you were jealous when he was touching that nasty-ass demon.

"Hmm ..." His eyes sparkle as he moves his lips toward my ear while slipping his fingers underneath the hem of the corset and brushing them against my sides. "You don't need to be jealous," he whispers. "We didn't really want Darla, and we were never going to do anything with her. We were just distracting her so we could slip some sleep mist into her drink."

"I know that's a lie ... I heard her say you guys hooked up with her before." As soon as the words leave my lips, I want to bitch-slap myself.

Damn tricky faeries! I just admitted I was watching them.

He chuckles lowly in my ear. "That was a long time ago, and Asher and I were both so fucking drunk and high we barely knew what we were doing. Trust me; if we had been sober, we wouldn't have touched her." He brushes his fingers across my side. "We're not into demons."

"Good for you." I roll my eyes. "You know I don't care, right?"

Another chuckle, and then he grazes my earlobe with his lips. "I think you might be lying again."

My heart sprints in my chest. "Just because you don't want to believe the truth, doesn't mean I'm lying."

"So, you're telling me that you didn't get upset when you saw Asher and I touching Darla?" he questions with a glimmer of amusement in his voice. "That seeing us with her wasn't what made your powers set off and knock everything onto the floor?"

"No," I say, cringing at the breathlessness of my tone.

"Then, why do you sound so breathless?"

"It's the corset. It's squishing my lungs."

"Liar," he breathes hotly into my ear. "But you're good at it. And I'm glad. It'll be useful during our thieving journey."

I press my lips together, staring at the wall behind Asher, refusing to say anything else that might reveal just how big of a liar I am.

East softly tickles my skin. "If you'd let us, we'll touch you however you want. I think even Arrow would, and he never participates in our sexual endeavors."

My gaze instinctively flits to Arrow, who's staring at

me with his brows knit, but then he rapidly looks away when our gazes collide and drags his hand over the top of his head.

"Do you want us to do that?" East asks, sketching a path across my waist. "Do you want us to all touch you like that?"

"Like what?" My voice is a bit shaky, but at least I get the words out. "I really have no idea what you're talking about since I never saw you touching Darla."

A deep chuckle reverberates through his chest. "You're good, sweetheart. Maybe one of the best I've seen in a while."

My heart flutters in my chest at his compliment, but I tell it to shut the fuck up. That we're so not going there, to a place where I actually get excited over a compliment from a faerie.

"Again, I don't know what you're talking about," I say evenly, causing the corners of Asher's lips to twitch.

"Hmm … Well, if that's the case, then I guess I better show you." He brushes his lips along the side of my neck.

Both tension and desire flare through my body, and I swallow hard.

"I don't need a demonstration." I internally cringe at how flustered I sound.

"You sure about that?" He kisses my neck again, slightly parting his lips to gently suck on my skin.

I squeeze my eyes shut as a soft gasp slips past my lips.

Goosebumps break out across my flesh as he traces circles along my hipbone—

"That's enough," Asher bites out.

My eyelids flutter open as East pulls back. Then I hurriedly smash my lips together, trying to hide my breathlessness, but the binding corset makes the rising and crashing of my chest painfully obvious.

"Yeah, you're probably right. I do need to stop," East says . "But only so *we* can do the demonstration properly." He splays his fingers across my hip. "Come on, Ash; you're just as much a part of this as I am."

"I don't want a demonstration." What I want is this needy desire to stop controlling my body. The problem is, I've never been touched like this before—never been touched much at all—and my body thinks it's been missing out on something.

Stupid hormones.

"I'm not going to do anything right now," Asher says flatly, although his eyes are saying the opposite, blazing with flames. "We have other shit that needs to be done, so get your hands off her and let's get the demon's soul out of her damn body before she wakes up."

It's like a cold bucket of ice water has been dumped over my head.

I wiggle out of East's arms and fold my arms across my chest. "You're taking her *soul*? Huh … Why?"

Asher's gaze bores into mine for a brief but intense

moment, then he yanks his eyes off me and focuses on the demon. "Because we need it to get into the vault."

"Which is what exactly?" I gesture for him to give me more.

"The place where the Steel books are kept," Arrow explains, his arm brushing mine as he steps closer to me. "To get inside it, we need some very specific items."

"Like a demon soul?" I still can't wrap my head around that. "I didn't even realize demons have souls."

"They do, but they're very small and withered." Asher crouches down beside Darla and tilts his head to the side as he examines her. "We're lucky she showed up, or else we would've had to track one down. This way saved us a lot of time and headaches."

"Do you guys have demons knocking on your door a lot?" I ask, adjusting the top of the corset.

"Not always, but sometimes." When I crinkle my nose, he adds, "Darla's a groupie. She usually shows up at least once during every tour stop."

"So, she follows you around to different planets?" I ask, and East nods. "How pathetic."

"I completely agree." East flashes me a wicked grin. "I'd much rather be doing the chasing."

I press my lips together, the spot on my neck where he sucked tingling a bit. "Not everyone who runs from you wants to be chased."

His brow elevates. "Is this another one of our life lessons?"

I press back a smile. "Maybe."

Curiosity sparkles in his eyes. "What about you?"

My brows furrow. "What about me?"

He slants forward, his voice lowering. "Do you want to be chased?"

I roll my eyes. "In your dreams."

His grin widens. "Do we really need to do this again? I know you're lying. About a lot of things."

I roll my eyes.

Asher glances at me then at East before shaking his head. "Are you done wasting time?"

East gives him a thumbs-up. "Yep, I'm good."

Asher heaves a sigh then rolls up his sleeves and adjusts his cuffs. "Then let's get this over with so we can get back here in time to transport to the arena."

"Relax, we'll have plenty of time." East places his hands on the demon's arm.

I've never seen a soul extracted from anything before, so I slant forward to get a better look as Asher leans over Darla's face—

Arrow enfolds his metal fingers around my wrist and rapidly steers me toward the hallway. "You don't want to be in there while they do that; trust me."

"Is it gross?" I ask as we stop in front of a shut door that I know leads to his room. Not that I've ever been in there before. I just glanced in once when I snuck into their vehicle to steal Asher's lamp.

Nodding, he pushes open the door. "When a demon drinks a soul, they drink it out of the creature's or human's mouth. But to get a demon's soul out of their body, you have to reach into their mouth and pull it out."

I shudder at the mental image of Asher reaching into Darla's throat. "I owe you a huge thank you then, because there is no way in hell I wanted to see that."

Arrow offers me a small smile, though his face is creased with tension as he pulls me into the room with him. "There are a couple of things I want to talk to you about, starting with that tattoo on your back." He releases my arm, walks over to a metal dresser, and opens the top drawer.

"Do you think it's something bad?" I take in all the different shades of metals and gadgets around the room, the orbed chandelier, the gleaming metal floor, and the massive four-poster bed welded with various metals.

His room is wicked cool.

"I think it might be a key to what you are." He bumps the dresser drawer shut, clutching a small, metal box in his hand. "Like a mark or something."

I blink in surprise. "Really?"

He nods then sits down on the edge of the bed. "Tattoos don't just appear out of nowhere. They have to be put on you." He sets the metal box down and pries off the lid. "And I'm not sure that the star on your back is a tattoo."

"It looks like one to me." I watch as he removes a rag from inside the box and starts rubbing it across the charred piece of bronzed metal weaved through the flesh of his arm.

"If you look closely at it, you can see it has a sparkly texture to it, and it's a bit elevated. Tattoos are usually made with flat ink stained into the skin." He scrubs harder at the spot. "Plus, those symbols inside the star aren't from any language I know. I'd like to find out if they mean anything."

"How do you do that?"

"I know a few Seeker Seers in the city. They might know something. But we need to be careful what we say to them about you. Or anyone for that matter …" He trails off as he looks up and notes me watching him. Then he swallows hard. "Darla burnt my metal with her flames. This is the only way I can get it off." He squirms a bit. "Sorry if it's weird."

Confusion weaves through me. "Why would it be weird?"

He shrugs. "Some creatures find cyborgs' habits a bit unsettling."

"You're just polishing your arm. That's not weird." I sit down on the bed beside him and take the rag from him. Then I dip it into the polish that's inside the metal tin before rubbing at the burnt spot on his arm. "See? Not a big deal." I smile, but it swiftly falters when I notice he is staring at me in astonishment. "Sorry," I say, figuring I crossed a line by not asking first.

I start to stand up and give him the rag back, but he seizes ahold of my wrist.

"No. Don't," he utters quietly.

I hesitate then slowly sit back down and start rubbing at the singed spot again.

His eyes track my hand as I drag the rag across the metal. I'm unsure what's happening, but his eyes convey a drop of fascination, so I continue polishing him for longer than I probably need to.

"I'm sorry I'm acting strange," he mumbles, yanking his gaze away from my hand. "It's just ... I've never had anyone polish me before."

I chew on my bottom lip. Wait ... Is this like porn for cyborgs or something?

"It's nothing sexual," he quickly adds, as if reading my mind. "It's just nice to be ... touched."

"Do you not get touched a lot?" Okay, this conversation could be heading to some very awkward territory if I'm not careful.

He shakes his head. "Most want nothing to do with my kind. Even my own kind doesn't want to get close to each other."

"So, you spend a lot of time alone?" How sad. A sadness I understand way too well.

"I did until I met Asher and East. Things changed when I joined the band. My life got more … hectic."

"In a bad way?"

"In a different way than what I was used to." He rotates to the side, bringing his knee up onto the bed between us. "It's weird because, while I'm on stage, I'm surrounded by a ton of creatures screaming out my name. And even when I step off, there're still so many creatures wanting to be near me. But somehow, I still feel alone most of the time."

"Maybe it's because you haven't found your person yet. Or, well, your creature."

His forehead furrows. "What do you mean?"

I set the rag down on the bed and twist toward him, keeping my feet on the ground to avoid my skirt riding up higher than it already is. "Before I met Jason, I spent a lot of time alone. And I mean, *really* alone. I didn't have any friends and my family was gone, and honestly, I was kind of afraid that, if I got too close to someone, I'd end up loving them and they'd die. But then I met Jason, and he wiggled his way into my life. We ended up becoming really good friends, and I found out that it was nice to have someone to talk to and to be there for me. And even though I always had to hold back a little when I was around him, he made me feel not as lonely."

Sadness flickers across his face. "The only creatures I'm close to is Asher and East, and honestly, I spend more time keeping them out of trouble than talking to them." He rubs at another burnt spot on his arm with his thumb. "I swear they're always getting in trouble."

"That doesn't surprise me."

He offers me a smile that doesn't quite reach his eyes. I know that smile. Have worn one similar many times.

"If you want, I can be your person." And yep, I've officially lost my damn mind.

What is going on with me lately? First, I let East kiss my neck, and now I'm offering to be Arrow's BFF? I think all this worlds traveling and craziness is starting to mess with my head.

"You're offering to be my friend?" He seems confused and a bit amused.

I shrug. "Well, you don't have to be if you don't want to. I just thought, since we're here, and I currently don't have my person, you could be mine and I could be yours." I scrunch my nose. "Although, neither of us are really people, so I think we may need another term for our impending friendship."

He chuckles softly, his silver eyes bright. "You're an interesting creature. You really are."

"Thanks … I think."

"It's a good thing," he assures me. "Trust me; I come from a world of boring and ordinary, and it's not great."

I give a pressing glance at my outfit. "I'm not sure I agree with you on this world being boring and ordinary, since I have to dress up like this just to blend in."

A tiny smile graces his lips. "You look nice, though."

"Are you sure?" I question. "Because Asher seemed upset when he saw what I'm wearing."

"That wasn't what he was upset about."

"Then, what had his panties all in a bunch?"

His brows knit. "Panties in a bunch? What does that mean?"

It's like the foodgasm conversation all over again.

"It's an expression that means he was acting super uptight," I attempt to explain.

He shakes his head. "Your world has very odd terms."

"How would they say it on your planet then?"

His lips threaten to turn upward. "That he was acting super uptight."

Smiling, I lightly swat his arm. "Whatever. I like human terms better. They're much more … interesting. Then again, I'm not even human, so maybe all the terms I'm using are wrong." A frown pulls at my lips as realization smacks me hard.

I'm not human.

I'm some weird-ass creature.

What if my kind is from another planet than the one I grew up on?

What if there's this whole world I don't know about?

But, if all this is true, then how did I end up in the human world and was raised by my human parents? And as far as I can remember, they always treated me like I was human.

Did my parents know what I am?

My whole life has been one, big lie.

"Just because you found out you're not human, doesn't mean your past doesn't belong to you," Arrow says sympathetically. "You're still you, and you can remain being who you are. You don't have to change, no matter what we find out about you."

His words bring me a drop of comfort.

"You're kind of good at this best friend's thing." I give him a playful yet accusing glance. "Are you sure you've never done it before?"

His lips twitch into a smile. "Nope, I can honestly say you're my first."

"What in the worlds are you two talking about?"

Arrow and I both jump at the sound of East's voice drifting from across the room, and then my gaze darts to the doorway.

He's standing there with a curiously amused expression.

"It's a secret," Arrow tells him. Then he trades a quick, amused look with me, and I grin.

"Yep, and we're not going to tell you," I add, smirking at East.

East juts out his bottom lip. "That's not very nice."

I lift a shoulder. "We're not trying to be nice."

East's frown deepens, then he leans back and calls out down the hallway, "Asher, Arrow and our lovely little pet are keeping a secret from us."

I roll my eyes. "What a little tattletale."

A ghost of a smile emerges on Arrow's lips. "Oh, I know." He takes the rag from me and sets it in the tin. "Usually, I'm the one he's tattling to."

"You should come up with some sort of punishment system for whenever he does it," I suggest with a conspiratorial grin.

"I'll only agree to that if you're the one who gets to punish me," East says as he ambles into the room.

"Sounds good to me." I tap my finger against my lips. "I'll just need a pair of iron cuffs, a dragon ash laced whip, and a bottle of hell fire liquid." Faeries are weakened by all the items I prattle off, so I expect East to get offended. But I should know by now to never expect anything from East other than flirty smiles and dirty remarks.

An impish grin etches across his face as steps closer to me until the front of his legs bump mine. "And how will you punish me with those?"

"Um … by using them on you?" *Why does he seem so pleased about this?*

His grin magnifies as he leans over me and places his hands beside my hips. "Harlynn, Harlynn, Harlynn, my innocent, naïve, little creature, I'm not sure what to do with you."

"Maybe back off," Arrow suggests with a shrug.

East's eyes glint with surprised delight, but his gaze remains on me. "And yet, despite your naïve innocence, you've somehow managed to wrap Arrow around your little finger."

I try not to squirm. "I have not. We're just friends."

"Really?" East is all sorts of amused as his gaze dances between Arrow and me. "He's never tried to be friends with anyone before. Usually, he avoids everyone unless we force him to socialize."

Arrow's silver eyes glaze over with irritation. "That's because the company you invite to our vehicle usually isn't worth getting to know."

"Yeah, probably," East agrees. "But I find it amusing how quickly you've gotten close to our little thief."

"I'm not yours," I point out in exasperation.

"It's okay," he assures Arrow, ignoring me. "It's good you like her since we'll be keeping her for a while. Maybe forever, if she gets attached."

I glare at him. "That won't happen."

East dramatically rolls his eyes. "We'll see."

"You're beyond annoying," Arrow tells him.

"But not beyond inaccurate." Grinning, East pushes back and offers me his hand. "Are you ready to go, my little creature?"

"Only if you stop calling me *yours* and *little creature*."

His smile is filled with trickery. "Then, what do you want me to call you?"

"Um, my name," I tell him like *duh*.

He dismisses my request with a flick of his wrist. "That's too easy."

I sigh. "And that's a bad thing?"

He nods in all seriousness. "Complications make life much more interesting."

"So, you're saying that me showing up in your vehicle and ruining your plan to get rid of Asher's father was a good thing?" I question with skepticism.

"You didn't ruin our plan. Just changed it a bit." He snatches ahold my hand and effortlessly hauls me to my feet. "You showing up in our vehicle was one of the best complications ever."

"Yeah, we'll see if you're singing the same tune after having to deal with me for a couple of weeks," I say, tugging the hem of my skirt down.

"*Months*," he reminds me with a grin. "We get you for at least a couple of months." He pulls me forward. "Now, let's get going."

Sighing, I let him guide me toward the door with Arrow trailing at my heels. When we enter the hallway, I reach back and grab Arrow's hand for no other reason than I don't want East thinking I'll just walk around, letting him hold my hand and pretending I belong to him.

Arrow doesn't pull away, but his metal fingers are rigid. Figuring I'm making him uncomfortable, I start to let go of his hand, but he laces his fingers through mine and holds on tightly.

I smile to myself. I don't even know why, other than maybe all of this chaos is making me lose some of my sanity. Then my smile fades as we walk into the living room and I see Asher and the demon aren't there.

I glance at East with my brows furrowed. "Where's Asher?"

"He took Darla to the prison," he replies, scooping up a few gold coins from off the counter and stuffing them into his pocket. Then he tosses a couple to Arrow. "We're supposed to meet him at The Bronzed Arch Center," he tells Arrow.

Arrow's lips sink. "Wait … We're not …" He grimaces as East nods. "I thought we weren't doing that anymore."

I glance between the two of them. "Doing what?"

Arrow rubs his forehead with the heel of his hand while East grins, tugging on a strand of my hair.

"We're doing a little PA," he explains.

"What's PA?"

"Personal appearance." Arrow is the one to answer, his hand falling to his side. "Which means we're going to stand around, taking photos and signing autographs."

"But I thought we were going to do things that'll help us get into The Vault," I say in confusion. "And Asher said you weren't doing anything for the tour until you were about to perform."

"That was the plan." East starts toward the front door, pulling me with him. "But then Maple, our band manager, called and told us we have to make an appearance."

"Oh … Should I just stay here?" And maybe, while they're out, I can snoop around a bit and see if they're keeping anything from me. Because it seems like they are. Like with that whole blood contract thing.

Wisps of East's hair fall into his eyes as he shakes his head. "It's too dangerous, especially when the worlds patrol might be after you."

"Hey, I have powers," I point out. "I'm not completely defenseless."

"I understand that." East's gaze sears into me. "But you need to learn to control your powers before you use them."

I see his point, but still … "I think to learn how to control my powers, I'll have to learn more about what I am, so shouldn't we—or at least I—be focusing on that?"

"*We'll* focus on that while we do some PA," East assures me as he opens the front door.

Bronzed sunlight spills inside the vehicle, making me squint.

"By signing autographs and taking photos?" I blink until my eyes adjust to the light.

"Are you doubting us?" East asks, highly entertained.

"No … But it seems like you guys are super busy, and since I'm not and I'm an excellent thief"—I plaster on an arrogant grin—"maybe I should just do this job alone."

East cocks a brow. "The next thing we need to get into The Vault is the essence of a succubus."

"Oh." Confusions winds through me, and I hate that it does. "What's an essence?"

"The outer layer of a soul," East explains with his brow still arched. "So, do you think you can do that? Do you think you can seduce a succubus into letting us borrow her essence for a bit?"

"Yeah," I lie.

East gives me a *really* look, to which I sigh.

"Fine, maybe I can't," I admit. "But still … it seems like I should be doing something else, besides standing around and watching you guys dazzle your fans."

"Oh, you will." He tows me out the door as he steps outside. "Because we also need an incubus's essence."

"Okay … Wait. What?" I skid to a stop, nearly falling on my ass as my heels slip against the slick ground. "How the hell am I supposed to help with that?"

He winks at me. "By doing what you do best."

"Steal it." I grin. "Sounds like fun. Well, unless I have to remove it like a soul." My smile dissolves.

"That's not what I meant." East taps his finger against his lips. "Okay, you'll be doing what you do second best."

I shrug, totally confused. "Be a smartass?"

He snorts a laugh. "You're the most adorable creature I've ever met." He traces his fingertip down the brim of my nose. "I meant you're going to distract him, sweetheart."

"Oh." I glower at him. "Hey, that is not my second-best talent."

His brows rise toward his hairline. "It's taken us fifteen minutes to walk out of this vehicle. And when the worlds patrol showed up, we were more distracted with your lips than the fact that there were hellhounds outside."

I pull a guilty face because he's so right. "I don't do it on purpose."

"I know." The most warming, adoring smile sparkles across his face as he tucks a lock of my hair behind my ear. "But you're still good at it."

My heart leaps in my chest from his compliment and from the way he's looking at me, and my breath quickens ever so slightly. And he more than notices, too, as my chest heaves and my breasts almost pop out of my top. Surprisingly, though, he doesn't comment on it.

"We should get going," he utters, his brows knitting, as if he's deeply puzzled.

That makes two of us. But I'm not about to ask him

what's bothering him since he'll more than likely embar-
rass me.

Instead, I focus on getting my breathing under
control as we start across the field toward the city that,
from the way these guys act, is extremely dangerous.

CHAPTER 19

THE CITY IS a few miles away from where we parked, and we have to take a winding path through the forest to get there. While nothing but metallic trees and bushes appear to be around, I have the strangest feeling of being watched. That feeling only amplifies the deeper we get into the trees.

"You doing okay, sweetheart?" East glances at me as we trek around the largest trees I've ever seen.

The coppery leaves glint in the golden-brown sunlight filtering through the polished branches above, making the entire forest appear shimmery and making my eyeballs wig out against the constant reflecting rays of light.

"Yeah, I'm fine." I blink a few times. "All this uneven, flickering light is just messing with my eyes a bit."

"I wasn't talking about your eyes ..." East scans me over. "You seem a bit uneasy."

"Oh." I clutch his hand as my boots slip against the ground. "I just have this weird feeling I'm being watched."

East's muscles ravel tightly as his gaze skims the trees.

"You think there's something out there?" Arrow asks, holding my other hand as he looks behind us then to the side.

East shakes his head, a crease gradually forming between his brows. "I can't see anything, but ..." He glances at me then at Arrow. "We know nothing about her powers, so for all we know, she could have a sensor built into her."

"A sensor that warns me when I'm being watched?" I ask. "Is that a thing?"

East shrugs. "It's not not a thing."

"There you go again, talking in riddles." I give a quick glimpse at the nearby trees as the watching sensation rolls over me again.

A familiar chill crawls up my spine, but I can't figure out what it is or why I'm feeling it.

"Relax. We won't let anything hurt you." East slips his arm through mine and yanks me closer to him.

Arrow does the same thing with my other arm, and then we start down the path again, all of us on guard, constantly looking around and tensing at every noise. The farther we walk, the more I begin to notice the lack of animals around, like bats, ravens, or wild horses. Back on my planet, the forest was filled with those types of creatures. Here, though …

"It's so empty here," I remark quietly as I fold my fingers around East's bicep and wrap my other hand around Arrow's arm. "I mean, where are all the animals and stuff?"

"There aren't any animals here," Arrow says, the gadgets in his elbows spinning as he digs a pocket watch out of his pocket to check the time. "Well, there're mechanical ones in the city, but they aren't like the animals on your planet." He puts the pocket watch away.

"We should really stop referring to it as *her* planet." East steers us down the left side of a fork in the path. "For all we know, she could be from someplace else."

"It's still where she can remember growing up," Arrow says. "Therefore, it's *her* planet."

"Where I can remember growing up …?" I glance up at him, my brows pulling together. "Wait. Do you guys think …?" I grind to a halt, forcing them to stop with me. "Do you guys think I've, like, lived longer than I can remember and have just forgotten a part of my life?"

The zero-shock factor on their faces lets me know it's exactly what they're thinking.

"Most paranormals don't age like humans," East explains reluctantly. "So yes, one of our theories about you is that you might be older than you think and you've somehow forgotten your life before you ended up on the human planet."

"I can remember most of my life," I stress. "All the way back until I was five years old."

"Then maybe we're wrong." East moves to walk forward again, but I refuse to budge.

"You are wrong," I tell him firmly. "I know my life. I have all sorts of memories of when I was younger and being with my parents, and no one's going to try to take those away from me."

"I'm not trying to take them away from you. We just …" He shuts his eyes and takes a deep breath, shaking his head before opening his eyes again. "We know for a fact that certain paranormals, especially very powerful ones, can tamper with other paranormals' memories. They can make you believe you experienced things that you never really did." He casts an apprehensively glance at Arrow, whose face is masked with startling agony. "And they can also take memories away."

Suddenly, this conversation is making a bit more sense.

Arrow told me that he can't remember much of his past. But that doesn't mean I believe my past and memories aren't real, or that I've forgotten a part of my life.

"I'm sorry for whatever happened to you"—I give Arrow's arm what I hope is a comforting squeeze then glance at East—"but unless there's some sort of proof that my memories were tampered with, I'm not going to think they were … I want … I need to hold on to the life I had with my parents." I subtly suck back the tears wanting to pour out.

East's expression softens as he molds his palm to my cheek. "Even if it ends up your memories were tampered with, the moments with your parents can still belong to you, okay?"

I nod, feeling too shaky to speak.

He offers me a consoling smile before lowering his hand and starting down the path again. This time, I follow.

Still, as we hike deeper into the trees, my mind lingers on what East said. What if my mind was tampered with? Why would a creature do that to me? And who did it? Did my parents know? Or was that life never even real? Was I just one day put into the human world with fake memories?

No. There's no way. Asher's dad taking my parents away and cursing me *did* happen. Asher confirmed that. But, what about before that? Was I born someplace else and just can't remember?

Gah! This is driving me crazy! I need to focus on something else before I have a panic attack.

A second later, my wish is granted when we emerge from the trees and into the outskirts of the city.

"Holy freakin' crazy trolls," I mutter as I take in the

coppery, towering buildings lining the brass streets, the abundance of cyborgs and creatures strolling around, and the stands filled with sparkly jewelry, delicious-smelling food, and lavish clothing.

A few vehicles are parked here and there, but most creatures are on foot. And everyone is dressed in steampunk attire, with gadgets, chains, buckles, leather, and lace decorating their clothing.

East smiles at my reaction. "So adorable."

I don't even care what he says at the moment.

I inch closer to him as we reach the streets, the air electrifying and smelling of baked goods. I instinctively take a deep inhale and, even though I had a pretty big breakfast, my stomach grumbles.

"I think someone's hungry," East muses as we weave through a crowd of what I'm guessing are vampires, since they have fangs and extremely crimson lips.

Then again, Darla had really crimson lips and she was a demon, so …

I press even closer to East and grasp Arrow's arm tighter.

"Don't be nervous," Arrow whispers in my ear. "We've got you."

I may talk a lot of smack about them never "having me," but this time I keep my lips zipped because, yeah, I'm kind of glad they have me right now. This place is crazy busy and super unfamiliar. It makes me uneasy, which leaves me feeling completely out of my element.

"Keep your head down," East suddenly mutters as we near a group of creatures, mostly female, who are decked out in matching leather corsets, striped skirts, and Ash East Arrow tattoos.

I choke on a shocked laugh as the guys duck their heads.

"Creatures actually tattoo you guys' band name on their skin?"

With his head low and his hair veiling his face, East reaches back and gently pinches my hip. "I find your shock insulting."

"I don't," Arrow says with his eyes fixed on the ground. "I hate that tattoo trend."

"I don't understand it." My heels *click* against the coppery sidewalk as we veer right and away from the tattooed groupies. "I mean, if you're going to get a tattoo, then shouldn't it be, like, personal and mean something?"

East tilts his head to look at me. "What's the star on your back mean?"

My brows crinkle as I glance at Arrow. "You didn't tell him?"

Arrow shakes his head. "I was planning on it, but everyone got too distracted with that Darla thing."

East slips his hand down my arm and laces his fingers through mine as he quickens his pace. "Tell me what?"

"I'll explain later." Arrow's gaze sweeps across another group of leather, trendily-dressed, tattooed creatures. "When we're not surrounded by creatures that could—and probably would—sell the story to a tabloid."

East takes longer strides as a creature wearing a long, black dress excitedly tries to push her way through the crowd toward us.

"It's Ash East Arrow!"

"Fuck … I really wish this planet had a back entrance," East mumbles, shoving creatures out of our way. "Maple should've set up a teleport session for us."

Arrow moves his arm away from my hand, but only to place his palm against the small of my back. "She probably didn't have time."

"No, she's just getting lazier with every tour stop," East disagrees. "I think, when we have time, we should sit down and discuss hiring someone new."

Arrow frowns. "We just hired her two months ago."

East throws a stressing look at him. "You know as well as I do that the only reason we agreed to hire her is because of who her father is."

"Who's her father?" I wonder, eyeing the bags of glittery, silvery cotton candy hanging from the roof of a candy stand.

They have glittery, silvery cotton candy here?
East glances at Arrow, who shrugs.

"We might as well tell her now," Arrow tells him. "Before Maple does, because you know she will."

East blows out a sigh. "I know, but I'm worried I'll scare our little mouse."

"I don't get scared easily," I gripe. "I didn't even freak out when I thought Asher's death poison was going to kill me. I was just mildly worried."

The edges of East's glimmering lips twitch. "True, but I can think of a couple of things that frighten you." He sinks his teeth into his bottom lip, his gaze flicking to my mouth.

"I'm not afraid of kissing you," I say indignantly. "I just don't want to."

"Is that why you gasped when I kissed your neck?" His insinuating gaze flits from my eyes to my neck then to my lips, and my stomach flutters.

Stupid, idiotic stomach.

"I didn't gasp because I wanted you to kiss me," I lie. "The corset was too binding."

"You guys are getting distracted again," Arrow murmurs. "And we're about to the Arch, so now would be a good time to tell her who Maple's father is, before Maple shows up and blindsides Harlynn."

East wrenches his gaze away from my mouth and sighs. "You're probably right—"

Someone shouts their band's name again, and he

abruptly spins sideways, squeezing into a very narrow alleyway.

I trip over my skirt as I struggle to rush after him, and Arrow ends up bumping his shoulder against the side of the building as he hurriedly makes the turn.

"Why are we taking this route?" Arrow asks as we sidestep down the alley. "It'll take us longer."

"But we'll have more privacy." East inches to the side. "And I don't want to walk in through the front entrance where everyone's lined up."

"We could've taken the back streets," Arrow mutters as he struggles to squeeze down the slender space. "I can barely fit through here."

"The back streets are too crowded." East glances over his shoulder at him. "If you want, you can go that way."

Arrow shakes his head. "I'm fine."

A smirk twitches at East's lips. "That's what I thought."

Arrow sighs but doesn't comment, focusing on getting through the alleyway instead.

East is a little less muscular, so he's not having as difficult of a time. And I'm much smaller, so I'm not struggling at all. But Arrow is a bit more broader and taller than East, probably due to the metal woven in his body, and his shoulders keep bumping into the walls.

"Maple's father is Asher's father's brother," East spits out suddenly.

I slam to a halt so swiftly that Arrow crashes into me.

"Fuck," he curses, bringing his hands down on my shoulders, his chest pressed against my back.

"Sorry," I mutter then glare daggers at East. "So, she's a genie?"

East shrugs, glancing at me. "Yes and no."

I give him a firm look. "I don't know what that means, so you're going to have to explain it."

"Her father is a genie, and her mother was a faerie, so she's a little of both," he says as he ducks underneath a stairway running down the side of the building and halfway into the alley.

"I didn't realize faeries and genies could procreate," I comment, lowering my head and struggling to crouch low, thanks to the corset.

"A lot of different creatures can procreate," East says, putting his hand on my head so I won't bump it on the bottom of the stairway. "It just doesn't happen very often."

Uneasiness bursts through me as I straighten. While I've warmed up to the idea of being around Asher, I in no way, shape, or lumpy ogre form want to be around another genie, especially another one related to the genie that cursed me.

I open my mouth to say just that when Arrow unexpectedly lets out a string of curses.

"Damn stiff arms," he grumbles.

I peer over my shoulder at him and my eyes widen.

He's stuck. And in the odd angle, half bent down and turned, his shoulders wedged underneath the bottom of the stairs.

"You're stuck," I say, laughter tickling at the back of my throat.

Do not laugh at him. It'd be so mean.

His silver eyes lock on mine. "Why do I get the feeling you think this is funny?"

"Because it is." East rests his chin on my shoulder while sliding an arm around my waist. "You should see yourself right now. Seriously, where's a camera when you need one?"

"It's not funny," I attempt to say with a straight face, but my voice is all wobbly.

Arrow gives me a dirty look. "Some best friend you are."

"Hey, best friends can laugh at each other," I protest, feeling awful. "I'm sorry. I really am. It's just that ..." I trail off, my eyes narrowing as Arrow grins.

"I'm just messing around with you, Harlynn."

I can't help smiling. "Your smile's really pretty." It really is.

Arrow shifts, trying to look away, but since he can't turn his head, I get a good view of his flushed cheeks.

"You made the cyborg blush." East kisses my cheek. "Bravo, you clever girl. Do you know how hard that is?"

I roll my eyes, but a smile threatens to turn at my lips.

Arrow quietly sighs. "Can you two quit joking around and get me out of here?"

"And how do you propose we do that?" East questions in amusement. "You're stuck underneath a stairway that's welded to a metal building. I mean, I'm strong"—he tilts his head as his gaze travels to the top of the stairway—"but not that strong."

"Can't you, like, make it vanish or something?" I ask, resting my hands on the railing.

"I could if I had some vanishing dust, but my stash is in the vehicle," East says. "If I go back, we'll be late."

"If I stay stuck, we'll be late," Arrow reminds him, wiggling his shoulders.

"I could always go buy some grease and slather it all over you," East proposes cleverly. "That might make you slippery enough that we can push you out of there."

"That sounds messy." I give the railing a little shake, unsure what I'm even trying to do.

East glides his hands up my arm, reaching up to grip the railing, too. His chest is pressed against my back, his breath hot on my neck. "We could always get naked and lather all of us up. Imagine how messy that would be."

I roll my eyes. "That wouldn't help Arrow get unstuck."

"No, but it'd be a lot of fun," he says wickedly. "And I did promise to give you a demonstration on the proper way to have an orgy. Although, it'd be more of a threesome."

"Will you stop flirting with her and go back to the vehicle to get some dust?" Arrow demands, his head bumping my thigh.

That's when I realize how close his face is to my lady parts and how high the hemline of my skirt is.

"Look, we're one step away from it already." East chuckles in my ear, his gaze fixed on where Arrow's head rests close to my upper thighs.

Irritated and a bit flustered, I move back to bump into him, but my ass ends up grinding against his man goodies.

"Fuck," Easts moans, his body stiffening against mine. "Please don't do that again. At least right now. It's too distracting and makes me want to spread open those long legs of yours and slip inside your—"

"Don't finish that sentence!" I shout, my body tingling with warmth.

Hot, I feel so scorching, as if I'm on fire—

Swoosh.

I skitter back, slamming into East as the stairway folds up and dissipates into thin air. Then the ground begins to shake, the alleyway widening as the buildings slide farther apart. Then, just as swiftly as it all happened, the air around us stills.

"What was that?" I whisper with wide eyes.

East holds me tightly against him while Arrow straightens, rubbing his head, his enlarged eyes mirroring mine.

"I think your power just made an entire stairway vanish and an alleyway widen," East states in awe.

I twist around to look at him. "But I didn't even do anything, except feel a bit … hot. But only because you embarr—frazzled me."

East steps back and taps his lips. "Correct me if I'm wrong, but it seems like, every time you unleash your powers, you're frazzled. Or, at least your emotions are running high."

I think back to how worried I was when I first used my powers, back when the worlds patrol had us surrounded. The second time, I was extremely irritated over East and Asher touching Darla. And this time, I was frazzled over East's dirty remark.

"That seems pretty accurate," I tell him. "But, what's your point?"

East props his shoulder against the wall. "My point is, maybe your emotions are what control your powers."

"But, what are my powers?" I wonder, readjusting the skirt. "I mean, so far I've only made the ground shake and a stairway fold up and vanish."

"And an alleyway widened," Arrow adds, dusting some dirt off his shoulder.

"True," I agree, noting the spaciousness around us. "But, what sort of power is that?"

"I'm not sure, but I'm really curious to find out what else you can do," East says then straightens and reaches for my hand. "But that'll have to wait until later. Right now, we need to get this little shindig over with so we can move on to more important things."

I start to take his hand, but then I pull back. "Wait. About Maple ... I'm not sure I feel comfortable being around another genie that's not Asher. And one that's related to Asher's father."

"Maple can't hurt you. Her powers are weak at best," East swears to me. "And even if she could, we wouldn't let her."

"I'm not really afraid of her hurting me," I divulge the partial truth. "It's just ... I don't know. I mean, I've barely gotten comfortable with the idea that Asher is related to the genie that ... that took away my parents. And now I'm supposed to be around another creature related to him ...?" I suck in a slow breath through my nose as my voice cracks. "Sorry."

"Don't apologize. It's okay to be upset." East brings my hand to his lips and grazes them across my knuckles. "We'll do everything we can to keep her away from you without it being too obvious. We can send her on errands. We do that a lot anyway. But I don't think it's a good idea to tell her to stay away from you. It'll just draw attention to you."

"Maybe you can give me something to do," I suggest. "Honestly, I'd rather be doing anything else than just sitting around."

"You won't be sitting around," East promises. "You'll be having fun."

"Doing what?" I ask dubiously.

Arrow's arm hums as he extends his hand forward and threads his fingers with mine.

I smile to myself. *He grabbed my hand first.*

"There's plenty of stuff to do backstage," Arrow says. "Just make sure not to leave that area."

Hmm ... "I know you guys said this city is dangerous, but so far, the only danger I've seen is from the too-thin alleyways."

Arrow's fingers tense around mine. "That's because it's daytime. It's during the night when we have to worry."

The way he says it, with such fear in his tone, sends a chill down my spine.

"What happens at night?" I dare ask.

He sucks in a shaky breath. Even East seems to quiver a little.

"It's when the monsters show their true selves," he whispers ominously.

CHAPTER 20

ARROW'S WORDS have me feeling all sorts of crazy uneasy, but I do my best to fake being okay, something I'm fantastic at. At least, I used to be. But either I'm starting to lose my awesome being good at being chill skills, or Arrow and East can read me well, because they keep checking on me.

"Are you sure you're okay?" East asks as he weaves us around what looks like a passed-out ogre blocking our path.

The road we're hiking up is slender and uneven, and while the population is sparser in this area, the few creatures loitering by the stands and bars are giving off a much darker vibe.

"I'm fine," I tell East for the umpteenth time. "I'm just

a little weirded-out about being on this planet. I mean, did you guys see that dude back there with the horns growing out of his forehead? He looked like the devil himself."

"Actually, I think he was one of his spawns." East's grip on my hand constricts as we near a large, bulky creature with scaly skin reclining against a lamppost.

I gulp. "Are you being serious?"

East nods, sweeping strands of his blond hair out of his eyes. "He has a lot of spawns. Don't worry, though; they can't hurt you unless you give them permission."

There are literally no words, and I only grow more speechless as the scaly creature's lips part and a lizard-like tongue snaps out, darting forward and nearly licking my cheek.

"Hey." East smacks his tongue away. "Touch her, and that disgusting tongue of yours will be cut off."

"And who's going to make that happen?" Scaly dude challenges through a hiss. "You or the little robot?"

East slows to a stop, his normally glittering eyes darkening like firestorm clouds. "I would be careful what you say, lizard."

Scaly dude trips back and scrambles inside a nearby bar.

"What was that about?" I wonder. Faeries aren't necessarily known for being the most frightening creatures, yet scaly dude looked scared out of his damn mind. "And how are your eyes doing that weird fiery thing?"

East blinks a couple of times, and the fire liquefies into smoke. "We should get going," he mutters. "We're already late."

From behind me, Arrow nods, his body rippling with tension.

My gaze dances between the two of them. "You guys aren't telling me something."

"Unfortunately, we can't tell you a lot of things yet," East mumbles, entwining his fingers through mine.

I wiggle my hand from his grip, cross my arms, and stare him down. "It's unfair to expect me to be okay with that statement."

"Who said anything about expecting you to be okay with it?" East asks.

"Well, um …" I frown. He has a point, but still … "You guys expect me to tell you everything, yet you keep stuff from me. Like whatever just happened with your eyes, or why Arrow got all twitchy when I told him I signed a contract with my blood." I hold up my hands as East's lips part. "It's cool. Keep your secrets, and I'll keep mine." I swing around him and stride down the zigzagging street, the heels of my boots *clicking* against the cobblestones.

Sure, I'm not certain where I'm heading, but I'm making a statement right now. That I'm tough and can take care of myself.

I only make it a handful of heel *clicks* before I get that feeling that I'm being watched again. Unlike in the forest, this time there are plenty of paranormals around that could be watching me. The question is: which one?

I discreetly scan the creatures strolling up and down the street, leaning against lampposts and buildings, and a few standing on balconies. Most of them appear distracted, but a few are glancing in my direction—

A towering creature with dark eyes, silver lips, and pale skin materializes in my path so swiftly that I nearly run into him. Thankfully, though, I manage to quickly slam on the brakes and regain my balance. Then I hurry to figure out what he is.

He's sporting an ankle-length, black cloak, and his dark eyes suddenly illuminate hauntingly beneath the shadow of his hood. I'm unsure I've ever seen anything like him, but the scent of darkness flowing off him seems strangely familiar.

"Easy, princess," he purrs. "Where are you going in such a rush?"

"Get out of my way," I say as calmly as I can.

His lips curl into a sly smirk. "It's been a long time since I've run into one of you that's feisty. Usually, your kind is submissive."

A zap of tension zips up my spine. "What do you mean by *your kind?*"

His eyes crackle like embers. "You don't know ... Interesting." He purrs the last word.

A shiver rolls through me. My first instinct is to twist around and see where in the hell East and Arrow are, but since I'm trying to prove a point that I'm independent, I keep my gaze on the creature in front of me.

"What do you know about me?" I dare ask, stepping toward him.

And why does he smell so familiar?

His eyes shadow over. "You're clueless. Master will be so pleased to hear that."

"Who the hell's your master ...?" My eyes widen as he dissolves into a pile of ash. "What the heck? I ..." I have no clue what just happened.

Wanting answers more than I want to prove my independence, I reel back around, planning to ask East and Arrow, but they're not there.

Huh?

Squinting against the sunlight, I skim the streets, balconies, and buildings, my bubbling tension erupting into panic. Every single creature, from vampires to cyborgs to faeries are watching me with interest.

"Shit." I spin around and dash down the road, keeping my gaze trained ahead, except for giving the occasional glances out of the corner of my eyes. So far, almost every paranormal I pass glances up at me, but none make a move to come near me. That doesn't bring me a damn drop of comfort as I aimlessly wander down the street with an abundance of faerie questions dancing in my mind.

Where did East and Arrow go? Did they just leave me? Or did something happen to them? And why is everyone gawking at me like I'm some rare, weird creature …?

A thought bitch-smacks me across the face.

What if that's exactly why they're staring at me? Because they know what I am. I mean, the guys said I had to be something rare and unheard of, so maybe these paranormals can see that.

"Dammit, why do I have to be so damn stubborn?" I curse myself for wandering away from East and Arrow as I make a sharp veer down a desolate alleyway and out of sight of the watchful eyes. Then I collapse back against the brass wall and take a deep breath. "Just calm down, Harlynn. Panicking isn't going to do you any good." Another breath in then out. "Get your shit together and make a plan."

The first idea that comes to mind is to go find Asher, East, and Arrow, but a part of me wonders if they ditched me. It's not like I wandered very far away, yet we somehow managed to lose each other. Yeah, I'm not buying it.

Maybe some more fans spotted them and they had to

duck into someplace nearby? Or maybe one of the para-normals lurking around did something to them? I don't know, though. I mean, lizard tongue dude seemed afraid of East. Plus, from what I've seen, the guys are perfectly capable of handling problems. Maybe they just got tired of handling mine.

Like a little bitch, reality rushes up and smacks me again.

I've brought nothing but problems into the guys' lives, and the only reason they ever brought me on this little adventure to begin with was for me to help them steal those objects. Now that I'm not human, I'm basically useless to them and have made it so the worlds patrol is probably tailing them.

Honestly, when I really analyze the situation, I don't blame them for ditching me. It wouldn't be the first time something like this has happened. Back when I first started living on the streets, I tried to befriend a couple of people so I wouldn't be totally alone. This was before I attained my awesome stealing abilities and my badass survival instincts, so no one really wanted me around.

My heart tightens at the memories of people telling me to leave, that I was slowing them down, that I was more of a problem than someone useful. After about the third or fourth time of that happening, I decided it was easier, at least on my pride and self-esteem, to take care of myself. So, I started teaching myself how to swindle, how to find shelter and food, and how to fight. And about a year later, I became the self-sufficient, badass mofo that I am today.

Remember that, Harlynn. You don't need anyone. You're tough. You can handle this.

Sucking in an inhale, I push away from the wall and square my shoulders. Then I leave the alley and start down the road, heading in the direction that leads back toward the entrance of the city. When I get there, I'll hike back through the woods, sneak into the guys' vehicle, and steal that demon's soul they stole earlier. Then I'll hack into their computers and find out what else I need so I can steal the Steel books. Sure, a lot could go wrong, and I highly doubt it's going to be that easy, but it's better than tracking Asher, East, and Arrow down and pathetically begging them to help me. No, I refuse to do that.

After I pull off my amazing plan and have the Steel books in my hands, I'll see if Asher is ready to dissolve the bargain. If not, I guess I'll still be stuck with him, East, and Arrow. Or, maybe I should say, they'll be stuck with me. But if I'm correct about East and Arrow ditching me, I doubt Asher will have a problem dissolving the bargain.

Still, as okay as I'm pretending to be, as I backtrack with my head held high, I can't help noticing the slight twinge gnawing at the center of my chest, right where my heart is beating. A twinge that feels an awful lot like heartache. Heartache over what? I'm unsure.

Or maybe I just don't want to admit the reason to myself. Admit that perhaps I was starting to like Asher, East, and Arrow just a little bit.

Admit that them bailing out on me hurts like an evil demon bitch.

CHAPTER 21

OKAY, so maybe I was a bit overconfident when I thought I'd just stroll on back to the guys' vehicle and put my plan into motion, something I learn when I run into my first obstacle. Aka a sassy elf and his droning cyborg sidekick.

"You look lost," the elf sneers as he emerges from the shadows of an alleyway nestled between a bar and a robotic arm repair shop.

The cyborg steps out behind him, the gadgets in his arms rotating as he crosses his arms and stares me down with shadowy eyes that are so much duller than Arrow's. And unlike Arrow, this cyborg lacks emotion, his expression blank, his eyes hollow.

The elf, however, is sparkling with glee as if he just stumbled upon a buried treasure.

I recall how East compared me to an elf once, at least

in terms of cleverness, but then added how I didn't look like one. I've never actually seen an elf up close, and while I prefer not to act vain, a bit of relief trickles through me knowing I don't resemble the … Well, how do I put this nicely? The icky creature standing in front of me.

Rounding in at an average height with wrinkly, damp skin, and a long, pointy nose, the elf isn't attractive. He also has a giant mole on his cheek where long hairs are growing out of it like whiskers. His brows look like caterpillars, and sharp, yellow teeth hang out from his grey lips.

"I'm not lost," I reply with confidence. "Now, please step out of my way, or else I'll have to make you. And trust me; I don't think that's going to be a pleasant experience for either one of us." I shudder at the mental image of having to put my hands on his moist-looking skin.

"You can try, but you won't succeed." He nods at the cyborg then gives me a shit-eating grin. "L's my bodyguard."

"Your name is L?"

When the cyborg nods, I shake my head.

Man, Arrow really is one of a kind, isn't he?

"What's wrong with L?" the elf prods.

"It's boring as fuck," I state bluntly, folding my arms and pretending to be way more chill than I am.

Dammit, why didn't I bring a weapon with me?

Because I was stupidly distracted by East and Arrow!

"Yeah? So what?" the elf replies, his face contorted in perplexity. "Cyborgs are boring as fuck and, therefore, need boring names."

"Not all of them are boring," I disagree. "And maybe if you gave him a better name, he'd be more exciting."

The elf rolls his eyes. "If you believe that, then you're more naïve than I first assessed."

"I'm not naïve at all," I argue, moving to step around them. "Now, if you'll excuse me …"

The cyborg moves lightning quick, blocking my path and grabbing my arm.

"You're not going anywhere yet." The elf circles around me, his cape trailing along the ground. "Not until you answer a couple of questions."

"I'm not doing shit," I grit out, trying to wiggle my arm from the cyborg's grip, but holy giants, he's strong.

"If you want to walk away from this, you'll cooperate." The elf stops beside the cyborg and flashes me a yellow, crooked-teethed smirk.

I roll my eyes. "Like that scares me. You're an elf. All you're good at is sneaking into places. You have no strength and hardly any powers."

He smiles darkly at me. "I have L, who is perfectly capable of ripping you apart with his hands. And he's very obedient."

I glance up at L, who's watching me expressionlessly.

"You know, you don't have to obey him. You could just walk away. Your life would be better if you did."

L doesn't utter a word.

I jerk on my arm again, and L's grip constricts, his fingers squeezing my arms so forcefully I wince. I lift my leg to kick him in the shin, but the impact against his metal leg rattles my entire body.

Cursing the liquid sky, my gaze snaps to the elf. "What do you want to know?" I snarl, wondering why my powers haven't manifested.

If East's theory is correct about my emotions bringing them out, then the ground should be quivering with my rage. But the air around me is still. Then again, my powers have been kind of flaky, surfacing whenever they feel like it.

When a cocky grin consumes the elf's face, I curl my fingers into fists.

"I want to know if you landed on this planet with the band known as Ash East Arrow," he says.

My brow arches. "What are you? A groupie?"

The elf snorts a laugh. "Fuck no. Not even close." He inches toward me. "Just answer the question, little lost lamb." He leans forward and sniffs my hair.

I slant away. "No, I landed here on me—"

I gasp at the cyborg wraps his metal fingers around my throat.

"Do not try to lie to me, little lamb," the elf warns,

poking me in the side. "Now, I'm going to ask one more time and you better tell the truth, or L's going to lose his patience."

I struggle for air as I glare up at L. Lose his patience? He looks bored out of his mind.

The elf paces the narrow width of the alleyway with his hands clasped behind his back. "Now, did you land on this planet with the band Ash East Arrow?"

"Maybe …" I gasp, reaching up and gripping the cyborg's hand wrapped around my neck. "So fucking what if I did?"

He grinds to a stop, grinning, clearly pleased. "So, you're friends with them then?"

I choke out a wheezy laugh. "Yeah, I don't do the whole friendship thing. It never works out well for me."

He narrows his eyes at me. "If you're not friends with them, then why are you traveling with them?"

"I'm their assistant," I lie through a wheeze.

The elf examines his fingernails. "Assistants never travel with bands."

"Well, I do." I stab my fingernails into L's hands in a lame attempt to escape.

"Just answer his questions truthfully so I can let you go," L tries to encourage.

"Or you could just let me go," I wheeze out.

He shakes his head. "I can't. He's my master."

That's the second time I've heard the term *master* used

in the last several minutes, and I'm starting to question if planet Steel has a master/servant rule in play. But, how does one get labeled as a master and who becomes a servant?

"I'm their assistant," I lie again, the world around me blurring as I grow lightheaded.

Silence grasps the air, except for the sound of my wheezing.

Dumbass elves. I'm going to pass out ...

The elf sighs. "Let her go."

"Are you sure, master?" the cyborg asks, his fingers remaining around my neck. "I think she's lying."

"Me, too, but it doesn't really matter," the elf says dismissively. "Whatever she is, she still has connections to the band. And right now, that's all we need."

"Okay." L suddenly loosens his grip, giving me hardly any time to react.

One second, my feet are dangling from the ground, and the next, the cobblestone is biting into my knees.

"A little warning would've been nice." I scowl at L as I stumble to my feet and dust the dirt off my tights.

He blinks confusedly at me. "What would I warn you about?"

"Nothing. Never mind." I reel around to run, but someone snags my arm. "Let me go," I demand, throwing a glare over my shoulder at L, only to find that the elf has ahold of me. I cringe at the sight of his wet fingers folded around my arm. "I answered your questions, so get your hand off me."

"We need one more thing from you." He tugs on my arm as he backs up down the alley with a delighted expression that makes my stomach churn.

L walks closely behind me, gently pushing me forward with his metal palm.

"L and I have been trying to track down Ash East Arrow for quite a while, but unfortunately, they have a protection spell on them that makes it so creatures like me have a hard time finding them."

"It protects elves from finding them? Because, from what I know, elves aren't a threat to most creatures. Well, unless you …" I bite down on my tongue as a revelation hits me.

Asher, East, and Arrow need my help to steal some powerful objects. And back when I broke into their vehicle, East mentioned he was worried the thief—aka me—might've been after their little rebellion collection. So, is that what this elf is after? They guys' collection of powerful objects? It makes sense. Elves are known for thievery and their desire to obtain powerful objects. But, how does this elf plan on using me to get to Asher, East, and Arrow's collection? Not that I'm about to ask him. No, the best way to play this is to pretend to be clueless and see if I can get him to accidentally spill his secrets.

"Unless I what?" the elf presses as we step onto the same street where I lost track of East and Arrow.

I lift a shoulder. "Unless you have an aversion to wrinkly, slimy skin."

He traces his tongue along his lips. "In my culture, the slimier the skin, the sexier you are."

I give a thumbs-up. "Good for you. But, in my culture, it means you're icky and should probably take more showers."

He roughly yanks me to his side. "Elves don't take showers. In fact, we rarely clean ourselves."

Vomit burns at the back of my throat. "Maybe L could hold on to my arm instead of you."

"Don't pretend like you don't like the feel of my wet skin against your flesh." The elf leans in, sniffs my hair, then lets out a fucking moan.

I dry heave. "Oh, my gods, stop. Just stop."

"You say that now, but if you went for a ride on Mr. Tinkles, you'd be screaming the opposite." He waggles his brows at me suggestively.

"Did you seriously just refer to your dick as Mr. Tinkles? Because it's a dumb fucking name." I waver then smile at him sweetly. "Then again, it seems like it'd belong to something small, so it's probably fitting."

Anger flares in his eyes as he delves his fingers into my flesh. "I assure you, it's very, very big."

I fight back a cringe that wants to sweep through my

body as his fingernails actually break through my skin. *I'm seriously going to need a virus shot after this.*

"Considering how small your hands and feet are, I'm going to assume you're lying to me, elf."

His lips twitch as he crowds my personal space. "How about we step into this inn and I'll prove it to you? You think you can handle that, little lamb?"

I have two ways I can approach this One, I can come back with a snide remark and continue letting him force me to go with him to where I'm guessing Asher, East, and Arrow are. Or two, I can challenge his request and hopefully distract him enough to bolt, find this Arch where the guys are, warn them an elf is looking for them, and then say peace out and go back to my mission of getting the Steel books for myself. Since I hate being forced to do shit, my gut instincts are telling me to go with option two. Not that I actually want to see Asher, East, and Arrow right now, but eventually, I'll have to.

"Fine, let's go." I smile and gesture at the inn. "Let's see what you've got hiding underneath those … stained pants." *Gag me.*

His brows rise in surprise, but he hastily shakes off the shock. "You're a dirty little thing, aren't you? I like it."

"Not as dirty as you," I mutter. "Or your Mr. Tinkles."

He either ignores me or doesn't hear me as he steers me across the street and toward the entrance of a two-story, brass building that has grimy windows, broken rain gutters, and a curtain for a door.

Lovely. This place looks like a whorehouse.

"Don't look so frightened. It's not as bad as it looks," the elf says as he ducks under the dusty curtain, pulling me with him.

As I take in the small room inside that has black ooze seeping from the cracks in the walls, I mutter, "I beg to differ."

Again, he makes no show of hearing me as he crosses the room, releasing my arm when we reach the front register where a rusty cyborg is standing and staring at the wall.

I sneak a peek over my shoulder at the entrance, debating whether to run now or not, but L steps through the curtain and positions himself in front of the only exit, at least as far as I can see.

Dammit! This is going to complicate my plan. But I guess I can always jump out the window when we get to the room, which sadly won't be the first time I've had to do something like that.

"I'd like one room for about an hour," the elf tells the cyborg—the innkeeper. "I'm going to show this lovely, little thing what she's been missing out on."

The innkeeper nods droningly as he reaches for a set of keys hanging on the wall. But, mid-turn, his gaze flicks in my direction and the strangest thing happens.

His eyes briefly widen.

Now, if it were any other creature, I wouldn't think twice, but cyborgs don't show surprise. Well, except for Arrow, but he's a rarity and has a heart, so …

"Here." The innkeeper slaps a key down on the countertop, his gaze flicking to me again.

"You seem awfully curious for a servant," the elf remarks, collecting the key. "Stop looking at her, or I'll report you to your master."

"He's not here," the innkeeper replies flatly, his eyes narrowing on the elf. "Your total is two steels. Please pay your fee and get on your way. I have other customers to attend to."

The elf's jaw ticks as he stuffs his hand into his pocket and slaps two steel coins onto the countertop. "I'm not leaving you a tip," he says, then grabs my hand and yanks me toward a slender, spiral staircase.

The innkeeper remains expressionless until I pass him. Then his expression softens.

"There's a secret tunnel behind the armoire in the room," he tells me. "Distract him then sneak out through it. It'll lead you to the alleyway in back. When you get out there, go to the Arch. You'll be safe there."

My eyes widen as I give a panicked glance at the elf, but he seems completely oblivious to what the cyborg said. That's when I remember I can hear in different frequencies, including cyborgs. But, how did the innkeeper know that? And how in the hell does he know I know Arrow? Unless they *were* looking for me? Still, why would Arrow tell some random innkeeper about my strange ability of speaking and hearing in cyborg frequency?

"Arrow is a friend of mine," the innkeeper adds, as if reading my mind. "I would send word to him if I could that you're here, but unfortunately, my master controls most of what I say and do. I can, however, let you know how to get yourself out of this mess, and from what Arrow told me, you should be able to."

Huh? When did Arrow tell this cyborg about me?

I open my mouth to ask, but the elf yanks on my arm so forcefully I nearly trip and land on my face. Thankfully, I grasp the railing of the stairway and stop that from happening, because seriously, this place is gross, leaking ooze from the walls kind of gross.

I hold on to the railing until we reach the top of the stairway. Then the elf starts down a hallway lined with numbered doors, towing me along with him.

The area upstairs just might be dumpier than the downstairs. Holes cover the walls; most of the lanterns are out, making the space dark; and the sounds of moans, both of pleasure and of pain, haunt the air.

I gulp down my jittery nerves, more than aware just how over my head I am.

Sexual stuff has never been my forte.

How am I going to get out of this?

Before I can attempt to come up with an answer, the elf stops in front of a door.

"Here we are," he announces cheerfully as he slides the key into the lock.

I stab my fingernails into my palms as he twists the handle, pushes open the door, and steps inside, already untying the collar of his cape.

I throw a glance around the hallway, debating whether I should bolt back down the stairs and try to get past L. For all I know, the innkeeper could've been lying about the secret passage and, if so, that means I'll be stuck up here with an elf who wants to screw me.

As far as I can tell, there're no windows around to escape out of, and while I like to think of myself as tough, elves do possess a smidgeon of magic. Then again, so do I.

If I only I could control it.

I take a deep breath and attempt to conjure up some shaky ground ninja powers, but again, nothing happens.

"Come on; don't be shy," the elf says to me as he plops down on the edge of the bed and starts unlacing his boots.

I'm not very trustful, especially with creatures I don't know, so it takes a lot of effort for me to lift my foot over the threshold and step inside that room. The moment I do, I know I'm putting almost all my trust in the innkeeper I barely spoke to.

Please don't let this be a mistake.

Once I enter the room, I close the door and assess the small space. No windows. Barely any furniture, other than a bed and an old, rotting armoire. The sight of it, though, gives me a tinge of hope that perhaps this is going to work out in my favor.

"Stop being so nervous and take off your clothes," the elf demands as he unbuttons his shirt. Then he moves to the button on his pants. "How about I introduce you to Mr. Tinkles? Maybe that'll relax you."

"Why would that relax me?" I question, loathing how nervous I feel.

"Because you'll get excited when you see it," he purrs, unfastening the button on his slacks.

Oh gods, is this really happening? Is this really going to be my first experience at seeing a penis?

No, don't let it get that far.

Think, Harlynn! Get yourself out of this mess!

I glimpse around the room, frantically searching for a way out, and my gaze centers on a lantern dangling from a wall hook. With enough force, it might be heavy enough to knock the elf out. But before I attempt to pull my ninja stunt, I need to have him distracted.

"Wait," I say as the elf starts to unzip his pants.

He freezes but doesn't remove his fingers from the

zipper. "Don't tell me you've changed your mind. And if you have, tough shit because we're doing this anyway."

There are so many, many things I want to say in that moment, but I swallow down those words—for now—and focus on my plan.

"I'm not backing out," I say in the most innocent tone I can muster. "I just want to know your name first. It might help me be less nervous."

He promptly shakes his head and unzips the zipper. "No names."

"Just your first name?" I ask while tracing my finger along my collarbone. "So I know what to shout out when you're fucking the shit out of me." Yeah, it physically pains me to say the last part without dry heaving, but I somehow manage.

His gaze drops to my chest and desire floods his eyes. "I guess I could do that for you, little lamb." His gaze locks with mine as he sticks his hand down the front of his pants. "You can call me Yellow."

"Your name is Yellow?" I question with doubt.

He nods, touching himself. "I was named that because Mr. Tinkles has this—"

"It's a really nice name," I cut him off, not wanting to hear the rest of his story. "And knowing it makes me so much more comfortable." Sucking in a shaky breath, I reach behind me and start loosening the ribbons on my corset.

Grinning, he stands up and pulls down his pants, struggling a bit to take them off.

Seizing the opportunity, I reach up, snatch the lantern off the wall, and spin around, preparing to throw it at him, but he's already in front of me.

He grabs ahold of my arm. "Yeah, you didn't think I saw you eyeballing that, did you?" he sneers, prying my fingers off the handle of the lantern. The lantern crashes to the floor a second later.

He's stronger than I thought

"I'm tired of playing your little games," the elf snaps, then shoves me backward onto the bed.

I scramble to get up, but he climbs on top of me and pins my arms down beside my head. He's pant-less, and I can feel his slimy skin touching me almost everywhere.

"Get off me!" I seethe, thrashing my body around. But he barely budges, his grip on my wrists tightening.

"You thought you had me so played, didn't you? Thought you could just push me around because I'm an elf." He leans down until his lips are a mere inch away from mine. "Newsflash, little lamb. I'm not a normal elf. If I was, I wouldn't have been assigned to work for Chasing Magic Industries and sent to track down Asher, East, and Arrow."

Chasing Magic Industries? What is that?

I could ask him, but I'm a bit distracted with getting him off me before Mr. Tinkles touches my leg.

"Fuck you!" I shout, stabbing my fingernails into his hands.

He only laughs in my face. Then he slams his lips against mine as he reaches down between us to do gods know what. I think I have a pretty good idea when I hear the sound of my skirt tearing.

I gag against the rotting taste of him and the feel of his fingernails scratch a path up my thigh. Panic chokes my throat, smothering me as he grinds against me. But beneath the fear, rage storms through me.

Controlled. All my life I've been controlled by a paranormal. Even when I lived on the streets, I was controlled by Five Smoke Magic's rules.

Control.

Control.

Control.

Will I ever be free—

The rage building inside me bursts and unleashes, my power waving over the room. But it doesn't make the ground quiver like I anticipated. No. Instead, the metal bars of the headboard uncurl and snake toward Yellow, wrapping around his arms and legs and jerking him off me.

"What in the worlds?" he gasps out as the bars drag him off the bed and onto the floor.

I scramble to the side of the bed and watch with wide

eyes as the bars cocoon around him, starting at his feet and working their way up his body.

"Get these things off of me—"

A bar winds around his mouth.

A slow smile spreads across my face as I rise to my feet. "Man, that looks really uncomfortable."

His eyes narrow as he tries to worm free, but he can barely move.

My grin broadens and grows when I note a small gap between the bars right where his Mr. Tinkles is.

Lifting my foot, I stomp down on it, and his eyes bulge as he lets out a muffled scream.

I smile in satisfaction, but part of it is all bravado. Deep down, I'm shaken and feel sick to my stomach. The taste of his lips on mine is branded into my mind like a hot iron against flesh.

"Remember this the next time you try to put your hands on someone without their permission. Remember what it feels like to be tied up against your will and there's not a damn thing you can do about it." I crouch down beside him. "It's a sucky feeling, right? The help-lessness." I place my hand on his forehead and pierce my fingernails into his flesh.

I'm not even positive why I do it, other than to maybe mark him like he marked my mind with this awful moment. Hopefully, he'll have scars on his forehead, and every time he looks in the mirror, he'll be reminded of this. If I were the killing type, I just might do that. But I'm not.

Instead, I stand upright, cross the room, and drag the armoire away from the wall.

Just like the innkeeper said, there is a tunnel hidden behind it, but if it leads to the alleyway, I'm unsure. It's too dark inside for me to be able to tell.

Usually, I plan my escapes better than this, but I don't have a choice this time. It's either go out this way or try to sneak past L at the front entrance.

So, summoning a deep breath, I step into the darkness, hoping the innkeeper wasn't lying about where the tunnel leads.

CHAPTER 22

Turns out, the innkeeper was being truthful, and only a handful of seconds later, I'm stepping out into the shadows of an alleyway. I waste no time getting the hell away from that inn and hightailing it down the street in the direction East and Arrow were heading in last time I was with them.

I can feel creatures watching me as I powerwalk, but I keep my head tucked down and try to ignore them, only glancing up to check around for the Arch. Eventually, I spot it curving from the streets and arching toward the sky like a giant horseshoe.

I quicken up my pace, and within a matter of minutes, I'm standing right beside the Arch.

Up close, it's massive and glints like starlight against the glimmering sunlight. I also notice it arches over a bronzed domed building that has a stage stretching across the space of land in front. An iron gate encloses the area, and the longest line of paranormals I've ever seen is formed in front of the entrance.

"Holy crazy trolls," I mumble as I take in the line. It has to be at least a couple of miles long, and all the paranormals standing in it look as crazed as the ones East, Arrow, and I passed while we were walking through the city. "Are all these creatures here to see Asher, East, and Arrow?"

I soon get my answer as everyone begins chanting, "Ash East Arrow! Ash East Arrow! Ash East Arrow!"

Awesome. How am I supposed to get past all these creatures? Because I'm not standing in this line. However, I know firsthand that security is going to be complicated to get by.

"Gods, I can't believe they're late," a vampire decked out in a leather dress and studded jewelry mumbles as she shoves by me, dashing toward the line. "I wonder what's going on."

Another vampire wearing leather and studs shoves by me. This time, I shove her back, annoyed. She shoots me a nasty look before hurrying after her friend.

"I hope nothing bad happened to them," she tells her friend, hugging a notebook to her chest. "Especially Asher." She lets out a blissful sigh that makes me roll my eyes.

So, the guys are late to their little PA thingy. Why? I guess I'll find out when I sneak backstage, because that's going to happen. I just need a plan.

Chewing on my bottom lip, I observe the streets, the line, and the gates. Then my gaze locks on an area located at the side of the building where a group of uniformed paranormals are standing. Security, I presume, which means that's where the entrance to backstage is.

Cracking my knuckles, I walk toward it, figuring I'll start with giving security my name and cross my fingers I'm on the backstage access list. If not, I'll have to come up with a better plan.

I slow to a stop as my gaze drops to my torn skirt and the scratch marks covering my legs. I look like a prostitute who just had sex in a graveyard. Not to mention the skirt is torn so high that I'm nearly flashing everyone. But a wardrobe malfunction is an easy fix. All I need is something to cover up with.

So, as I pass by a faerie sporting an indigo cloak, I snag it off her.

"Hey, what the heck?" She whirls around, scanning the paranormals around her as I slip into the crowd.

Once I get the cloak on, I shove my way through groups of paranormals and up to the side entrance. Truthfully, I doubt my name is going to be on that list, so imagine my surprise when a polished cyborg waves me through before I even say my name.

"Harlynn Merringten, right?" he asks but doesn't wait for me to answer before grabbing my arm and plucking me from the crowd. Then he marches toward a set of metal doors, motioning for me to follow. "Everyone's been searching for you."

"Um …" I shuffle after him, highly aware all of security is eyeballing me. "Wait. How do you know who I am?"

He glances over his shoulder at me as he wraps his fingers around one of the door handles. "Asher, East, and Arrow have everyone looking for you. They handed out a picture from the database and are even offering a reward. Not that I can actually accept it. My master won't allow it."

There's that word again …

"Why're they looking for me?" I lower the hood of my cloak. "They're the ones who left me."

His coppery brows crinkle. "That's not what I was told." He yanks open the door. "Come on; I need to get you to them. They've been refusing to go out and sign autographs until you're found. And things are starting to get really out of hand out there." He swings his hand at the line of paranormals that are now chanting, "Hurry up! Hurry up! We want Ash East Arrow now or we'll tear the place down!"

"They seem like lovely fans," I say sarcastically as I step inside the building.

The cyborg offers me a mechanical smile, and then his gadgets buzz to life as he hikes down the metal-lined hallway trimmed with steel doors and bronzed lighting. I trail after him, basking in the quiet atmosphere. But about halfway down, that peaceful silence turns into full-blown chaos.

"I don't give a shit if they want me to go out!" Asher shouts. "I'm not doing it until we find her!"

His raging voice is echoed by a loud crash, then smoke funnels from underneath a door.

"Sounds like a genie is having a tizzy tantrum," I utter, confusion flowing through me.

Is Asher talking about me? This makes no sense. Why would East and Arrow ditch me only for Asher to worry about me?

The cyborg gives me a strange look as he stops in front of the door where the smoke is funneling from. "You're very brave to say something snarky about a genie while you're in earshot of him."

"Want to know a little secret?" I ask then raise my voice. "Asher is a total softy"

The shouting stops.

A hum of a gadget later, the door is swung open and Asher steps through the doorway. He's dressed in black jeans and no shirt, his tattoos and scars visible. He slams to a stop when his smoky gaze lands on me. He blinks several times, not saying a word, simply staring at me.

The longer he stares with fire blazing in his eyes, the more I squirm. The worst part, though, is how crazily my heart leaps in my chest, like a cracked-out unicorn that just found out they can make rainbows.

Oh, shut the hell up, heart. You don't want to go there. Neither does Asher. And remember the curse!

"So, I heard you guys were looking for me," I break the silence, crossing my arms and feeling very self-conscious.

That self-consciousness only amplifies when Asher's gaze tracks down my body and zeroes in on the scratch marks on my legs. The muscles in his jaw spasm as he reaches for me. With how intense he looks, I expect him to grab me, but he gently wraps his fingers around my wrist and carefully pulls me into a very nicely decorated room.

A hologram hangs on the far back, dark red wall, the screen showing the view of outside. The domed ceiling is painted with shimmering gold stars, a long table covered with food and drinks runs along the side wall, and a guitar is perched in the corner. Covering the floor, though, is what looks like shattered glass, probably from the crash I just heard. And beside the glass is a leather sofa where a curvy woman is sitting. She has her legs crossed, her blonde hair is pulled into a tight ponytail, and her purplish-blue eyes are assessing me with disdain.

Wait. Is this an aftershow woman ...?

"Maple, get out," Asher orders as he tows me across the room with him.

Maple? The half-genie, half-faerie who's related to Asher and, more importantly, Asher's father?

I stiffen, my mind racing with conflicted thoughts on whether to get the flying wizards out of here or not. Part of me really wants to leave and get away from this genie. On the other hand, after spending some time alone on this planet, I'm not too eager to go back out there on my own. Then again, I'll eventually have to woman-up if I want to continue with my plan of finding the Steel books by myself.

"*Now*," Asher warns when Maple stays put.

Maple's eyes enlarge, but she quickly collects herself, smoothing her hands across her skirt and straightening her shoulders. "I'm not going anywhere unless it's to lead you out onto that stage."

"You'll do what I tell you." Asher snatches up a glass filled with amber liquid and takes a long sip. Then he slams the glass down and, grasping my hand, spins toward Maple, who hasn't budge. "Don't make me curse you. Remember, you work for me, not the other way around."

Normally, I'd be making all sorts of remarks about Asher's very genie-like temper at the moment, but I really want Maple to leave, so I keep my trap shut.

She glares at me like this is all my fault. "Fine." She

stands up, adjusting the bottom of her dress. "I'll go round up East and Arrow and let them know you're little"—she crinkles her nose at me—"pet, or whatever the heck she is, has been found."

"I'm not a pet," I protest, putting a hand on my hip.

She smirks, flipping her hair off her shoulder. "That's what all the groupies say."

"I'm not a groupie or a pet. And you're the one who's obeying Asher, so who's the pet?" I let a sassy grin spread across my face.

Smoke funnels in her eyes as she fists her hands at her sides. "How dare you talk to me like that—"

"You will not touch Harlynn. If you do, I'll curse you with the darkest of curses," Asher warns in an eerily low tone, eliciting a shiver from me. "Now get out before I have security come remove you."

Maple blinks, the smoke in her eyes fizzling. "But I—"

"Now," he cuts her off, releasing my hand and storming toward her.

Gritting her teeth, she reels around and stomps out of the room, slamming the door behind her.

Asher frees a deafening exhale, the stiffness in his lean shoulders loosening. "I think East is right. We need to fire her."

"But she seems so lovely." Sarcasm seeps through my voice.

Asher gradually turns toward me, his eyes smoldering

as he drags his gaze down my body to my legs. I expect him to ask about the scratches, so I'm thrown for a turn when he strides toward me, stealing the distance between us in the snap of a wish, and seals his lips to mine.

I gasp as he parts my lips with his tongue and slips it into my mouth while moving his hands to the small of my back.

Clutching his arms, I start to push away from him, but as the taste of sparkling wishes, dark curses, and warm cupcakes flood my mouth, I pull him closer, clinging to him and allowing his lips to erase some of the memory of Yellow's kiss.

Asher groans, sliding his hands to my hips then down to my thighs. "*Et solicitus fui. Damnare tam anxius fui. Non possum facere quod semper iterum,*" he mutters between kisses.

"What the heck … does that … mean?" I gasp between kisses and trying to breathe, but he only deepens the kiss, pulling me closer.

A moan escapes me, and I lift my leg to climb up him, craving something I can't quite understand. Then, gripping my legs, he guides me away and breaks the connection of our lips.

"Who put those scratches on your legs?" he demands, his chest rising and crashing as he breathes heavily.

"I …" I blink a few times, realizing how dazed that kiss made me. *I really need to focus.* "It's kind of a long story." One I'm not sure I want to tell him. Well, at least not the part where Yellow tried to …

I swallow down the lump in my throat. I'm not sure if I want to talk about what Yellow did to me aloud, but I do need to warn Asher about Yellow looking for him and him being part of Chasing Magic Industries—whatever that is.

Asher softly tucks a strand of my hair behind my ear. "I've got time."

He's acting weird, too affectionate, like that time I woke up in bed after passing out in the compartment. And like that time, his gentle, caring mood feels awkward as fuck. I need the cold, snide, bossy Asher to come out so I can feel comfortable again.

"You sure about that?" I point at the hologram where fans cover the streets and bang against the gates, chanting his name.

"I've got time," he repeats, moving his fingers back up my body and curling them around my hips. Then he picks me up, urges my legs around his waist, and strides toward the sofa.

"Put me down," I protest, wiggling to get down.

He only tightens his grip and plops down on the sofa.

I move to stand up, but he circles his arms around my waist.

Grimacing, I twist sideways in his lap. "Look, I've had a really shitty day, and I'm not in the mood for your genie games." As the memory of Yellow pinning me to the bed sears through my mind, I shift my weight, put my feet up on the cushion beside us, and cover my exposed legs with the tail of the stolen cloak.

His pierced brows furrow. "What do you mean by my genie games?"

I give him an unimpressed look. "The ditching Harlynn genie game."

His forehead creases. "I never ditched you."

I smooth my hand over the creases in my skirt, pretending like I don't care about what I'm about to say. Though I do. Too much. And it's terrifying the hell bats out of me. Not to mention it's very risky for me to be emotionally attached to anyone, even a cocky genie, a flirty faerie, and a sweet cyborg.

"But Arrow and East did," I say then sigh. "It doesn't really matter. I kind of get why they did it. And I was going to just go back to the vehicle and do my own thing so you guys could do yours, but something got in my way."

He gapes at me then shakes his head. "Do you seriously believe they ditched you?"

I give a half-shrug. "It's the only reason I can think of that explains why East and Arrow just took off and left me in the street." I glance at the door as that twinge in my heart hits again.

Maybe I should leave. I'm getting way too emotional.

He cups my chin and turns my head toward him, his eyes sparking with spritz of sparks. "No one ditched you," he says softly but firmly. "East and Arrow were walking down the street with you, and then, suddenly you weren't there. They didn't see you leave or anyone take you, so we assumed it had to be some sort of spell. But magic can't transport you off the planet, so we knew you had to still be on Steel. East and Arrow notified me immediately, and I sent every creature I could trust to look for you. And Arrow and East have been going around the city, talking to every acquaintance Arrow has here, but no one had seen you."

He traces his fingers along my thigh where the scratches mark my skin. "I would've gone out to look for you myself, but since you knew we were going to be at the Arch, we decided it'd be better if I waited here in case you showed up. It was driving me crazy, though, just sitting around and doing nothing." His gaze drifts to the glass covering the floor, and then he shakes his head, focusing on me. "I guess it was good that I stayed, since you're here now." He gives me a bizarre look that almost resembles being impressed. "I don't know why I'm surprised. You're clever. I should've known you'd find your way here."

I like the idea of what he's saying, probably a bit too much, but still ... "I never saw anyone looking for me."

"Well, it's true. There're a ton of paranormals that

were—and probably still are—looking for you." A crease forms between his brows. "If you couldn't see any of them, though, then I'm going to assume whatever spell was put on you kept you from being spotted or maybe found. Magic can be tricky like that. We can probably find a witch who could run a tracing spell on you and find out exactly what happened so we can get to the why."

I'm still not sure if I'm buying his explanation. "But other creatures could see me. And I know for sure this elf, a cyborg, and weird-looking creature could."

Asher tilts his head to the side. "Do you know what the weird creature was?"

"No, I'd never seen anything like it before."

"What features did it have?"

"Dark, glowing eyes; silver lips; and pale skin ..."

As Asher pales, a bundle of nerves jolt through me.

"What is it?"

"What you're describing ... I think I know what it is." The worry in his tone sends fear lashing through me.

I almost don't dare ask. *Almost.*

"What is it?"

He snakes his arm around my waist and draws me closer. "Amongst my kind, they're known as Wishing Shadows."

"I've never heard of those."

"That's because they're rare."

I quirk a brow. "Rare like I'm supposed to be?"

He shakes his head, his lips quirking. "You, little thief, are the rarest creature I've ever crossed paths with."

"Well, this Wishing Shadow seemed to know what I am, so—"

I let out a squeak as he abruptly stands up with me in his arms.

"Hey, I thought we discussed this whole carrying thing."

"Yeah, and it was a discussion you lost." He starts to step forward with me in his arms, but then he freezes, as if conflicted whether to walk or stay put. Wisps of grey and blue smoke billow in his eyes as he stares off into empty space.

"Why are your eyes doing that?" I ask.

He doesn't answer, appearing lost and terrified.

A terrified genie? This has got to be bad.

"What exactly is a Wishing Shadow?"

He blinks, his gaze shifting to me. "They're ... genies without powers."

I relax a glitter drop. "Then I don't think that's what this thing was since he disappeared into a pile of ash."

He grinds his jaw from side to side. "That's because they do have powers."

"But you just said they didn't," I gripe. "You're being completely contradicting."

"Yeah … I should probably explain it better." But he looks as if that's the last thing he wants to do.

I motion for him to go ahead. "So, get at it."

He chews on his bottom lip, hesitating. "I don't want to frighten you."

"I never get scared." Usually, that's the truth, but not today when I was with Yellow.

No, when he held me down, I thought … Well, I was scared things were going to end worse than they did.

"Never say never, Harlynn. There's always a first for everything." He huffs out a stressed breath. "And maybe this won't frighten you, but it'll definitely upset you."

I ignore the ball of fear forming in the pit of my stomach. "Doesn't matter. I still want to know. And you better hurry up because I've got my own important things to tell you."

Curiosity sparks in his eyes. "Like what?"

I promptly shake my head. "Nope. You go first."

His gaze bores into mine, flames igniting and shadows casting over his face as he tries to intimidate me.

"Stare me down all you want, but I'm not caving." I flash him a haughty grin. "Your constipated, intimidating look has zero affect on me."

He shakes his head, mumbling, "You're such a handful." Then he exhales heavily. "Wishing Shadows are genies born without magic. They're also servants in our world, and usually get assigned to serve one genie during their lifetime."

"What is with you paranormals and having servants?" I interrupt. "Because today, I've met three cyborgs who said they couldn't do certain things because their masters forbid it."

"About half the cyborgs on planet Steel are servants, and it's like that on other planets as well. But planet Steel is the worst, mainly because cyborgs can be programmed to obey," Asher explains with a hue of sadness in his eyes.

"Is …? Was Arrow ever one?" I ask softly.

Asher rubs his pale blue lips together then slightly nods. "He was, but it was a long time ago."

I recall something Arrow said to me. "Did you rescue him from being one?"

His eyes spark in surprise. "Why would you think that?"

I shrug. "Because Arrow mentioned you rescued him."

He studies me closely. "What else has he told you?"

"Not too much. Just a little about this planet, and I can tell he doesn't like it here very much. Oh yeah, and he told—or, well, let me feel—that he has a real heart."

His lips part in astonishment. "Arrow let you feel his heart beating?"

I nod in puzzlement. "Yeah … Was he not supposed to?"

Asher shakes his head in disbelief. "No, he can tell

whoever he thinks he can trust with the secret. It's just that he's only ever told East and I."

Arrow trusts me? I smile at that.

"I like that he trusts me. And don't worry; I won't tell anyone. I like Arrow. Kind of always have. Well, except for when I thought he ditched me."

He slips his tongue out to wet his lips. "I'm not worried about you telling anyone. I know you're trustworthy enough. You've more than proven that."

His words send the stupidest warmth through my body.

Stupid, traitor body. Seriously, it needs to stop reacting this way over Asher, East, and Arrow. I mean, for starters, they're paranormals, but I guess I am too, so …

I mentally shake my head at myself. None of this matters. Even if I decided to get past the fact that they're paranormals, I still can't let myself feel too much for them.

"Then, what're you worried about?" I ask, shoving the warmth in my body aside.

"Hmm …" He sucks on his lip ring. "I think I might need to talk to Arrow before I say anything else."

"Sounds like you're keeping a secret from me," I speculate.

"I'm keeping as many secrets from you as you are from us," he challenges, carrying my gaze. "Do you want to exchange one of yours for mine?"

I shake my head. "No, not really." Which is mostly the truth. The only main thing I haven't told Asher is about Yellow, but I plan on getting to that just as soon as he tells me more about this Wishing Shadow. Well, minus the part about what happened in the bed.

"Okay then," Asher says simply.

"Okay," I reply, a bit confused.

Why is he being so agreeable?

He shifts my weight then sinks back down onto the couch. "So, are you going to tell me how you got those scratches?"

I instinctively cover the scratches with my hand. "I will when you tell me more about this Wishing Shadow thing and why it seemed to know what I am."

A sigh puffs from his lips. "Fine, since you're clearly not going to listen to my warning and drop this, I'll tell you." He gives a short pause, giving me another chance to back out, and I make a great show of pressing my lips together. He sighs again. "There's really not that much to tell, other than they mostly become servants and can sometimes channel their master's power if the master permits it."

"No wonder he was able to wither away," I mumble. "And come to think of it, I lost track of East and Arrow when he popped up in front of me, so maybe he's the one who casted a spell on me. That is, if genies can do those kinds of spells." I eyeball Asher over. "From what I understand, you can basically cast any spell you want as long as it's in the form of a wish or curse."

"That's not quite how it works," he tells me stiffly. "Each genie has their own unique abilities, which means that the Wishing Shadow you crossed paths with must belong to a genie who has an ability to make a creature untraceable to others."

"What's your ability?" I wonder, loathing how curious I sound.

Since when am I curious about genies?

His eyes darken as he slants toward me and puts his lips beside my ear. "I can do many things, little thief, and one of these days, I'll show you."

I slant back to meet his gaze. "No thanks. I'm not a fan of curses or wishes."

He leans closer again, his lips brushing my ear. "I can do a lot more than just cast spells and curses … Lots and lots of amazing things that'll ruin you in the best way possible." He traces his teeth along my earlobe, and my shoulder shudders upward.

"Stop … Stop trying to distract me," I warn, the breathlessness in my tone completely cringe-worthy.

He chuckles huskily then drags his teeth along the sensitive speck of flesh again. "I'm not trying to distract you." He bites down on my earlobe, and a cry fumbles from my lips.

Not a painful cry. No, the noise that leaves my lips is needy and desperate and crammed with desire.

Fucking tricky genies. He's definitely up to something.

But two can play this game.

"I know you're trying to distract me," I snap, shifting around and swinging my leg over to the other side so I'm straddling his lap. "Now fess up and tell me more about this Wishing Shadow." I place my hands on his shoulders and push him back, pinning him against the couch.

A voice whispers in the back of my mind that I'm being awfully ballsy right now, being this demanding to a genie. He could very well turn the tables around on me at any cursed second. But, for some reason, I'm not worried. Why? Who the crazy vampires knows, other than maybe I'm starting to trust him.

Trust. What a dangerous word. It makes me uncomfortable just thinking about it.

His eyes darken with smoke. "Little thief," a warning rings in his tone. "You're playing with fire right now."

"Actually, it looks like I'm playing with a genie." I dazzle him with a cocky smirk as I push on his shoulders harder. "And you're currently losing."

His eyes crackle, sparks showering in the pupils. "I'm *letting* you win," he says in a low tone.

"That's what I'd say, too, if I was getting my ass kicked—"

I gasp in surprise as he snags ahold of my hips, lifts me up, and flips me around, lying me down on the sofa.

I start to get back up, but he lines his body over mine, moving his fingers quickly to unfasten the tie of the cloak.

"Hey," I whine as he tugs the cloak off and tosses it aside, leaving me feeling very vulnerable in my torn skirt.

"Now, what was it you were saying about me getting my ass kicked?" A smug grin tugs at his lips as he positions his hands beside my head and lowers his lips toward mine.

My breath gets caught in my chest as his mouth nears mine. After what just happened with Yellow, all sorts of conflictions are coiling through me. Want and desire. Fear and nervousness.

I should push him off me. Should stop this. There's a reason I haven't kissed a ton of guys.

Think about the curse, Harlynn. Get your emotions in check.

I open my mouth to tell him to back off, but he pauses on his own, his lips a sliver of an inch away from mine.

"I want you to tell me where those scratches came from and why your skirt's torn," he says, his breath dusting across my lips.

When I shake my head, he swallows audibly.

"Was it …? Did the Wishing Shadow touch you?"

"What? No." I shake my head for added emphasis. "He

didn't do anything really. Just said my kind were usually submissive, and that I wasn't. He also said his master would be so pleased to hear that I'm clueless about what I am. Then he puffed away into a cloud of ash ... Oh, and he smelled familiar, which I thought was pretty weird, since I'm almost positive I've never met one of his kind before."

"What did he smell like?" Asher asks, but he doesn't sound that interested, as if he already knows.

"Darkness. Which honestly, I didn't even realize I knew what darkness smelled like until then." I pause, assessing him. "You know this Wishing Shadow, don't you?"

"No—"

"How do you expect me to tell you where the scratches came from when you won't tell me the truth about this?" I cut him off.

He sinks into silence as he either absorbs my words or tries to conjure up a good lie. "I'm afraid you'll try to run if I tell you," he finally admits.

"If I did, I'd die, since I'd be backing out on our bargain," I remind him with a hint of bitterness.

Sure, Asher and I are getting along better, but when it all comes down to it, I'm being forced to be here with him, Arrow, and East.

Controlled.

Always controlled.

Like earlier today ...

His eyes suddenly widen. "Little thief, calm down."

I realize I'm shaking and try to get my body to chill the frosted demons out, but it has taken on a mind of its own apparently.

"You're shaking so badly," Asher mumbles, rotating to the side so he's no longer hovering over me. Then he places two fingers to my pulse while searching my eyes. "You're scared."

"I already told you, I never get scared," I grit out through the chattering of my teeth.

What's wrong with me? It's like someone has pushed a button in my head that powered off my ability to remain calm even when I'm not.

"I know what fear looks like. And you're afraid."

"I'm j-just cold."

He splays his fingers across the side of my neck. "No, you're beyond warm."

I shake my head in denial, wrapping my arms around myself.

"What happened to you?" he demands in the softest tone.

I smash my lips together as tears burn my eyes.

For reals, Harlynn. You're going to start fucking becoming a crier now of all times?

"Shhh ..." Asher whispers. "Try to relax. I'm going to take it away."

I blink at him, lost, and he gulps, his eyes wide with … horror?

More fear bursts through me at the sight of him terrified.

What's he about to do?

"Relax," he repeats as he slips his hand down along my collarbone then lines his palm to the center of my chest.

"What're you doing?" I whisper as an orb of light reflects from his skin.

"Taking the pain away," he murmurs, his glowing eyes fixed on mine.

A heart-knocking moment later, glittery warmth spills through my veins, my skin coating with it.

"Breathe," Asher demands gently.

I suck in an inhale, and the pressure that was building in my chest alleviates.

"Again," he says, taking a breath himself.

I mimic his move. *Air in. Air out. Pain in. Pain out …*

The tears in my eyes dry as my body stills.

"What was that?" I whisper as I stare up at him in awe.

The glowing around his skin and in his eyes dims. "That was one of my abilities."

"Oh … Well, it was …" I rack my mind for a word that won't make me sound too impressed but impressed enough, not wanting to overly stroke his genie ego. "Wonderful." I cringe. That so wasn't the word I was looking for.

Shockingly, his lips remain in a thin line as confliction dances across his expression.

"Are you okay?" I ask worriedly.

Nodding, he bends his arm and lowers his head toward mine. "Yeah … I'm fine." His eyelids lower, and then he delicately brushes his lips against mine, giving the softest caress of a wishful kiss.

A shaky breath quivers from my lips as I wind my fingers around his biceps. Worry creeps through me.

While quick and soft, this sort of kiss is the dangerous kind. The kind that could put both our curses into play.

I need to stop this now!

I start to protest when his lips softly touch mine again and a content moan eases from his. My heart does this weird leaping thing as my fingers unconsciously wander up his arms and slip around to his shoulder blades, my fingers piercing into his skin as I struggle to remain in control of my emotions.

An uneven moan falters from Asher's lips. "We should … We should stop. I shouldn't have … I can't …" He dips his lips and kisses me again, this time with a bit more force.

I groan as my mind spins out of control. I'm being very stupid right now, for so many different reasons. But I swear the longer he kisses me, the better I feel. Maybe because he's using his magic on me? I should care that he is, but … I don't know. It's making me feel so much better.

"Har, we should stop," he breathes between kisses.

Har? He called me Har? I hate how much I like it.

I nod in agreement with every intention of putting a stop to this, but I end up winding my legs around his hips, as if I've lost the ability to think rationally.

He groans, grinding his hips against mine as he kisses me again.

I gasp against his lips as the strangest, and I'll admit wonderful, sensations burst through me. A tremble rolls through my body again, but this time for a different reason.

He pauses, pushing back a margin of an inch, question marks flooding his eyes. "Har, have you …?" He trails off, reluctance masking his face.

I swear he can see my inexperience written all over my face, and like an idiot, a flush creeps across my cheeks. It's so fucking annoying that I react this way. Out of all the things to get embarrassed over, this is what my mind chooses?

"You want me to stop?" he asks with confliction.

I will my head to nod because, for one, we *so* don't need to be going down this road. And two, I'd like to try to salvage some of my dignity. Instead, I roll my hips against his.

Bravo, Harlynn. Way to look like a needy, horny succubus.

But I'm not even positive it's completely about being needy. Part of me likes the feel of Asher against me because it makes me forget that Yellow tried to touch me like this.

"We should … I don't …" Asher breathes raggedly.

A sputtering genie? Never thought I'd see one of those—

He rocks his hips against mine, and a startled gasp fumbles from my lips as I dig my fingernails deeper into his shoulder blades. Groaning, he repeats the movement, his gaze relentlessly locked on mine.

"We should stop," he keeps muttering underneath his breath, yet his hips only seem to rock faster.

I move with him, desperation, desire, and panic coursing through my veins. My emotions are running all over the place, like a broken meter. I can barely sort through them. Barely comprehend what I'm feeling. Tears pool in my eyes again, but I hold on to Asher, hold on to the only thing that's not letting that fucking memory of Yellow consume my mind—

Asher abruptly jerks back, jumps off the sofa, and rushes toward the door, but then he pauses halfway across the room and clutches his head. His back is to me, but I can see his shoulders rising and falling, and I can hear the sharp intakes of his breath.

I feel equally as rattled as I sit up and struggle to get my breathing under control, my mind crammed with a clusterfuck of confusion.

What just happened? And why did Asher stop? And why do I feel both relieved and disappointed that he did? Not to mention embarrassed.

When he makes no effort to say anything or turn around, I get up and, ignoring the shakiness of my legs, start to step toward the door. "I'm just going to go out in the hallway for a bit," I mutter.

He turns around, his brows knit. "Why?"

"Because I think we could both maybe use a break from each other." I can barely look him in the eye, feeling stupid and disgusted with myself.

I practically attacked him.

As I squeeze by him, he captures my arm.

"I don't want a break," he insists, capturing my gaze. "What I want is for you to tell me why your skirt's torn and why you were trying to distract yourself by grinding your hips against mine. Not that I'd mind any other time, but I don't want you to be upset when we mess around. I want you to have a clear head." He tugs on my arm, pulling me closer, his eyes swirling with smoky flames. "So you can feel everything I'm doing to you."

My breathing starts to quicken, but I take a subtle breath and calm myself down. "I don't know why you're making a big deal out of my skirt being torn. It just got snagged on something. That's it."

"You're lying," he states. "I can smell it all over you."

This isn't the first time he's said something like that to me.

"I thought we already established that I'm a pro liar," I remind him. "So maybe your little sniffer, lie detector thing is broken."

"I can also smell elf on you," he adds, disregarding my remark. "You mentioned one was able to see you. And a couple of cyborgs. Who exactly were they?"

"Who exactly is the Wishing Shadow?" I challenge.

He shakes his head. "You go first."

"Nope."

"Little thief …" he starts to warn.

"Bossy genie," I talk over him, and he shakes his head, but his lips threaten to turn upward. "Look, if you want me to tell you what happened, you have to tell me first. There've been too many times when you've managed to talk around giving me a straight answer, like how you never explained why I look familiar to you." I don't bother mentioning I figured the answer out on my own. That's a secret I'm going to hold on to for now.

He shakes his head several times, the flames in his eyes burning brighter, which probably means he's pissed off. "You drive me absolutely crazy. Do you know that?"

I shrug. "Wouldn't be the first time someone's said that to me, and I'm sure it won't be the last."

"Not if I can help it," he mumbles.

"What the hell does that mean?"

"Nothing." He shakes his head, tugging me toward him until our bodies our flushed. Then he places his hands on my hips and holds me tightly. "Before I tell you who the Wishing Shadow is, I want to remind you of our bargain and what'll happen if you break it."

"I don't need a reminder of my debt to you," I say resentfully. "I'm perfectly aware that I can't leave you guys until I've stolen the objects."

"Good." His lack of caring annoys the crap out of me.

I glare at him. "Now that we got that stupid reminder out of the way, you can tell me who the fuck this Wishing Shadow is."

His grip on me intensifies. "It's … He's my father's servant."

CHAPTER 23

Maybe I should've put two and two together and figured that out on my own. Perhaps, deep down, I already knew the answer but was naively hoping I was wrong. Doesn't really matter, though. Not right now anyway.

"I need to leave." I step back, but he delves his fingers into my hips, stopping me.

"You can't run away," he says. "The bargain we made will kill you if you do."

"Then dissolve the bargain," I grit out, shoving against his chest in a lame-ass attempt to get away from him.

He swiftly shakes his head. "No. That bargain is the only thing keeping you from running away."

"Who cares if I do?" I scoff. "I'm not even useful to you anymore. In fact, I cause more problems than anything else." I gesture at the hologram showing a view of the outside to try to prove my point. "Look at that crowd. They're so pissed off that you guys aren't out there. And the only reason you're not is because of me."

"I don't give a shit about that crowd," he growls out. "What I care about is you being safe. And you're safe with us." His voice softens as he briefly caresses my cheek with his knuckles. "You can't run away from my father, little thief. If he wants to find you, he will."

"You think I'm worried about him finding me?" I gape at him. "I want him to find them, Asher. I want to get my revenge, not run away." I force down the shakiness rising in my throat. "I've wanted my revenge since the day he took my parents away."

His tension reduces, but he keeps his hands on my hips. "I want that, too; trust me."

"Then, why aren't you going after him? I mean, you're a genie and you're powerful."

"Because my father's more powerful," he strains out. "He's more powerful than any other genie still alive. That's why East, Arrow, and I have been trying to collect these objects—to gain more power so we can go up against him and the rest of his follower and actually stand a chance." He moves his hands from my hips to cup my face. "I understand your need for revenge—I feel it myself—but I'm not about to risk my own life or East's and Arrow's to try to get it." He looks me straight in the eyes. "And I'm not going to let you risk yours to try to either." He skims his thumb along my cheekbone, and I detect the slightest bit of wobbliness in his hand. "My father has taken away too many creatures that I care about. I'm not going to let him take any more away from me."

Vulnerable, pained genie. That's definitely, *definitely* something I thought I'd never see. But actually seeing it … seeing the emotions reflecting from his eyes … it's a lot to take in.

"Who …? Who did he take away from you?" I whisper.

I don't really expect him to answer, so he startles me when he says, "Some of my friends back on my planet … East's brother and sister … my mother …" He pauses for a beat then mumbles, "The possibility of you."

My brows tug together, and my lips part, ready to ask questions, but he steps back, rubbing his hand across his face.

"I really should find a way to get out there," he mutters, glancing at the hologram. "Before they break the gates down."

Understanding his pain all too well, I decide to let my questions drop for now.

"Asher," I say as he turns for the door. "I'm sorry about your mom."

He stiffens as he folds his fingers around the doorknob. "You don't need to be sorry. It's not your fault."

I wrap my arms around myself. "I know, but I know how hard that has to be for you."

He glances over his shoulder, and we exchange a silent, meaningful look that puzzles me to no end. And I'm not even going to try to decipher it. If I did, then I have a feeling I might be giving in to my curse just a little bit.

"I'm going to go see if anyone knows where East and Arrow are. I'll be right back." He pulls open the door and moves to leave.

"Wait," I call out, and he pauses. "Before you go, there's something I need to tell you. Something about what happened while I was out on the street."

He faces me then moves back into the room, closes the door, and waits patiently for me to explain.

It takes me a conflicting moment, but once I open my mouth, the words just pour out of me as I start to tell him everything.

CHAPTER 24

OKAY, I end up not telling him everything. I mean to. I know that maybe I should have. But when I get to the part where Yellow takes me up to that room, my stomach churns with nausea and I damn near vomit on the floor. So, I stop, bottle the words up, and shove them down, letting them mix with the pain and disgust. It's unhealthy —I know that—but I can't seem to get past the revulsion, remorse, and embarrassment.

"What happened when you got up to the room?" Asher prods when I trail off mid-story.

We're sitting on the sofa, close but not close enough that we're touching, with the sounds of chanting from outside still filling the air around us. The more I tell him about what happened, the more worked-up he gets. I'm worried he might explode at any given moment.

I shrug, picking at my fingers. "Apparently, aside from being able to shake the ground, widen alleyways, and make stairways vanish, I can also make the bars on a headboard come to life and snake around elves. After that, I just snuck out the tunnel that Arrow's cyborg friend told me about."

Asher's eyes pop wide. "Since when can you widen alleyways and make stairways vanish?"

"Oh, did Arrow and East not tell you about that?" I ask, and he shakes his head. "Well, it happened on our way here, when Arrow got stuck underneath a stairway and couldn't get out."

"That's … That's really impressive." He stares at me in wonderment. "I wonder what else you can do."

"I'm not sure, but I think East's theory about my emotions bringing out my powers is right. Although, I think I really need to start working on controlling them better because, a lot of times, they just happen or won't work at all."

"It's probably because you haven't used them in a while, if ever," Asher clarifies, draping an arm along the back of the sofa. "Powers work a lot like muscles in terms that they can weaken if they're not frequently used, so if they're dormant for a while, they don't work properly until you rebuild your strength."

"I guess that makes sense." I recline back, adjusting my torn skirt. "But, how can I use my power and rebuild their strength if I have to rely on my emotions setting them off?"

"I think, when we find out what you are and where your powers stem from, you might have an easier time controlling them."

"And when exactly is that going to be?"

"You mean, when are we going after the books?" he asks, and I nod. "As soon as we get the soul of an incubus and succubus, and Arrow hacks into the city's system to get a layout of The Vault."

"Why do you need the souls anyway? And what about this Chasing Magic Industries? What are they? And why are they hunting you? And what about the worlds patrol?" I frown as the shouting from outside grows louder and more demanding. "It seems like we're drawing an awful lot of attention right now, which you said you wanted to avoid."

"We'll be fine. As far as we can tell, the worlds patrol hasn't been able to track us here. And they haven't put a bounty on all of us," he attempts to reassure me, but nervousness resides in his expression as he casts a glance at the hologram. "As for the Chasing Magic Industries, they're basically a group that oversees the theft of magical objects, and while we've put up a protection spell around us to keep them from easily tracking us down, every so often one of their lackeys manages to get close. But this elf, he won't be able to find us, even with all the noise going on outside. Besides, there's always a bit of chaos when we're on tour. Usually, it's for an encore, but this isn't that much different."

I attempt to tell if he's lying, but he's the portrait of indifference at the moment. "Would Yellow have been able to find you if I had led him to you guys?"

"Possibly." He gives a short pause. "But you didn't." It's not a question, but I shrug anyway.

"It's not a big deal. I mostly did it because he was bossing me around, and you know how much I hate that." I fight back a squirm and the need to cover up the scratches as his gaze descends to my legs.

"You never told me where you got these from."

"It's not a big deal. I just scratched them on some rough brick when I was walking down that tunnel to get out of the inn."

His gaze snaps to mine. "These aren't scratches from bricks. They're scratches from fingernails."

"How would you know?" I quip in an attempt to avoid the truth. "Are you an expert on scratches?"

"Actually, I am," he mumbles, scratching at the scars on his chest.

"What happened?" I reach to touch his scars, but mid-reach, I withdraw, comprehending how dumb of an idea it would be.

"You tell me what happened here first, and then I'll

tell you." He delicately sketches his finger along one of the marks.

I shiver as both desire and nausea crash through me, and the entire floor quivers as well. Bottles on the table *clink* together and a cup tumbles off, shattering even more glass on the floor.

Asher's jaw ticks. "What did the elf do to you?"

"Nothing," I enunciate in a clipped tone. "So just drop it."

"No. You're going to tell the truth."

"No, I'm not." I bite down on my tongue as I realize my mishap.

"So, you *are* lying," he says, not smugly but with annoyance. When I refuse to say anything else, he spreads his fingers across my knee and pulls me closer. "Why won't you tell me?" His tone is shockingly sooth-ing, which only seems to infuriate me more.

"Because it's none of your business," I bite out, putting my hands on my legs to cover the red marks. "And it doesn't even matter. I handled the problem myself. End of story."

Asher's gaze is unyielding. "Did he …? Did he touch you?"

"No, not really." I squirm, frazzled and irritated amongst a buttload of other things.

His gaze zeroes in on my legs again. "If he didn't

touch you, then why are there fingernail scratches all over your legs?"

"Oh, my gods," I growl out. "You're seriously not going to drop this, are you?"

The fucker has the nerve to shake his head.

I curl my fingers inward, stabbing my fingernails into my palms. "Fine, you want the fucking truth?" I don't wait for him to respond, my anger controlling me. "Yeah, the stupid, disgusting elf forced me down on the bed, ripped my skirt, scratched the shit out of my legs, put his lips on mine, and tried to force me to … well, I'm sure you can guess. But my powers kicked in and the bed yanked him off me." I'm breathing profusely by the time I'm finished, but I'm too riled up to give a shit. "I fucking handled it. I'm not helpless. I can take care of myself. I don't need to talk about this with anyone." I'm unsure who I'm even trying to convince—him or myself. "Are you fucking happy now?"

He shakes his head from side to side, his eyes blazing like a wildfire, his body shaking. "No," he bites out as the walls and floor begin to quake.

At first, I think my powers are surfacing, but then I note how the trembling coincides with the intakes of Asher's breath.

"Stay here," he growls, jumping to his feet. Then he storms across the room, the entire place jolting with his pounding steps.

"Where are you going?" I call out as I stumble to my feet.

"To take care of something." He yanks open the door. "Just stay here. I'll be back in a second." He steps out and slams the door behind him.

The shaking gradually settles after a couple of seconds tick by, and then I move to chase after him. But when I jerk on the doorknob, the damn door won't open.

"Did he fucking lock me in here?" I snarl, hammering my fist on the door. "Asher, open the damn door!"

Silence is my only response.

Cursing my stupidity, I turn around, slump against the door, and shut my eyes as the past few hours roll over me. Taking it all in is exhausting, and I feel so drained. Drained from the day's events. Drained from Asher's mood swings. Drained from using my powers.

Like when I was in the compartment, my eyelids slowly grow heavy and my body sags toward the floor as exhaustion takes over.

CHAPTER 25

I FEEL fingers stroking my cheek, tantalizing tickles that make me so peaceful. So damn content ...

Wait ... I'm having the strangest sense of déjà vu ...

A heartbeat later, it clicks. I've been in this situation before, when I woke up after passing out in the compartment and Asher was stroking my cheek.

I blink my eyelids open, expecting my gaze to collide with the genie's fiery eyes. Instead, I meet East's glittery gaze. His eyes lack the luminosity they usually do, though.

"Hey." His voice is gentle. So is his touch as he traces his fingertips along my cheekbone. "You passed out on us again."

I blink my vision into focus. "I think I may have overused my powers for the day." I peer around. I'm lying on the leather sofa in the same room I passed out in, and my head is resting on East's lap. He has his shirt off, his glittery wings are on full display, and the rings on his fingers feel cold against my warm cheeks. "How long was I out? I'm guessing not too long since I'm still in the same room."

"It's only been about an hour." East splays his fingers across my cheek. "How are you feeling?"

"A little tired." I yawn. "But that's how I felt the last time I woke up from this little crashing from using my magic thing."

"That's not what I meant." He smooths his hand over the top of my head. "I meant, how are you feeling after the incident with Yellow?"

The edges of my mouth tug downward. "Asher told you about that?"

He nods. "But only because Arrow and I dragged the truth out of him after we caught him storming away from here, looking like he was about to commit murder."

"Who was he going to try to murder?" I ask, stretching out my legs.

East's brow curves up. "You don't know the answer to that already?"

"I ... Wait ... He wasn't going after Yellow, was he?" I shake my head. "I already told him I handled it."

East gapes at me like I'm insane. "Of course he was going after him, and I probably should've let him." He bounces his leg, jittery and irritated and completely un-East-like. "The only reason Arrow and I talked him out of it is because, the moment Asher would've found Yellow, our spell would've disintegrate and Chasing Magic Industries would be able to track us." His jaw clenches. "I probably should've just let Asher do it, though. It's driving me crazy that I didn't. I should've helped him do it. What happened to you … is partly my fault anyway, for not watching you more closely."

I blow out a heavy breath. "East, no one should've gone after Yellow. And this isn't anyone's fault. I'm the one who wandered off. If I hadn't, then the Wishing Shadow wouldn't have been able to put a spell on me." I sit up, sweeping my hair out of my face while lowering my feet to the floor. "And you guys don't need to protect me. I can protect myself perfectly fine."

"Killing Yellow isn't about protecting you from him. It's about him putting his hands on you and trying to force you to …" He works his jaw from side to side. "He deserves to have his fucking fingers that marked your legs broken off his hands." Like in the street right before I ran into the Wishing Shadow, his eyes darken like thunderclouds. "And anything else that touched you."

"Nothing else touched me." I scratch my wrist and tug at the hem of my skirt. "Well, I mean, his body did when he was pushing me down …" I swallow down the burn rising in the back of my throat. "But I mean his … thing

... didn't ..." I blow out a shaky exhale, staring down at the floor. "I really don't want to talk about this anymore."

His fixes his finger underneath my chin and tilts my head toward him. His gaze sears into me, which is a little odd. Usually, Asher is the one with the intense stare.

"I know you don't want to talk about it, and I'll stop if you need me to, but I want to say one more thing." He scoots toward me, sliding his hand behind my back, his wonderful sugary scent engulfing my nostrils. "Eventually, you should find someone you trust to talk to about it. Keeping stuff like this bottled up ... it'll eat you away inside."

A protest is already working its way up my throat, but the way his tone has shifted—lowering, quieting, darkening with pain—makes me pause and assess him. The storm has left his eyes and is replaced by a despairing, haunted shadow.

Did something happen to him?

As if reading my mind, he says, "A very, very long time ago, back when I still lived on Shimmerland, my life wasn't nearly as amazing as it is now." He attempts to convince me that he's okay with a dazzling grin, but without the typical, wicked glint in his eyes, it looks all sorts of wrong. And when he takes a deep breath, the smile fizzles. "When I first left Shimmerland and that not-so-amazing life behind, I refused to talk about what happened to me. I bottled it up, pretended. I was really good at pretending. So good I almost had myself fooled that I *was* okay. But the thing is, eventually, buried emotions have a way of digging themselves up and all that shit I was hiding … well, let's just say I refer to that part of my life as my dark time."

His words send a chill down my spine, but that doesn't make wanting to talk about what happened to me today any easier.

I stare down at my hands. "I just want to forget about it for now, okay?"

"That's fine." He places a hand on my knee. "Just know I'm here whenever you need to talk. And I'm an excellent listener when I need to be. And I … I understand."

I nod. "Thanks." My gaze flicks up to him, and he offers me an easy, warm smile, not an ounce of flirting evident. The look seems out of the ordinary on him, yet not necessarily in a bad way. He appears less mischievous and more honest, and that makes me feel more comfortable around him.

Between kissing Asher, my choice to befriend Arrow, and now this bonding moment with East, I feel like I'm getting in way over my head with these guys.

I think I need a break and maybe some fresh air …

"Where are Arrow and Asher anyway?" I ask, desperate for a subject change.

He stares at me for a spark of a second before

pointing over my shoulder. "They're outside, taking care of the mob."

I peer back at the hologram and find that the line weaving around the building has shrunken and the chanting has shifted into excited squeals and bubbling excitement.

I glance back at East. "Why aren't you out there?"

He grins, but his eyes lack luster. "Because I was on sleeping princess duty."

I point a finger at him. "Don't you dare start calling me princess."

When his eyes flicker with delight, I sigh, too aware of how much I missed the look of it.

"You know what? I think I'm going to." He slides closer to me until his hip is pressed against mine. "With how high maintenance you are, it's far more fitting than sweetheart."

My jaw drops. "Hey, I'm not even close to being high maintenance."

A smirk creeps across his face. "Hate to break it to you, princess, but from the moment you stepped foot onto our vehicle, you've done nothing but bring havoc into our lives." When I glower at him, he chuckles. "Relax, we love your havoc." I cringe at the word *love*, but he doesn't appear to notice. "And I have a feeling you're going to bring a lot more, but in the best way possible."

I attempt to keep glaring at him, but it's difficult when

he's sporting a genuine, glittery smile. "Well, just so you know, it's a two-way street. My life was completely dull until I got stuck with you guys' dumb asses." I'm such a fucking liar. My life was never dull. But I'm trying to win an argument.

I brace myself for a snide remark, but all he does is offer me his hand. Confused, I lay my palm in his, and he lifts me to my feet.

"Where are we going?" I ask as he starts toward the door.

"I figure we could go backstage and watch Asher and Arrow dazzle our fans," he explains as he opens the door. "And get you some fresh air."

Fresh air sounds nice, but …

My gaze travels down to my torn skirt. "I think I should probably put a cloak on first."

East slows to a stop, his gaze tracking mine. Then a deep frown etches across his face, swirls of storm clouds funneling in his eyes.

"Why do your eyes do that?" I ask the same question I did the first time I witnessed the change in his eyes.

And just like the first time, he avoids answering me.

"Let's save that story for later, okay?" he mumbles through a weighted breath. "We've already had too much darkness for one day."

I gulp down the fear threatening to take hold of me. Usually, dropping stuff isn't my style, but since he didn't force me to talk about Yellow, I can at least return the favor.

"I can fix your skirt for you, if you want me to," he says, and I eagerly nod, more than ready to get rid of the reminder of what happened today. But then he hesitates, nibbling on his bottom lip. "I'll have to touch the torn spot to fix it, though."

"Oh." My gaze descends to the shredded area. "It's fine."

"Are you sure?" he double-checks, and I nod, though my anxiety seeps through. "Just tell me if I need to stop," he utters, slowly extending his hand toward me.

I'm more afraid than I want to admit and that pisses me off. Fear? Is it going to become a part of my life more now, all because some dipshit elf thought he could do whatever he wanted with me?

Fucking elf. If I ever cross paths with him again, I hope I've learned to control my powers by then. That way, I can punish him exactly how I want to.

"Sweetheart." East freezes, worry creasing his face. "Do you need me to stop?"

Not wanting to let fear control me, I shake my hand then grab his hand and place it on the ripped hem of the skirt. "Do your magic, faerie." I snap my fingers at him. "Chop, chop. We haven't got all day."

A small smile touches his lips. "You're amazingly brave and strong." He places one hand against the hem of my skirt while reaching up to cup my cheek with the other. "And don't ever let anyone tell you any differently."

Feeling uneasy at the compliment, my lips part with a snarky retort, but he beats me to the punch as his grin morphs into a full-blown smirk.

"That probably won't be too much of a problem," he says. "Since, over the next two months, you're going to get attached to us and want to stay with us forever."

When my lips twitch in annoyance, his smirk magnifies.

Normally, when he insists I'll end up never wanting to leave them, I retaliate with a remark of denial. But, since that never seems to get me anywhere, I decide to go at it from another angle.

"Well, if that really happens, then I guess you'll be forced to tell me I'm amazing every single day," I quip with a grin.

He mirrors my grin as he slides his hand from my cheek to the back of my neck and inches forward, the tips of his boots clipping mine. "Oh, we're going to do a lot more than that." He skims his fingers over the nape of my neck, and my eyes widen as breathtaking tingles sprinkle down my skin.

I'm not even sure whose magic causes the sensation—his or mine—so I smash my lips together and pretend it didn't happen. *Pretend, pretend, pretend.*

I realize that, over the years, I've pretended a lot. It

makes me wonder if I'll ever have to stop pretending. Makes me wonder if the curse can ever be broken.

I chew on my thumbnail. "East … if you guys ever do get rid of Asher's father, will that break the curse?"

Remorse flickers in his eyes. "Unfortunately, even after a genie dies, the curses they casted while they were alive don't die with them."

"Oh." Disappointment crushes down on my shoulders.

"We'll find a way to break your curse," he promises. "Asher's already mentioned a few ways he believes could help."

I force a smile, wishing I could believe him. But the truth is, if Asher already knew a way to break a genie's curse, then wouldn't he have broken his already?

Yeah, I have a feeling I may very well spend the rest of my life silently drowning in my buried emotions until they dig themselves up, and then …

Well, if that ever happens, then the poor soul I fell in love with is going to be the one who suffers for it.

CHAPTER 26

AFTER EAST FIXES MY SKIRT, we make our way backstage, which is a spacious area that runs along the back of stage where Asher and Arrow are schmoozing their fans. Columns and curtains divide the two areas, and creatures wearing badges a lot similar to what I wore back when I was part of the staff are all over the place. Most of the staff members act squirmy and swoony when East appears, staring at him like he's some sort of god. But he ignores them and guides me to a gap just along the left side so I can peer out at the stage.

Asher and Arrow are sitting behind a marble table in the center of it, signing album covers and chatting with the two female vampires in front of them who look beyond flustered. Honestly, I didn't realize vampires could be flustered, but apparently, they can.

Just behind the two flustered vampires is a group of leather-dressed faeries, their glimmering skin inked with *Ash East Arrow*. And behind them are a bunch of tattooed pixies. And so on and so on.

So many creatures are here, and I want to pretend I'm not amazed at what I see, try to remind myself of how I felt about paranormal bands back when I thought I was human, but holy crazy chaos trolls, it's hard not to stare at all the madness in awe.

"There're so many creatures here," I mumble. "I don't even know what three quarters of them are." That realization makes me frown.

Here I thought I knew a lot about paranormals. Turns out, I was wrong. But I guess Asher's un-genie-like nature already made me start to realize that.

East moves up behind me and loops his hands around my waist, a move a lot of the staff members notice and frown at.

I could wiggle away, like I normally do when he crowds my personal space, but I don't want to make a scene. And truthfully, I'm sort of getting used to his touching, much to my dismay.

"Are you impressed?" he whispers in my ear, his bare chest pressing against my back.

"Kind of." The truth is, I'm beyond impressed, but East doesn't need his ego stroked any more than it already is.

Even right now, the creatures around us look like they're one flirty smile away from getting down on their knees and worshipping him.

"Kind of?" He lightly pinches my side. "How you wound my ego, sweetheart."

I roll my eyes. "I think your ego can handle it."

He chuckles, pulling me closer. "So, which ones are the creatures you don't know?"

"Well, there're the ones with all the eyes on their heads," I say, trying to discreetly point at a group of them, yet they all turn to look at me, causing me to inch closer to East.

"Those would be seeing demons," he explains. "And they're staring at you now because they see everything and saw you point at them."

Worry crawls through me. "Are they dangerous?"

"Most demons are, but they wouldn't dare touch you when they know you're with us." He stares at the demons until they look away.

"I'm not with you. I'm *stuck* with you."

He merely laughs.

I sigh in exhaustion. "You're the most persistent person—*thing* I've ever met."

He freezes, and so does every creature nearby, all of them gaping at me.

Okay, what'd I do now?

"A *thing*?" East says with a hint of shocked amusement. "Did you just call me a *thing*?"

"Um … yeah?" I shrink against him as a couple of the bigger creatures glare at me. "Why are they staring at me like they … like they want to, like, bitch-slap me or something?"

"Because you called me a thing." His sounds fully entertained now. "Which is quite close to the worst dirty insult you can throw at a paranormal. It's basically like calling a human a whore."

"Oh." I frown. "I didn't know that. I just thought it was like calling you a dude or something."

He laughs quietly, his breath caressing my ear. "Sometimes, I love how innocent you are."

"I'm not innocent," I growl. "I've done a lot of bad stuff in my life."

"I'm sure you have, but you're also very innocent with a lot of things. It's okay, though. It's things like your innocence, feistiness, cleverness, and general lack of regard about whether you piss me off or not that makes you so appealing." He caresses his lips against my cheek. "That and the fact that you're unbelievably fucking gorgeous."

I stupidly flush like a dumbass, swoony groupie, but thankfully, he can't tell. Or, well, I think he can't. But then he reaches forward and strokes my cheek with the back of his hand.

"I also love that you blush," he murmurs. "It's been ages since I've been around another creature who has something else besides lust in their eyes."

"I'm not blushing," I lie indignantly.

"It's also fucking cute when you lie. And how you never seem to get flattered no matter how much a compliment you. You're a tough crowd to win over."

It's at that exact moment someone from the crowd spots East and me and squeals, "East!" at the top of his lungs.

Within seconds, more paranormals have spotted him and, like earlier, they start to chant, "East! East! East! We want East!"

Asher is in the middle of autographing a vampire's forearm when he pauses to glance behind him. Then Arrow twists around in his seat, and both their gazes instantly find us.

The look on Asher's face is unreadable as he motions for East to come out while pushing back from the table and rising to his feet.

"I'm going to trade places with Asher for a bit, okay?" East swings around in front of me.

"You can all go out there together," I say. "I don't need a babysitter."

He gives me a tolerant. "I'm going to trade places with Asher for a bit," he repeats then tucks a strand of my hair behind my ear, a move that earns me the reward of several dirty looks from both staff members and the fans outside.

Yep, that's me. Harlynn Merringten, making friends everywhere I go.

When East turns around and steps out on stage, the crowd goes wild with roars, shouts, and even a few creatures send magical fireworks up in the air, which I'll admit is kind of cool. And East eats that shit up, throwing his hands up in the air and encouraging everyone to shout louder.

I roll my eyes, not a bit surprised. *Just like I told Asher earlier. An attention whore.*

Then again, Asher said he grows tired of it, and East seems good at pretending. At least, from what I can tell. Maybe this is all an act. It's really hard to tell, and I don't even know why I'm analyzing it so much. Why I'm becoming so interested in them.

I really need to get my head back in the game ...

As East reaches the middle of the stage, Asher walks off. His fierce gaze is locked on mine as he strides toward me. Then he laces his fingers through mine and, without missing a beat, hauls me with him as he hurries toward the back area.

While a few staff members looked shocked when East appeared with me, every single creature backstage that spots Asher holding my hand nearly trips over their feet.

"They seem shocked to see me with you," I remark as

Asher steers me toward a set of sheer curtains hanging on the far back wall.

"Probably because they can't figure out what you are." He gives a short pause. "Well, that and I don't usually walk around holding hands with other creatures." He quickly clears his throat, as if uneasy with his last comment.

"Not even aftershow women?" I question with cynicism.

He glances over at me, cocking a brow. "You seem awfully obsessed with the idea of me, East, and Arrow being with aftershow women."

I'm secretly relieved he's acting like his normal, snarky self again. I can handle the cocky, sassy Asher way better than I can handle the upset or compassionate version of him.

"I'm not obsessed," I stress. "I was just making a simple, and I'm sure, accurate statement."

"No, a completely non-accurate statement. We never bring anyone backstage." With that, he ducks behind the curtains and steps into an enclosed space that gives us some privacy from all the staring. Then he releases my hand and spins around to face me, his gaze sweeping up and down my body before locking in on my skirt. "Your skirt's fixed," he mumbles, fiddling with the hem.

"East fixed it with magic before we came out here." I

scratch my wrists, getting squirmy over where the conversation is heading.

Asher's gaze skates to mine, and that compassion that makes me stupidly uncomfortable is reflecting from his eyes. "I'm not going to make you talk about what happened or ask you any more questions for now. I just wanted to …" He dithers, looking contemplative. "I wanted to apologize for freaking out on you earlier and locking you in the room. I only did it because I didn't want you following me."

I gape at him. "You're *apologizing* to me?"

A crinkle forms between his brows. "Yeah … Why do you sound so surprised about it?"

I give a half-shrug, leaning back, the curtain brushing against my back. "It's just … I didn't think genies apologized. Especially to humans."

"You're not human," he reminds me. "And I've apologized to you before. But you're right; I don't do it very often."

As his words start to sink in, I grow extremely twitchy. "You don't need to apologize. What you did wasn't bad, and I think you meant well." I drum my fingers against the sides of my legs as uneasiness festers inside me. "I want to say, though, that you don't need to go after Yellow. It's too risky." For several different reasons. "One day, *I'll* get my revenge on him." I plaster on a smile, trying to lighten the mood. "In case you haven't figured it out yet, I'm kind of a grudge holder."

He tucks a lock of my hair behind my ear. "No, Harlynn, you're really not."

Between the use of my real name and the way he stares at me with the strangest, almost endearing look on his face, my comfort level plummets even more. Fortunately, the crowd starts yelling Asher's name.

"You might want to get back out there." I seize the opportunity to have a moment alone because, holy hell, if he keeps looking at me like this, I may very well try to bolt.

And I'd really rather not do that while we're on Steel, especially since the sunlight is slipping away.

"They're fine," he mutters, tilting his head to the side as he continues to stare at me with utter fascination and a bit of confusion.

As the chanting grows louder, I sigh.

"Ash, will you just go out there? I'll be fine by myself for a little while. I'm more used to being by myself than I am being around others." When his lips twitch in amusement, I frown. "What's so funny about what I said?"

He rolls his tongue in his mouth, fighting back a smile. "Nothing. What you said … it was actually kind of sad." His smile evaporates.

"Don't you dare pity me," I warn, crossing my arms.

"And if you didn't find it funny, then why were you grinning like an idiot?"

"I wasn't grinning like an idiot," he denies. "I was merely a bit amused."

"About what?"

"About the fact that you called me Ash."

"Oh." I feel stupid for giving him a nickname, but I play it cool, trying to salvage what little dignity I have left. "I don't see what the big deal is. East calls you that all the time."

"He does, and so does Arrow. No one else."

"Well, sorry, I guess." Although, I still don't get what the big deal is. "I'll try to stick to calling you genie dude or cocky asshat from now on."

He grins, amused, and then closes the space between us. "Call me whatever you want. I've been called a lot worse." He reaches up and traces the pad of his finger along my bottom lip. "Personally, though, I liked hearing *Ash* come from your lips." His lips kick up into a grin as a shaky exhale fumbles from my lips. But then his grin dissipates as the crowd continues screaming out his name. "You're right; I probably do need to go back out there, just for a little bit."

"Go," I encourage, more than eager to get a break from him, from East, even from Arrow. And during that break, I'll take some time to repeatedly kick my own ass until I get my shit together and start acting like the old

Harlynn who didn't let little touches, smiles, and apologies fog up her judgment.

He nods with reluctance. "Stay backstage, okay? No wandering off." He grabs the curtain and pulls it open. "I'll let all the staff know you're with us so no one will bother you. If they do, yell for us."

I roll my eyes. "Stop being so paranoid. I can take care of myself."

His gaze flits to mine. "I'm not being paranoid. I'm trying to keep you safe. Now, please behave." With that, he folds his fingers around my wrist and tugs me out behind him as he strides forward.

He only releases me when we near the entrance of the stage. Then, with one final, concerned look in my direction, he makes his way back out to his fans, who shout in excitement.

Despite how much I want to wander off, I stay behind stage like I promised Asher I would. While I never did see him tell any of the staff members about me, no one tries to bother me, so I figure he either had Maple do it or used some sort of weird genie communication power on them.

Occasionally, Asher, Arrow, and East all glance in my direction, as if making sure I'm staying where I'm supposed to be, which begins to drive both myself and their fans insane.

"Who's that girl you keep looking at back there?" an

attractive, red-headed succubus asks Asher as he glances back at me while signing his name across her shirt.

"A friend," is all he says. Then he hands her back her marker and motions for the next fan to move up.

The succubus glares at me before shoving a vampire waiting in line out of her way and stomping off toward the exit gates.

A friend, huh? So that's what I'm supposed to be? It's a little weird—the idea of being friends with paranormals. Then again, I'm a paranormal myself. Besides, it's not like we're really friends. I'm sure that's just a cover up for what I really am.

Which is what, Harlynn?

I grimace at my thoughts, realizing I don't have an answer. Realizing, I'm still fairly unsure of why Asher, East, and Arrow are keeping me around.

"That girl's staring at you," a vampire with long, blonde hair stage-whispers to East as she has him sign her arm.

"What girl?" East replies without glancing up.

"That girl behind stage." She gives an insinuating glance in my direction. "Is she a stalker? Maybe you should have someone remove her."

East caps the marker then gradually twists around in the chair, looking at me, his eyes shimmering with mischief.

I give him a dirty look, like *don't you dare bring me into your drama.* But that only seems to make his eyes shine brighter.

"That pretty girl right there?" he asks the vampire with his gaze fixed on me. "The one with the gorgeous eyes and killer legs."

I fire a glare at him, and his lips quirk.

"Um … I guess so." The vampire shifts her weight, nervousness edging across her pale expression.

"Hmm … Stalker or not, I think I might keep her. She'd make a delectably delicious treat later after the show." He winks at me, to which I respond with the middle finger.

He chuckles, facing the vampire again, whose jaw is hanging to her knees. After she wanders off with confusion written all over her face, he goes back to signing autographs and charming his fans.

East is really entertaining to watch and is beyond charming, but I'm not too surprised by that. Asher is a bit moodier, but sporadically puts on an alluring smile that makes everyone go crazy. And Arrow is exactly like how I imagined him to be—quiet and kind, offering a small smile here and there, but not the real smile I've witnessed a couple of times.

I'm not sure how long I stand there watching them, but eventually, a human-like creature approaches me. He looks around my age, is tall, with blond hair, and he's wearing a staff badge.

"Hey," he greets me. "I was told to come see if you wanted anything to eat." My stomach chooses that exact moment to grumble, and he chuckles. "Never mind. I think I have my answer. Just tell me what you want, and I'll go get it for you."

I crinkle my nose at the idea of being served. "I can go get it myself. Just point the way."

"Are you sure?" he checks. "It's sort of my job to serve the band members."

"Yeah, but I'm not a band member," I point out. "And I'm not really a fan of being served."

He gives me the kind of smile that screams human. Could it be that he is one? "Fair enough. But at least let me show you where the food is." He winks at me, his eyes briefly illuminating.

Okay then. Definitely not human.

I start to follow him, but pause, remembering the promise I made to Asher. "Wait. Is the food backstage or somewhere else?"

He points at a section of curtains not too far away from where we're standing. "It's just back there."

"Thanks. I think I can find my way on my own." Not that he seems like a bad guy, but not knowing what sort of creature he is makes me uneasy.

To my relief, he nods and walks off, leaving me to go get food by myself.

I quickly walk back to where he pointed and duck

behind the curtain, ready to dive into some yummy food. But being hungry becomes the least of my concerns when I realize nothing is behind the curtain but a door. Worry prickles through me, and I reel around, ready to hightail it back to my safe spot right beside the stage, when a hand is slapped across my mouth and a body is pressed up against mine, the stench of darkness flooding my nostrils.

I try to scream, but I'm jerked backward, farther away from the curtain and into a small room that I'm assuming is behind the door.

"Shhh …" the Wishing Shadow whispers in my ear. "No one's going to hurt you, princess."

I bite down on the fucker's hand then kick him in the shin, but it barely fazes him.

He pulls me deeper into the room that is lit up by a single, flickering light. A chair is in the corner, and chains and cuffs have been strapped to the arms and legs.

Panic soars through me as he guides me into the chair. I immediately start to stand up, but the cuffs snap around my wrists and ankles, by magic I'm guessing.

Taking a deep breath, I open my mouth to scream, but no sound leaves my lips. As the severity of the situation weighs down on me, I swallow hard.

"Relax, princess." The Wishing Shadow steps in front of me. "Like I said, no one's going to hurt you."

He's wearing the cloak he had on earlier, but the hood

is lowered so I can see his face better. His features are striking, not just in the sense that he's gorgeous in a scary, intimidating sort of way, but his face is also familiar. A click of a moment later, I figure out why.

He looks kind of like Asher.

Sure, his lips are silver instead of blue, but they are full and shaped like Asher's. His eyes are the same shape, too, but glow with embers instead of flames. And his hair is equally as dark, but chin-length instead of short.

"Who are you?" I whisper, digging my fingernails into the arms of the chair as frustration boils through me.

Why can't I scream or at least talk louder? Is he using magic on me? Borrowed magic from Asher's father? That thought makes a foul, sickening knot form in the pit of my stomach.

He crouches down in front of me and rests his arms on my legs. His skin is unpredictably warm. "Do you really not know the answer to that? Because, creatures can usually see the resemblance right away."

I will my voice to come out smooth. "You're Asher's father's Wishing Shadow."

His brows elevate to his hairline. "Okay, that was not what I expected you to say." He eyes me over inquisitively. "Just how much has my brother told you about his life?"

My eyes enlarge. *Brother?*

His lips curl. "Did he not mention that part?" When I

frown, he tacks on, "Don't take it personally. No one in the family ever talks about me. I'm kind of a disappointment, being what I am and all. Then again, my father's disappointed in everything except for himself." He angles his head to the side and studies me. "Except for you. He seemed positively pleased when I told him that I'd found you and that you were still as clueless as you were the first time he met you."

Anger bubbles underneath my flesh, blinding rage that makes me want to shred this Wishing Shadow apart with my bare hands.

"You should take me to him," I whisper lowly. "Let us get reacquainted." Then I can finally get my revenge.

Now that I have powers, that could very well happen. Then again, I can't control them very well. Like right now, I can't even get them to manifest.

Come on, powers. Free me! Turn this chair into a snake.

The stillness in my body causes my frustration to intensify.

Dammit! What's the point in having powers if I can't even use them when I need them?

The Wishing Shadow's silvery lips twist into a grin. "As much as I'd love to give you the opportunity to get your revenge on my father, that magic of yours is pretty much useless right now."

"What do you know about my magic?" I question, pausing my escape.

"Now, what would be the fun in just telling you?" Amusement twinkles in his eyes, yet sadness somehow haunts his face.

"It'd be fun because it'd give you the opportunity to help me learn more about my powers, which would help me be able to control them better, which might lead to me being able to take your father down, which will not only eliminate his disappointment in you—you know, seeing as how he'd be dead and all—but it'd also free you." The latter I'm unsure about, but I'm attempting to bull-shit my way out of this, and I'll put money on him wanting to be free. No one wants to be a servant.

He momentarily studies me. "You're an … interesting creature."

"Why does everyone always say that?" I scoff, jerking on the chains.

A smile touches his lips that makes him look less scary. "Because you are." He watches me struggle to get free in utter fascination. "You won't escape, no matter how hard you pull on those things."

I continue to try anyway, throwing my weight forward. "Clearly, you've never chained up an awesome and very clever thief before."

His smile expands. "You're amusing. Almost makes me wish I didn't have to do what I'm about to do."

An icy chill spills across my flesh as the door behind him swings open. Maple steps inside, a devious smile consuming her face as she takes in the chains securing me to the chair.

"Not so feisty now, are we?" she sneers, crossing her arms and smirking.

"When I get out of these chains," I say in an eerily calm tone, "I'm going to wipe that smirk off your face with my fist."

Her nostrils flare, while the Wishing Shadow busts up laughing, but the noise is shaky and raspy, as if it's been ages since he laughed.

"Maxton," Maple warns, "you will not laugh at me, or else I'll make sure your father curses you with a decade's worth of silence."

He rolls his tongue along his teeth, his jaw ticking, and his fingers curling inward. "Fine," he grinds out, the embers in his eyes sizzling.

"So, your name's Maxton." A conniving smile pulls at my lips. "Good to know."

"And why's that?" He seems authentically curious.

I lean closer to him, so close our noses nearly touch. "Because it makes it easier to track you down *when* I get my revenge."

His eyes smolder, and an unsteady breath eases past his lips, his gaze briefly dropping to my own lips. Then he quickly shakes his head. "You say that like you're going to escape."

"Oh, I'm going to." I slant back in the chair and let a

lazy grin spread across my face. "Just you wait."

Yeah, I'm so full of shit. I have no clue how I'm going to get out of here since I can't scream and magic is binding these chains to me. But that doesn't mean I can't pretend and make him squirm a bit.

Of course, he seems more intrigued than squirmy to me, so perhaps I'm not pretending as well as I normally do.

"Let's just get this over with." Maple ambles toward me, adjusting the bracelets on her wrists. "August wants her off the planet and into his hands before the sun goes down."

"Who's August?" I comprehend my mistake as soon as Maple grins.

"The genie who's going to own you soon." Her grin enlarges when I gulp.

"He's my father," Maxton says, measuring my reaction thoroughly.

Maple smacks her palm upside his head and hisses, "Stop telling her things. All she needs to know is that she'll belong to a genie soon and that she'll have to obey him."

The muscles in Maxton's jaw spasm. "Please don't hit me."

She smacks him again, harder this time. "I can do whatever I want to you. Anyone can." When she slaps him yet again, I cringe. "And there's not a damn thing you can do about it." She hits him again and again, and he winces but makes no effort to stop her.

A strange sensation coils inside my gut. Yeah, Maxton put a spell on me earlier and brought me here to do gods know what, but I think he may have no control over his actions. Him not hitting or yelling at Maple more than proves that. Well, either that or he's a freakin' patience guru.

"Stop hitting him," I say, shocking all three of us.

Maple freezes, her hand suspended in mid-air. "Do you seriously feel *sorry* for him? *Him?* A Wishing Shadow?" When I don't answer, she cackles with laughter. "Oh, my gods. And this is the creature August thinks can save him? How pathetic."

Huh? Save him? Save him from what?

"I'd be careful," Maxton warns quietly. "She may be naïve, but she's extremely powerful."

Maple's gaze skims me over, then her lips curl. "I think I'll be okay." Then she strikes Maxton in the head again, this time with her gaze fixed on me. "I think she may not like violence, though. That's odd. Her kind is usually so used to it." She hits Maxton in the face, and he flinches. "That's okay. We'll get her used to it. And we'll be doing her a favor with where she's going." She reaches out and slaps me across the face.

"Fucking genies," I growl out as my cheek stings. "What the hell is wrong with you?"

"Watch it, Maple," Maxton cautions, his face contorted in pain as he stares at my cheek, which I'm sure has a big, huge, Maple-sized handprint on it—the chick has freakishly large hands. "The orders were to bring her back unharmed."

"A little slap on the face isn't going to hurt her." Her palm collides with my cheek again.

Rage pours through my veins, potent, hot, and scorching. My ears ring as my jaw pops. But beneath the pain, a bit of magic flickers. Not a lot, but enough that I can almost taste it.

"Back off." Maxton lets out a shaky exhale through his nose, his fists balled. "Up until a couple of hours ago, you weren't even a part of this. I'm not even sure why August brought you into this. I have it handled."

Maple rolls her eyes and crosses her arms. "Like August actually trusts you. You may be bound to him, but he knows, if there is ever a chance for you to free yourself, you'll take it. And in the condition he's in, he can't risk it." She whacks Maxton across the head again. "He's lucky she"—she gives a glance in my direction—"ended up with your brother so I was able to step in and help."

"Why wouldn't she have ended up with Asher?" Maxton glances at me with a bit of spark back in his eyes. "It was Destiny after all, and Destiny always wins."

What the hell is Destiny? I want to ask, but Maple hits

him again, in the shoulder, and this time, it's hard enough that I hear a bone crack.

He cries out in pain, clutching his arm. "Fuck, I think you broke a bone."

"Well, if you weren't so pathetically weak, that wouldn't have happened," she snaps, moving to strike him again.

"Stop!" I shout, my magic stirring to life. "Stop being such a freakin' bitch."

Her blazing eyes zero in on me. "You wouldn't feel sorry for him if you knew what is going to happen to you when he brings you to August."

They keep saying *when* they bring me to August, as if he can't come to me. I wonder why.

"*If* he brings me to August," I correct as my magic currents through my veins. "But I have a feeling that's not going to happen."

She plasters on a cocky smirk. "Then you're even stupider than I thought."

"And you hit like a pixie." I flash her a clever grin and am rewarded when she punches me in the jaw.

Sure, it hurts like a motherfucker, but her hits ignite anger inside of me, which seems to be powering up my magic.

"I take that back." I work to keep my voice even, the pain getting to me. "You hit like a human."

That comment makes her snap. She reaches to punch

me again, but then she suddenly stops and reels toward Maxton, smacking his broken shoulder repeatedly. He remains crouched on the floor, taking every blow with a wince. He never tries to retaliate. Never says much of anything, and I start to figure out that my original assumption was right. He's bound to August and can't do much of anything. That revelation causes a storm to brew inside of me, lightning bolts of energy channeling through my body, and the room around me quivers like thunder.

"What's happening?" Maple asks, lowering her hands to the side as she glances around in puzzlement.

Maxton's gaze glides toward me, a delighted shock glinting in his eyes. "I think our little qui furabatur is more powerful than my father anticipated."

Qui furabatur.

Qui furabatur.

Hold on to that word, Harlynn.

"Well, she needs to stop it." Her gaze cuts to me, and then she grabs a fistful of my hair. "Stop that." When the room continues to quake, she yanks on my hair so hard my eyes water. "Stop that now, or you'll be punished."

"No." My voice comes out louder this time, which means I'm regaining control over myself once again.

Taking a deep inhale, I open my mouth and belt out the loudest scream I can. Unfortunately, magic pours out, too, and mixes with the scream, causing smoke, mist, and glitter to launch across the room and shatter the walls and floor.

My eyes widen as the chains around my arms and legs evaporate into dust, and the floor splinters apart and opens up.

Maple screams as she tumbles into the hole, and then I gasp as I start to fall in after her, but Maxton snags ahold of my hand and jerks me to the side.

"Thanks," I mumble, even though he probably did it so he can bring me to his father.

That is *so* not happening.

Pushing to my feet, I skitter around the seemingly bottomless hole in the floor, ready to bolt, but I slam to a stop when I catch sight of the backstage area.

Columns are tipped over and crumbled; the curtains are gone, lost in the howling wind probably; the roof is partially collapsed; and the staffing members are fleeing toward the streets with the fans, who are crying out in fear. And onstage, where Asher, East, and Arrow were sitting, it is now abandoned and cracked in half.

"They left me?" I whisper, that twinge in my heart rising again. Or did they? I twist back around toward Maxton then instantly stumble back at his nearness. "Did you make me invisible again?" I demand, regaining my footing.

He rolls his eyes, inching toward me. "Like I could. You just sucked almost all my power."

I match his move and step back, my feet bumping into a tipped over column. "I did not."

"You did." The tail of his cloak swishes across the floor as he slowly moves toward me, his eyes dull and shadowed over. "It's only temporary, though, so you'd better run."

"Is that a threat?"

"No, it's a warning."

"Oh." I hesitate, unsure what to make of him.

He frowns. "Harlynn … You need to run …" His eyes widen as the embers awaken. "*Now.*"

Since my power has gone silent again, I don't wait for him to tell me twice. I spin around and run across the stage and toward the street. But as I arrive, I find a giant crack in the floor is blocking my path.

I screech to a halt. It's too wide to jump across and stretches as far as my eyes can see. The stairs that lead off stage have buckled, leaving about a three-story drop to the ground below.

"Shit." I whirl around, then stumble back as Maxton rushes at me, his eyes possessed by the embers.

Sidestepping him, I rush down the side of the crack in the floor, jump over a tipped over column, and swing around a large piece of ceiling.

"How long is this fucking crack?" I mumble as I search for the end. "Come on—"

Fingers brush my back, but I don't peer over my

shoulder to see how close he is. Instead, I increase my pace.

As I round a column that has managed to stay up, I slam into a solid object with so much force that I nearly fall back on my ass. I doubtlessly would've, but arms are then encompassing my waist and pulling me forward again.

Blinking, I peer up and realize that the solid object I ran into is actually East.

"Are you okay?" he asks with unfamiliar worry.

I bob my head up and down. "But Asher's brother is right behind me. He's the Wishing Shadow that casted a spell on me earlier today, and he's here now because he wants to take me to Asher's father."

"Not wants to. Has to." Maxton's emotionless voice sails from over my shoulder.

Tension ripples through East as he swings me around and positions himself in front of me.

"Max," East says calmly with his hands positioned at his sides. "Come on; you know you don't want to do this."

"Even if that were true, you know I have no control over this," Maxton bites out, winding around debris as he stalks toward us. "I have to take her to him."

"And why can't he come get her himself?" East wonders, pressed protectively against me.

"You know I can't tell you that," Maxton responds. "Now move out of my way before I have to make you."

"I can't do that," East says in a disheartened tone. "You know I can't let you take her."

"Then we'll have to fight," Max replies, his voice mirroring East's.

"I know." East releases a loud breath. "I'm so sorry, Max. I really am."

I peer over East's shoulder just as Maxton takes a step toward us, rubble crunching underneath his boots.

"Me, too." Remorse overflows his eyes.

This might just be the most depressing conversation I've ever witnessed.

"Sweetheart," East calls from over his shoulder. "I need you run. Head back to the vehicle and wait for Arrow and Asher."

"I'm not just going to leave you here by yourself," I say, shaking my head.

"I'll be fine," he assures me. "You worrying about me is cute, though. I think I'll add that to my list."

What list?

Before I can ask, he reaches back and gently nudges me backward. "Go."

I glance at Maxton, who has a pained look on his face as his hands crackle with electric-blue bolts of magic.

"No. I'm not leaving you."

"Little mouse." A warning rings in East's tone. "This isn't up for argument."

I snort a nervous laugh. "It's cute you actually believe

that." I move to dodge around him, hoping upon hope that my powers will surface again.

If not, I'm so screwed. But I'm not about to just walk away and let East get fried by Maxton's magic, and gods know what else, all because August is after me for whatever reason.

As I step to East's side, though, someone circles an arm my waist. At first, I think it's East, but then the scent of cupcakes graces my nostrils.

"I don't think so, little thief," Asher says as he lifts me up until my feet no longer touch the ground.

"Hey, put me down," I gripe, pushing against his chest.

His gaze connects with mine for a heart-fluttering second, and then he whispers, "I'm sorry."

"Sorry for what—"

The question gets ripped from my lips as he throws me in the air.

I gasp as I sail across the broken stage and brace myself for impact. Instead of hitting the floor, though, Arrow appears out of nowhere and catches me in his arms.

"Take her back to the vehicle!" Asher shouts from across the stage. "Don't make any stops. You need to get her there before the sun goes down."

"I will!" Arrow yells back with a nod.

"Arrow," I warn, grasping his shoulder and trying to wiggle from his arms. "Don't you dare—"

I squeak when he slings me over his shoulder and takes off, running away from Asher and East.

"Traitor," I seethe, pounding my fist against his back, which kind of hurts because of the metal. "Friends are supposed to have each other's backs."

"They're also supposed to protect each other, which is what I'm doing right now." His robotic skills must kick in, because he starts to effortlessly leap over columns and fallen pieces of debris, the gadgets in his body humming to life.

"You can't do this," I protest, clutching the back of his shirt as he reaches the mob of creatures chaotically rushing down the street. Panic laces the air, along with the buzzing of electricity. "This isn't Asher and East's battle to fight. And I'm stronger than you think." I swallow a shaky breath as tears sting my eyes. "I'm the one who brought the whole building down and made Maple fall into a bottomless hole. I can handle this, so take me back." I'm not even completely sure what I'm fussing over—me fighting my own battles or the worry that East and Asher are going to get hurt.

The latter frightens me more than it should.

"No." The firmness in his tone is foreign. "And don't talk about what you did ... not until we get to the vehicle." His voice softens. "Okay?"

A thousand protests are about to burst from the tip of

my tongue, but they are cut off by the sound of an intercom clicking on.

"Attention citizens and visitors of Steel. Due to the current situation going on at the Arch, the mayor is putting the entire planet on lockdown. No creature is permitted to leave or enter the planet until law enforcement has done an investigation into the cause behind the collapsing of the Arch. There will also be a curfew enforced until further notice. All creatures must be in their homes before dusk. Thank you for your cooperation."

As the intercom buzzes off, the creatures around us quicken their paces, pushing and shoving each other as they scurry down the street.

"The collapsing of the Arch …?" I sweep my hair out of my eyes, lift my head, and look back in the direction we came from.

My jaw drops.

The Arch is no longer stretching toward the sky but lying in pieces on the ground.

"Please tell me no one got hurt," I whisper in horror.

Oh, my gods, I did this.

I broke a city.

Holy fucking shit, I really am dangerous, just like the worlds patrol said.

"Everyone's fine," Arrow says, quickening his strides. "Harlynn, don't say anything else, okay? Not until we get back to the vehicle. It's very important."

As shock whips through me, striking me speechless, all I can do is nod.

CHAPTER 27

BY THE TIME we reach the forest, the last of the golden sunlight has slipped away from the sky, which has nervousness edging through me.

"Should we be worried?" I ask, peering around at the towering trees and bushes, the bronzed moonlight casting an eerie glow off all the metal.

"We're fine," Arrow insists. He still has me slung over his shoulder, but I haven't protested for a while. In fact, I've been pretty quiet due to the shock that bitch-slapped me across the face when I realized I knocked the Arch down. "The monsters I was referring to earlier mostly hang out in the city." He gulps. "They're part machine and feed off weak creatures ... But they shouldn't come out here. Not when it's so underpopulated."

I smash my quivering lips together. "What about the curfew?"

"We'll be okay. We're almost to the vehicle." Despite his words, he increases his pace, taking longer strides.

We remain silent and on edge for the rest of the journey back to the vehicle. My mind mostly lingers on Asher and East, and if they're all right. Questions also flood my thoughts, like what qui furabatur means. Since Arrow urged me to be quiet, though, I haven't dared ask yet.

Finally, after what feels like hours, we arrive at the vehicle. Arrow hurries inside, sets me down, and then locks the door. When he turns around, my lips part, but he places a finger against his lips and shakes his head.

"Turn security on," he announces to the empty room.

A series of *clicks* sound through the air, and then he rushes down the hallway, peering in all the rooms.

"What're you looking for?" I whisper as I inch toward the hallway.

"I'm just making sure no one's here." He exits Asher's room and walks back down the hallway toward me. "Usually, I'm not too worried, since East puts up a seal every time we leave, but you were kind of a slap of reality that maybe his magic doesn't protect the vehicle as well as we thought." He stops in front of me with a trace of worry in his eyes. "Not that any of us are upset that you were able to get through his magic. We're glad you're here." Rubbing his lips together, he brushes his brass knuckles across my cheek, only to hastily pull away.

"Asher mentioned you thought East and I left you in the street. I just want you to know we'd never do that. We don't want to ditch you. We looked everywhere for you. I'm just glad you crossed paths with Steelford."

"Steelford …? Wait. Is that the innkeeper that told me where the tunnel was?"

He nods. "I told some of my old acquaintances about you; gave them a description in case they spotted you. That's how he knew who you were." He presses his lips together in a thin line. "Asher told me what happened at the inn. I'm so sorry."

I scratch my leg. "You don't need to be sorry. It wasn't your fault."

"We brought you to this planet, knowing it was dangerous, and promised you that you'd be safe, so it is our fault."

"It's not your fault," I repeat, but he only shakes his head.

I sigh, not really giving up, but putting a tack in it for now.

"So, what do we do now? I mean, how long do lock-downs usually last?"

He hesitates, fiddling with a gadget on his arm. "Usually, until law enforcement closes the investigation."

"So, until they find out it's me and captures me?"

Awesome. Now I'm going to be a prisoner on planet Steel.

"They're not going to capture you," he promises determinedly. "No one saw you use your power."

"Maxton did," I point out miserably. "And Maple. But I think … I think she might be dead."

Oh, my gods, I think I may have killed her with my powers.

Yeah, she may have been an evil wench, but the idea that I killed a creature is making my stomach churn with guilt. And here I thought I was a revenge badass.

Arrow surveys me with his silver eyes. "What exactly happened?"

Blowing out a deafening exhale, I entwine my fingers through his and pull him toward the sofa. We sit down beside each other, and then I proceed to tell him what happened while I was backstage, all the way until the floor opened up, swallowed Maple, and I ran.

He remains silent, listening to each word I utter. By the time I'm finished, he's grown unsettlingly quiet. In fact, he's been quiet since I reached the part in the story where Maxton said, "*qui furabatur.*"

"What does *qui furabatur* mean?" I ask, breaking the silence.

Arrow hesitates then nervously laces his fingers through mine, his fingers notably shaking, but that's usually how he is, so I'm unsure what to make of it.

"It means magic stealer." The worry in his tone sends fear trickling through me.

"Is it …? Is it what I am?"

He swiftly shakes his head and scoots closer to me.

Well, at least he doesn't seem afraid of me.

"There're a handful of creatures that can steal magic from other creatures," he explains. "Most of them are rare, though."

"Like me?" I ask, and he gives a nod. "So, how do I find out which one I am? And why does Asher's father want to get ahold of me? Maple acted as if he was sick or something and needed me to help him."

"I really don't know," he tells me. "The Steel books should give us some answers, at least to what you are. But with the city being on lockdown, we're going to have to be extra careful about stealing them." He casts a worried glance at the door for the tenth time in the last hour.

"They're going to be all right, right?" I ask, squeezing his hand and drawing his attention back to me. "Asher and East, I mean."

He nods with a rigid smile. "Of course."

"You're a terrible liar, Arrow." I sigh heavily, wiggle my hand from his, and then lower my head into my hands. "This is all my fault."

"Hey." Arrow splays his metal fingers across my cheek then angles my head back up. "None of this is your fault, Harlynn, so please don't think that."

"Yeah, it is. Maxton's only here to get me and take me to August. The Arch collapsed because of me. We're here because of me."

"Asher, East, and I chose to come to this planet. And Maxton is only here because August is a power-hungry psychopath. And the Arch?" He lifts a broad shoulder. "Everyone does a little bit of damage when they first get their powers." When I raise my brows, he adds, "The first time East got his powers, he turned an entire kingdom into glass. And when Asher first got his wish granting powers, he accidentally wished for an entire planet made of water."

"Wait. You're not saying he …?"

"Yep. He's the reason we have planet Water in our universe. Not that anyone gives him credit for that—his father took it—but we know the truth."

I shake my head in shock. "Why water, though?"

He chuckles, his eyes crinkling around the corners. The look is damn near mesmerizing. "He had a thing for mermaids back then and thought, if he could create a large pool of magical water, he could have all the mermaids he wanted. But he was still learning how to control his magic and ended up creating an entire planet that became overpopulated very quickly."

"Wow. That's really impressive. Seriously, kind of badass, accident or not." Suddenly aware that my guilt has lessened a bit, I wrap my arms around him. "Thank you, Arrow."

He places a trembling hand against my back. "For what?"

"For making me feel a little better." I hug him tighter. "You're kind of good at this friendship stuff."

He frees an unsteady breath then leans into my hug. I start to smile to myself when a loud *bang* echoes through the vehicle.

"All right, if she's handing out hugs, I definitely think I should get one this time."

The sound of East's voice has relief washing over me, but I try to contain my happiness as I pull away from Arrow and twist around on the sofa.

He's standing in front of the open front door, strands of his blond hair askew, and his pant leg is a bit torn. Other than that, he appears unharmed.

"Where's Asher?" Arrow asks, rising to his feet.

"He'll be here in a bit. He's finding a safe place to put Maxton." East's gaze sears into me as he crosses the room. "You, lovely creature, have caused quite the commotion across this planet."

I push to my feet, adjusting the hem of my skirt. "I didn't mean to. I was just trying to get away from Maxton and Maple, and then …" I frown. "I feel awful."

East dismisses me with a flick of his wrist. "Don't. This planet was a dump anyway."

"I actually think it's kind of pretty," I say. "Well, the scenery is anyway."

"That's because you've only been to a total of three planets." East halts in front of me and crosses his arms with an oddly stern look on his face. "Before we go any further with this conversation, I need to say something."

I roll my eyes. "Don't you always?"

His lips quirk. "Yes, but this is important." He forces a frown and points his finger at me. "The next time I tell you to run, you run. No arguing. Not about that."

I poke him in the chest. "You don't get to tell me what to do. If I want to stay and fight my own battles, then I'm going to. And it was really fucked-up that Asher threw me at Arrow, and he took off with me. That's not fair."

"It's completely fair." He lowers his voice as he slants closer to me. "If we want to protect you, we can."

"If I want to protect myself, I can," I retort with my arms crossed.

"I know." His gentle tone throws me off balance. "But until you learn how to control your powers a bit, you have to let us help you."

My jaw twitches at the word *help*, but I bite down the urge to snap at him, knowing he's right. The collapsing of the Arch proves that. Proves I can't control my power very well right now.

"Fine," I manage to get out. Then, scrounging up every

ounce of gratitude I can muster, I put my arms around him and give him a hug. "Thanks for helping me."

He instantly circles his arms around my waist and pulls me closer. "You're welcome. And this hug makes it worth almost getting my ass kicked."

I pull back to look at him. "You almost got your ass kicked?"

He wavers. "Asher's brother channels his power from his father, who's probably one of the most powerful creatures to exist, which means Maxton can be very powerful. Fortunately, for our sakes, we have you." He brushes his hand along the bottom of my chin.

Puzzlement webs through me. "But I didn't do anything except collapse the Arch."

"And get the planet put on lockdown, which means that Maxton is currently not connected to August's power. Well, until the lockdown is removed." East places a hand against the small of my back and steers me toward the sofa. "We also learned a little bit of information from Maxton on our way here." He pulls me down with him as he sits down, and Arrow takes a seat beside me, his knee resting against mine. "Starting with the reason he casted a spell on you earlier instead of snatching you away and taking you to August. It also helps us understand your powers better."

My interest piques. "What's the reason?"

"You were channeling too much magic from the creatures around you, and he couldn't get past the barrier you apparently put up around yourself. So, instead, he casted an invisible spell on you, hoping to isolate you. Except, your powers made the spell a bit wonky, and he ended up only isolating you from us. I'm guessing that happened because of your little ability to reflect magic sometimes."

He slides an arm around my shoulders and draws me closer to his side, his bare chest radiating warmth. I should push away, but I'm too tired to care at the moment.

"The room he pulled you into backstage had magic-proof walls, so he was hoping that might help. Unfortunately for him, but fortunately for us, you stole some of Maple's powers."

"But, what does that mean?" I try not to breathe in his scent, but I do, and I hate how much it relaxes me. "How can I just steal creatures' powers and do weird things with it?"

"That question will probably only be answered when we find out what you are." East sketches his finger along my shoulder as he briefly stares off into empty space.

"Can't you just ask Maxton if you have him now? Because he seems to know." I shiver from his touch, but he barely notices.

Something's wrong.

He blinks, focusing on me. "Sadly, Maxton has been cursed into silence and obedience. While he can't be connected to August's magic right now, he can't really talk too much about August's secrets, unless he finds a loophole, and that could take more time than we have. That's why Asher is taking him to a secluded location right now. That way, he won't be near you when the lockdown gets removed."

"Oh." Disappointment crushes my chest, along with a bit of pity for Maxton.

I realize right then and there how much I've changed over the last couple of weeks of being with these guys. How I've gone from paranormal hater to paranormal sympathizer and friend.

So freakin' weird.

"Don't worry; we'll figure this out," East swears, molding his palm to my cheek. "We'll figure out what you are and why Asher's father is suddenly after you. I promise you, we will."

I tilt my head back to meet his gaze. "Why, though? You guys don't have to help me. I just don't get it."

East trades an unreadable look with Arrow then fastens his gaze back on me. "Because it's what we do."

"You risk your lives to help random strangers?" I question with my brow raised.

He shakes his head, his eyes glittering. "We risk our lives to help our friends."

I crinkle my nose. "Are we really friends, though?"

He presses his hand to his heart, pretending to be

offended. "That's the second time you've wounded my heart today."

"I'm not trying to wound your heart. I'm just stating the truth." I recline back on the sofa. "We barely know each other. Not long enough to be friends anyway."

"Knowing someone forever doesn't make them your friends; trust me. I became friends with Asher almost the moment I met him, while barely making a connection with faeries I knew for decades beforehand. Same goes for Arrow—I bonded quickly to him." He pauses. "And you." He grins when I scowl. "Face it, sweetheart; we get along way too well not to be friends."

I roll my eyes. "We do not."

He disregards me. "And I'm betting, at this rate, we'll be lovers by sunrise."

I roll my eyes so damn hard they nearly get stuck in the back of my head. "You're so delusional." But he's wearing on me. A smile twitches at my lips.

"You know what I think you need?" He winks at me. "A little sugar."

Thinking he means sugar in the form of kisses or some dumb shit like that, I open my lips to protest, but then he sticks his hand out in front of him and his palm sparkles, forming a small bag of glittery purple cotton candy.

"Asher mentioned you like it," he tells me when I make no move to take it.

I'm surprised Asher remembered that story and feel stupidly touched. Still, I scrutinize the bag of cotton candy.

"Is that real?"

East smiles widely. "Of course it's real. My magic is one of the realest among the faeries."

"I have no idea what that means," I say, but I tentatively open the bag anyway because I'm too starving to care. Then I reach in and peel off a fluffy chunk. "If this, like, makes me fall asleep or something, I'm going to kick your ass when I wake up," I warn, lifting the piece of cotton-like candy toward my lips.

"My magic rarely works on you," he reminds me with a twinkle in his eyes. "And an ass-kicking from you seems more like a treat than a punishment." Smirking, he makes a big show of reaching for the cotton candy. "Maybe I should lace it with my magic."

I tuck the bag behind me. "No way." Then I pop the piece of candy into my mouth and let out a moan as the sugary taste dissolves into my taste buds.

East sinks his teeth into his bottom lip as his gaze dances from my lips to my eyes. "Good?"

I bob my head up and down. "It's the best I've ever tasted. Although, I've only had cotton candy one other time, but this stuff is way better."

His eyes sparkle brighter. "I'm glad my magic tastes delicious to you. I should feed it to you more often."

I'm not even positive why, but my cheeks warm with heat.

Shifting my weight, I stuff another piece into my mouth to stop myself from saying anything stupid.

East's grin broadens. "Is your mind going to the gutter?"

"No," I lie, more warmth rushing to my cheeks.

Chuckling, he tugs me to him and brushes his lips across my forehead. "You're adorable."

"If you say so," I murmur against his chest that smells similar to the candy currently dissolving in my mouth. For a mind-losing minute, I consider licking him just to see if he tastes the same. Then I mentally kick my ass and lean away. "So, what am I supposed to do now?"

"For now, you'll hang out on the vehicle for a while until this investigation blows over. And until we can find out if Maxton and Maple are the only ones here who are helping August," East says, wiping a drop of cotton candy off my lips with his fingertip.

I'd probably seize the opportunity to bite his finger, except his words remind me of something very important.

"The reason I walked back toward where Maxton was in the first place is because this blond male creature with illuminating eyes came up to me and told me there was food back there," I tell East and Arrow. "There wasn't any, so I'm guessing he was helping Maple and Maxton."

"Was he staff?" East asks worriedly.

I nod. "Yeah, he had a badge."

East frowns deeply. "It was probably an acquaintance of Maple's."

I stick another piece of cotton candy into my mouth. "I should also probably mention that I think … I think I may have accidentally killed her."

East shakes his head. "Maxton told us what happened, and there's no way that fall killed her, unfortunately." He slumps back on the sofa. "She's probably going to show up sooner or later if we don't find her first."

"We should check the magic repair shop tomorrow," Arrow suggests. "If she's hurt, she'll be there."

East nods in agreement. "You and I will go at dawn."

"And if she's there, what're you going to do?" I wonder, stuffing my mouth with more cotton candy.

"That's for us to worry about," he says, and I respond with a dirty look. He grins. "I'm really, *really* glad we get to keep you."

I let my head bob back as I groan. "You're not keeping me."

He just keeps on smiling, totally amused.

Rolling my eyes, I go back to stuffing my mouth with more sugar. "You think you've won this argument, but you're wrong."

"We'll see," is all he says, shooting Arrow a conspiratorial grin.

I give up, which means I must be super tired.

East flashes me another grin before focusing on Arrow. "I think, while we're out tomorrow, we can also work on getting those incubus' and succubus' souls."

"But I thought you said you wanted me to get the incubus's?" I interrupt through a mouthful of sugary deliciousness.

East trades a cautious glance with Arrow then looks at me. "I think we can probably handle it."

I lick a drop of cotton candy off my lips. "Look, I know I fucked up with the whole knocking down the Arch thing, but I'm good at stealing stuff, and I want to help with this."

"You can help steal the books. I just don't think it's a good idea to make you seduce this incubus so we can get his soul." He traces a finger down my jawline. "We'll find another way to get it."

I glance between the two of them, and Arrow tries to offer me a reassuring smile while East continues to stroke my jaw.

"What's going on?" I demand. "Because something is."

East looks at Arrow again then sighs, looking back at me. "We just think that, after the incident with Yellow, it might be easier on you if you don't have to flirt with a creature that's going to get handsy."

Confusion whisks through me. Hardly anyone has tried to do something to make things easier on me. In fact, I've spent the majority of my life feeling as if the world is against me. Suddenly, I don't feel that way, and that makes the strangest, most uncomfortable sensations twirl through me.

"I need to go … do something," I mutter, rising to my feet then bolting out of the room.

I haul ass to my bedroom, lock myself inside, and collapse to the floor. Tears burn my eyes like dirty, little bastards. I try to suck them back, but a few manage to escape.

I don't even know why I'm crying. It's not like Jason has never done nice things for me or tried to make my life easier. He has … a couple of times. I have to admit, though, that most of the time, I was the one helping Jason. Like when he got in trouble with the underground mafia, or the tons of times he pissed someone off and I had to step in and fight for him. Plus, every time we needed something, I was the one who stole it.

I wipe the tears from my cheeks but more trickle out.

The sad truth is, while I thought Jason and I were best friends, being here and being so open with these guys, being able to talk about my curse with them, them helping me without expecting anything in return is very new to me. And that new feeling not only makes me realize I've never had a really close friendship, but also makes me painfully aware of how emotionally attached I'm getting.

I need to get my act together and keep this friendship from progressing into anything else. If I can't and I end up feeling too much, I'm going to have to bail and protect them like they've been protecting me.

"Yep, if at any moment I feel like I might be tapping into that curse, I'm going to bail," I vow, trying to convince myself that the possibility of that happening is probably pretty low.

After all, they're paranormals, and I just can't see myself falling in love with one. Plus, there's a long way between liking someone as a friend and loving them ...

I hope.

CHAPTER 28

ASHER

"ARE you sure these chains will hold me?" My younger brother, Maxton, asks as I secure the last of them to his wrists.

We're in a cave out in the middle of the Steel forest. I hauled him out here to keep him as far away from Harlynn as possible so that, when the lockdown is removed, we'll have plenty of time to leave before he can get to her. Because he's going to try the moment he has our father's powers back. He has no control over it; hasn't since he was born a Wishing Shadow and our father deemed him his servant.

That day was awful. I cried. My mother cried and begged him not to, tried to curse him into not being able to.

He killed her for it, right in front of me, and watched as she died in my arms.

Yeah, our father is a fucking cruel bastard—always has been—which is why I've been gathering powerful objects that will hopefully help me kill him.

"Hopefully," I reply as I rise to my feet and dust off my hands.

The truth is, I don't know if the chains will hold, but as long as Maxton isn't being controlled, we don't have anything to worry about. My brother is a kind man underneath the scars, torture, and decades of being controlled.

"You better be certain." He leans against the rock behind him, bends his legs, and rests his hands on his knees.

"I'm as certain as I can be."

I turn to leave, hating having to leave him like this, but I don't have a choice. Any second the lockdown could be removed, and then he'll have more power than me.

"You should make sure to cover up that mark on her back," he suddenly grits out.

I glance at him confusedly. "Huh?"

"The star on Harlynn's back…" He swallows forcefully then strains out, "It…Just keep it hidden."

"Okay." I wish he could tell me why, but I can see on his face that he's struggling to speak right now. "Thanks." Even though it pains me, I turn to leave, torn between wanting to stay with him and wanting to get back and make sure Harlynn, East, and Arrow are okay. With the lockdown going on, it makes me anxious being away. "I'll come back tomorrow morning to bring you some food and check on you."

"Don't bother," he mumbles miserably.

"I'll be back tomorrow," I repeat then start to walk away.

"I know a way to get around your curse," he whispers so softly that, at first, I think I hear him wrong.

I pause, twisting back around. "What did you say?"

He lifts his head to meet my gaze. "I said, I know a way to get around your curse. You know, the one our father put on you that'll eventually make that lovely creature I met today die."

"The curse won't happen if I don't let it," I remind him.

He carries my gaze. "He sealed your curse with Destiny. There's no way of getting rid of it."

"Then I guess you really don't know a way to break it," I point out, turning to completely face him.

"I never said *break it*," he says. "I said *get around it*."

I eye him over, questioning if he's toying with me or not. Maxton himself wouldn't, but if our father has even an ounce of control over him, he would. "How do I get around it?"

He chews on his bottom lip, contemplating. "I'll tell you, but I need a favor first."

"What?" I ask warily.

He lowers his head and takes a deep breath. "I want you to kill me."

I gape at him. "You're fucking joking, right?"

When he lifts his head and looks at me, I can tell he's not. He wants to die.

"I can't live like this anymore." His voice cracks. "This isn't a life, Asher. This is hell."

"I can't kill you," I whisper, shaking my head.

"Even if it meant Harlynn could live and that you could finally fall in love?" he questions. "Think about it, brother. You could finally be free from this curse, and I could finally be free from mine."

I shake my head, stepping back. "I promised that, one day, I'd find a way to free you. I'm working on it now." *With the objects*, but I can't tell him that and risk word getting back to our father.

"Dad is planning something awful with her," he croaks out, his face bunched in pain as he strains out forbidden words. "If you get rid of me, it'll make it harder for him to get to her."

"I can protect Harlynn without killing you," I insist, balling my hands into fists at my side. "I won't do this. I'm going to save you like I promised the day Mom died."

"You can't save me—he's too strong," Maxton grits

out, tears flooding his eyes. "Please ... please agree to put me out of my misery, and I'll tell you how to get around the curse."

Shaking my head, I whirl around and stride toward the front of the cave. "I'll be back tomorrow with some food."

"Please think about it!" he cries out. "You don't have a lot of time! Please, Asher! Come back! Do this for me!"

His words fade as I run out of the cave, running away from him like a coward.

No, I can't do it. Can't watch another creature I care about die.

But what about Harlynn? Because, if my father did seal the curse with Destiny, then me falling in love with her will happen. And then she'll die.

Rage boils under my flesh as I realize that, in the end, I may very well have to make a decision I don't want to make.

One that might get someone I care about killed.

ABOUT THE AUTHOR

Jessica Sorensen is a *New York Times* and *USA Today* bestselling author who lives in the snowy mountains of Wyoming. When she's not writing, she spends her time reading and hanging out with her family.

For more info:

Facebook: Jessica.Sorensen.Author

Facebook group: Sorensen's Stars

Instagram: jessica_sorensenauthor

jessicasorensen.com

ALSO BY JESSICA SORENSEN

<u>Capturing Magic:</u>

Chasing Wishes

Untitled (coming soon)

<u>Tangled Realms:</u>

Forever Violet

Untitled (coming soon)

<u>Harlynn's Mystery Investigations:</u>

Sugar Cookies & Zombie Secrets

Untitled (coming soon)

<u>Mystic Willow Bay Vampires</u>

Untitled (coming soon)

<u>Mystic Willow Bay Mysteries Series:</u>

The Secret Life of a Witch

Untitled (coming soon)

<u>Enchanted Chaos Series:</u>

Enchanted Chaos

Shimmering Chaos

Untitled (coming soon)

My Cursed Superhero Life:

Grim

Cursed

Maddening

Undead

Untitled (coming soon)

Guardian Academy Series:

Entranced

Entangled

Untitled (coming soon)

Monster Academy for the Magical:

Monster Academy for the Magical

Untitled (coming soon)

The Shattered Promises Series:

Shattered Promises

Fractured Souls

Unbroken

Broken Visions

Scattered Ashes

<u>**The Fallen Star Series:**</u>

The Fallen Star

The Underworld

The Vision

The Promise

The Lost Soul

The Evanescence

<u>**The Darkness Falls Series:**</u>

Darkness Falls

Darkness Breaks

Darkness Fades

<u>**The Death Collectors Series (NA and YA):**</u>

Ember X and Ember

Cinder X and Cinder

Spark X and Spark

<u>**Standalones:**</u>

The Forgotten Girl

The Illusion of Annabella

Confessions of Luna & Grey

Rules of a Rebel & a Shy Girl

The Honeyton Mysteries:

Chasing Hadley

Falling for Hadley

Holding onto Hadley

Untitled (coming soon)

The Sunnyvale Mysteries:

The Year I Became Isabella Anders

The Year of Falling in Love

The Year of Second Chances

Lexi Ashford Series:

The Diary of Lexi Ashford

The Diary of Lexi Ashford: The Agreement

Untitled (coming soon)

The Unraveling Mysteries Series:

Unraveling You

Raveling You

Awakening You

Inspiring You

The Art of Being Friends:

The Art of Being Friends

The Rules of Being Friends

Untitled (coming soon)

The Coincidence Series:

The Coincidence of Callie and Kayden

The Redemption of Callie and Kayden

The Destiny of Violet and Luke

The Probability of Violet and Luke

The Certainty of Violet and Luke

The Resolution of Callie and Kayden

Seth & Greyson

The Secret Series:

The Prelude of Ella and Micha

The Secret of Ella and Micha

The Forever of Ella and Micha

The Temptation of Lila and Ethan

The Ever After of Ella and Micha

Lila and Ethan: Forever and Always

Ella and Micha: Infinitely and Always

Breaking Nova Series:

Breaking Nova

Saving Quinton

Delilah: The Making of Red

Nova and Quinton: No Regrets

Tristan: Finding Hope

Wreck Me

Ruin me

<u>Unbeautiful Series:</u>

Unbeautiful

Untamed

www.ingramcontent.com/pod-product-compliance
Lightning Source LLC
Chambersburg PA
CBHW030956190726
48285CB00004BB/1338